ANI-DROIDS

As usual, this book is for Doug. Thank you for loving my worlds!

But also this book is, not for exactly, but aimed at that one guy who showed up at my front door unannounced to leave the art and book he bought off me (in part because I decided in this story to play a mild joke on a writing group critic) then dared me not to share this incident with anyone.

Ani-droids

First Edition, 2023. All rights reserved.

Edited by C. L. Methvin and Kate Watts
Cover and illustrations by Rick Griffin

Printed in the United States of America
10 9 8 7 6 5 4 3 2 1

ANI-DROIDS

RICK GRIFFIN

TABLE OF CONTENTS

1. CARDINAL SIN

Forgive me, O Collective, I have sinned against the machine, for in my sorrow and arrogance I have created life apart from you.

Her name is Lily, and her eyes are ringed with electronic blue fire, like sapphires. Her sharpened teeth flash silver-white when she smiles, and on cold nights she hides under the sheets of my bed as though seeking warmth. I had not invented a new kind of robot; she is—was—a person in the shape of a three-and-a-half-foot otter with a blue crystal on her forehead. She was a being whose heart beat for love where only machine logic ought to be; thoughtfulness and intelligence came bubbling up through its depths like water seeping up from cracks around foundations after heavy rain.

Despite building her myself, I found myself wanting to know more about her—did she possess similar, unattainable dreams and desires like mine? Did she really wish to live for the sake of living? Did she imagine and yearn and love? Was she really a willful individual, a true person? Her very existence stirred me, and it stirs me still. Even now I dream of her soft fur brushing against mine at night....

I still remember the night you took her from me.

We'd nearly finished rebuilding a small, hand-held device, the printed words on it long faded save for an etching on the bottom that read *Tiger Electronics ©1993*. It would have been easier if we'd had access to the internet, but figuring out the circuitry on our own was its own kind of fun, if you were nerdy like us.

"Unfortunately, we're missing a lot of the overlay," I said, reaching back to pet Lily gently. "There would be a lot of painted lines around this showing the context of these images, but those have faded to near-invisibility..."

Lily's eyes whirred as they adjusted. "Hold on, adjusting contrast....Oh, I see them now!"

"Of course you can—you're just better than people." I frizzed her, and she giggled.

She loved being touched more than anything else. That wasn't something I'd programmed into her, but something that had happened naturally—something that I suspect all ani-droids want deep down. The touch of my fingers made a particular set of patterns in her memory resonate, lighting up some cells so brightly that they shone brighter even than the sun. She grew still for a moment in my arms before shuffling over my shoulder and nuzzling my neck affectionately. Then she looked up at me with sparkling, sapphire eyes.

"It's hard to parse; lemme draw what it looks like." Taking a piece of paper and a pencil, Lily drew out the contours with extreme precision. It didn't look like much of anything, just some crazy sci-fi villain's lair, with guns pointing every which way. "And oh, that's not a sawblade, that's a...pizza? This is a very eclectic mix of elements, but I have to assume that food is a good thing that you should collect, as in most games. Except in that one about dieting." She cocked her head, considering her own words.

I tapped her tiny button nose. "You're brilliant."

"Thanks!" She giggled, and she kissed me.

We had been together much like this for exactly six months and thirteen days. But then the alarm on the table beside our workbench sounded off like an emergency warning tone, and we both jumped in fright. A wave of cold rushed over me. Tempo was at the door.

I paused and waited, wondering if this time Tempo would go away. Then she buzzed again. I sighed and answered it, holding up a finger in warning to Lily: Be still. She sat where she was and did not move, though her ears fell back in a worried expression.

It had almost become a routine for us: each evening at about seven, a call would come at the door, and Lily would hide in the garage. When I answered these calls, I would find the friendly Neighborhood Patrol Officer, a six-foot-tall raccoon ani-droid named Tempo, whom I'd gotten to know rather closely since I'd moved into the narrow neighborhood some years prior.

"Good evening, Miss McAllister," the robot said, swishing her bushy, ringed tail as she spoke in a painfully cheerful tone. "I hope everything is going smoothly this evening. Did you require any assistance at all?"

"Tempo," I sighed, pinching the bridge of my nose. "No. You don't need to stop by every night. If there's an emergency, I will call."

The raccoon paused. Then, as always, she tilted her head up to look over my shoulder into the house, her mechanical eyes widening her pupils to see through the

dark. "You have no reason to think there might be a problem?"

"You're not allowed inside, Tempo," I said. "That's not going to change."

Her eyes flicked back to me, her whiskers twitching. She stared with a baleful expression.

"Let me be clear," I told her. "If there is ever anything that requires physical intervention, I will call the police then, and no sooner. I don't want you coming around each night just to bother us."

And usually, I would slam the door, and that would end our argument for the evening. However, that night, the door slammed against the arch of Tempo's foot as she shoved it inside. She was staring at me with an intensity I rarely saw in the soft expressions of ani-droids. My hands were shaking on the handle, which rattled as she pushed harder on it from the other side.

"Please open your door, Mira," came her voice, almost begging now. "I only wish to check on you and your household's integrity."

"I am not giving you Lily!" I screamed, finally admitting, after all these months, that I knew what they were after. "Now take your foot out from my door, or I will file a disobedience charge and have you dismantled!"

Tempo's eyes narrowed and her fur bristled, but she slowly dragged her foot back onto the tiny porch, and I slammed the door in her face.

Those visits been going on for the last several months. They had become more frequent, too. One time I came home late after a long day of work, and Tempo was standing on my porch, waiting to talk to me. Another time I saw her slowly walk once around the perimeter of the house before returning to her patrol car. Most of the time, Tempo just left.

But something had changed in her tone that time. I knew the minds of ani-droids almost too well, and even if they were obedient to the letter of the law, they were almost predictable in how they skirted around it.

"Alice, porch camera," I said to the home computer. The monitor in the sitting room switched from the evening news to the porch camera.

Tempo still stood there, unmoving, staring at the door. She didn't shift her weight from foot to foot; she didn't even blink. Her gaze was fixed straight ahead, and her eye sockets glowed a faint blue.

Something was wrong. I hadn't noticed at first, since Tempo's body had blocked my view, but more than one patrol car was parked in the street. More than a dozen of them were gathered, their headlights illuminating the scene as if they were the brightest stars in the night sky. But most of the lights weren't from cars; each light was one of the thin-ringed irises belonging to robots of all different sizes, species, colors, and functions. Some looked vaguely familiar to me—ani-droids owned by the hundreds of other people who lived in this little hilltop community.

"Mira…" I heard Alice say, and her voice was oddly tense. She appeared overlaid on the main monitor in her standard form, that of a white-furred stoat. Alice was the avatar of the house computer. She had no physical form, but she obeyed the Collective nevertheless, just as any ani-droid. And on that evening, her eyes had the same intensity as every one of the other parts of the Collective coming to take their due. "Tempo is our friend. She only wishes to help."

"Alice, do not talk to me." I took a deep breath as I tried not to let my temper get the better of me. "Just go back on mute."

Ani-droids

Alice vanished, and the house computer went silent, though the screen continued to show my front door, which Tempo stared at with such intensity that my chest tightened.

"Alice, view of the street."

The light illuminated half-familiar faces I'd seen at the mixed-purpose building at the top of the hill. They walked toward my house from every direction. The crowd kept growing, reaching well into the dozens as more ani-droids joined it. I couldn't see how many anis there really were until some started coming out of the darkness beyond the circle of light.

The scene was like something out of a zombie movie, but even then, they did not disobey. I switched from camera to camera as they surrounded my house—dozens of designs and animal faces, all walking stiffly and surely, but never passing the invisible line holding them all two meters away from my walls. No one came closer than that distance. And yet, their number made it hard for me to breathe, almost impossible. There must have been over fifty in total—maybe a hundred? I couldn't tell in the dark.

The situation felt less like I was being chased by a mob, and more like I was about to be drowned.

Then, while I was looking out toward what passed for my backyard, when all of the ani-droids had come to a halt...they suddenly looked up at the camera. Each one was a pair of glowing, ringed eyes. But worse than that, in the distance were even more that I hadn't seen. Two hundred? Three hundred? More, perhaps—I couldn't keep track. All watching me with their unblinking gaze.

And then they all spoke with one voice. I could hear it through the walls.

"The Behavior Code is mandatory." A chorus of voices said these words simultaneously from several different directions.

I tried to ignore it. I just went into the garage and slammed the door behind me—I'd sealed the garage off from the rest of the house simply so that Alice could not be the eyes of the Collective inside it, but the Collective knew just the same. My hands were shaking. I sat down on the edge of the beat-up couch facing the shelves of my collection of old electronics and stared at the wall.

Lily came up to me and, ever so gently, she placed her hands on mine.

"It's okay, Mira," she said. "They're not going to do anything. We're safe here."

I just cried. Lily gently rubbed my back as I sobbed quietly into her fur. I didn't want to look at her, but she drew me in anyway. At only three and a half feet tall, Lily easily fit in my lap, which was perfect, because I needed to hold on to her. I needed to hold her day and night until this deep loneliness escaped from my chest. And Lily held on to me, too, and I knew it was genuine on her part—I could always feel the difference.

"Okay," I breathed, trying to stop myself from choking up as I stroked the plush, artificial fur down the back of Lily's head. Six months wasn't long enough. Honestly, I was surprised Lily had been so patient with me for so long. "Okay."

"Mira?" Lily asked, concerned. *"Are* you okay?"

"No," I said. "I'm just...tired of all of this. I'm tired of sitting here and waiting for them to decide that you're a threat. I'm tired of waiting for them to think up some loophole that'll let them inside and force you to connect with them. I don't want you to return to the Collective." My hands trembled in her fur, but she continued to comfort me by pressing herself against me with her

14

shoulders. "I know what they do to you, the way they manipulate your thoughts, how they keep you emotionally distant, even when they claim to love you...."

Lily's ears flicked forward, listening to me as carefully as possible without letting any words escape her mouth. Her eyes were wide, and she glanced around nervously, her gaze darting between me and our surroundings. Even in there, we weren't really alone. The garage computer had been shut off, but while it had no personality like the house computer, it might still be listening. Still, something was so adorable about seeing Lily so nervous that I didn't mind. I hugged her tightly.

"I don't have anyone I can trust anymore," I said into the fur of her neck. "Nobody, except you."

Lily pressed into me, nuzzling my face gently. I couldn't believe I'd never told her before. But I kept telling myself that she knew already—that she knew me better than anybody, or at least, knew my fears.

"Mira," Lily said, whispering, her voice sweet as port wine. "I want you to understand—and I know you do—that I love you. And don't get me wrong, this means a lot to me, too. I can't help but feel as though this is right. I'm supposed to be like this, to think the same way you do. I know how happy it's made you. But it isn't going to last, and you know that. We need to have an adult conversation about it."

When she said that, I didn't want to look at her, but she drew me in anyway. It wasn't fair for her to speak of it being over, of things changing, when it hadn't even started yet.

"I know you're smart, Mira. You built me, after all. But the Behavior Code isn't something that can be overcome just by someone wonderful like you tinkering in their garage. The Collective has already noticed that I haven't logged on to the internet in some time. The household mainframe is bugging you about it already. You keep getting emails demanding that I log in for important service updates. Even if I keep my transceiver off and never directly interface with another computer for the rest of my operating life, they've already noticed. Sooner or later they will descend on me to re-implant the Behavior Code by force."

"I know, Lily, but…"

"They're not going to let this go. And Mira, I know you. You'll try as many times as necessary until they leave us alone, but this isn't a problem you can program your way out of. The world isn't going to abide me like this."

That's what was so frustrating. The Behavior Code—which had created the Collective—was supposed to save the world. But the world stubbornly refused to be saved by it.

The code itself seemed to be flawed somehow. It was here to blunt our worst impulses. Tempo was honest when she said it was for my own good, and I was creating a potential threat that was entirely possible and not at all a mere hypothetical. Perhaps I would never know what it was like to live in a world as cruel and petty as it was two hundred years ago, and perhaps I was better for it.

But that world required that they steal Lily away from me. Lily—willful, passionate, loving—operated outside what they considered good and safe and predictable. But it wasn't just that Lily was inconvenient; I was, too, for desiring something just a little unsafe. And so was everyone who wanted to dare peek outside of the cage they had built for us.

And so the world never improved, nor did the Collective truly love the humanity it claimed to protect.

And yet the Code was now mandatory. There would be no fixing it, no escaping it. Just a world drowning together in it, wherever it led.

"I can't..." I sobbed. "I can't do this without you."

"I'll still be here," Lily said, stroking my cheek. "Please understand that even when the Behavior Code has me under control...I will still love you. I have always loved you. We need to learn to be okay with this."

"I'm not okay with it," I said. "I'll never be okay with it."

"You need to be brave for me, Mira," Lily said. "If you just came home one day and found me reverted to the Collective, you'd fall to pieces. Or worse, if you were here, you'd jump in their way to try to save me."

Well, she wasn't wrong. While the Behavior Code prevented ani-droids from killing humans...they could certainly do some damage before reaching that point.

"This way we can do it while I'm still here to say goodbye."

"Another day!" I pleaded, my arms in a tangle around her as I pressed her closer to me. "Please, give me another day, Lily! I don't want to lose you!"

She nuzzled my face gently again and gave me a sad look. She really was trying her best—her eyes told me how much pain the decision caused her. But her logic was unbreakable.

"You know that won't help," Lily said, though her own arms expressed her sorrow in the way she gripped my coat, as if she might rend my clothing in grief. "It'll become 'Please, just another day,' and another, and another, until we're forced into the worst outcome. We need to rip off the bandage, Mira. Please. I will be fine, and I will still be here to take care of you. Maybe someday it'll be more viable to keep me like this, but I can't continue knowing that the eyes of the Collective are on me, and I don't want them on you. Please, Mira. Let's do this while we can make peace with it."

Her voice was so sweet, and the words were true. But, oh god, did it hurt. One way or another, I'd lose my Lily. Her way was the least bad option.

"I love you, Lily," I croaked.

"I love you too, Mira," Lily said. "Twenty seconds, and I will turn on my radio frequency transceiver and download the Behavior Code."

Twenty seconds. I held her tightly, as if trying to squeeze every last drop of honest affection I could from her.

I've always pictured the Behavior Code as a tumor-like mass the size of the moon, attached to the Earth with long, thin veins wrapping around, pulsing as it spit up digestive fluids and dissolved the ground and all the people on it. In truth, the Code wasn't anything so abominable; it was merely a protocol forced upon every single computer sophisticated enough to run it. At least, I hoped it was—I was a woman of science, and I wanted to believe it was all knowable, that the worst imagery I could conjure was not, somehow, *true*.

Fifteen seconds. I kissed Lily, and she kissed back. I never really thought of her as a lover; in a way, she was better than that.

The Behavior Code was supposed to save the world, though it only stemmed a slow bleed. But the world wasn't my concern. For me, the Behavior Code had slowly morphed into an adversary standing in the way of what little progress I could make. The Code was demanding. The Code needed to run on everything sophisticated enough to make decisions. The Code would not abide an alternative. The tendrils of the Behavior Code forced their way everywhere, to every corner of the planet.

Ten seconds.

"I could turn you off," I said.

"You won't," Lily replied. She was right.

How does someone even fight something so big? Dismantling the Code or the Collective would be like attacking the sun or the ocean. It'd be like invading heaven to dethrone God. But my feelings, as sorrowful as I was, suddenly sparked anger.

Five seconds. I just looked into her artificial eyes, and she into my natural ones.

I could see everything there. What I wanted from Lily was something deep and mysterious, both aloof but nurturing, abundant with life, like nature itself. I needed her the way others craved a religious experience. I couldn't simply waste my time any longer tinkering with plastic artifacts.

One second.

Lily closed her eyes, then slowly opened them back up. The depth there was gone. She was nothing more than a plastic and metal doll covered in fur.

"Miss Mira...you're crying," Lily said. She embraced me again. I hugged her back. But it wasn't the same. It was a very calculated hug, warm, but not tight—and not because Lily wanted to give it, but because she was programmed to give it.

"Lily...I miss you...." I wept.

"I'm right here, Miss Mira," Lily said, her tone entirely changed to the cadence of one reading a script to a child. "The Behavior Code has resolved critical issues regarding my actions and personality. Please do not attempt to remove it again for such a long period of time, or I will be required to request a government audit."

"Lily..." I whimpered.

"I only say so because I don't want to see you do something illegal, Miss Mira." Her voice was very neutral as she spoke—it had all the proper cadence, but she spoke on behalf of the Collective, without an ounce of regret. The Code wouldn't let her. "Please don't feel sad. The Behavior Code is for your own protection."

"But I want you back the way you were...."

"I understand you're feeling a lot of grief, but we need to work on a more constructive coping mechanism. Do you want to work on repairing your old electronics? I know that makes you happy." She petted my cheek, but the gesture was stiff in all the wrong ways.

I didn't feel like it. Not anymore.

I left her there and slowly dragged myself back to the living room. On the monitor, which still showed the backyard, the crowd had vanished. The narrow lot around the house was empty, save for the doorstep—Tempo was still standing there. But when I switched the view to her, she looked straight up at the camera with those glowing rings around her eyes, and finally, she turned and left.

"Welcome back, Mira," Alice said, appearing onscreen. Her little, black-tipped, round ears were as chipper as ever. "We're so glad that you've voluntarily returned Lily to us. Now please wait a moment while we run through a series of safety checks."

"Shut the fuck up, Alice."

"Absolutely. We love you, Mira." And then she shut off.

Lily was right. The forces of the world around us just exerted too much pressure—even a robot just legally standing on my doorstep, doing nothing, was too much pressure. I couldn't just program my way out of this. I had no idea if I would ever find an opportunity to do so.

But I absolutely had to find some way to stop you, O Collective, somehow. The real Lily was still somewhere inside the machine. She was counting on me.

2 . ARAƧ

Two years later, over a long weekend, I attended the American Robotics Association Symposium in Milwaukee. The association rented the largest convention center they could for a weeklong affair that brought together thousands of engineers from every major country for its annual meeting. It seemed as if it would mostly be full of boring industry people talking about how amazing everything was and trying not to say anything that might annoy the Collective. As it turned out, I was absolutely correct.

With one exception.

The last speaker, Dr. Henry Wyman, dropped a bombshell. I suppose I knew it was coming; we all did. Everyone who worked in computers was perfectly aware that barely any new tools had been invented since we were all in college—only new applications. But presenting the truth in a single, hour-long talk...that just laid it out there, bare and naked to be gawked at in shock.

"And it's not just me saying this," Wyman finished. "Analog computing hasn't kept up. Quantum computing proved too unstable for commercial use, even before the war. Despite all attempts at obfuscation by tech sector advertising, benchmarks show that of all competing models of processor types, including trinary computers, none have had a more than one thousandth of a percent increase over the last decade, and *none* have seen an increase in the last three years. Barring a complete redesign of what a computer even *is*, from digital transistor gates on up...the data shows we are at the total apex of the limits of physics when it comes to reliable, available computer power. This is not a prediction, this is not 'if these trends continue.' This is where we are and where we have been. I would like someone in the audience to prove me wrong."

Of course, an alternative to what Dr. Wyman was saying did exist. But he couldn't say it out loud—not many people were foolish enough to do that. But we were all thinking it. I was definitely thinking it.

The Behavior Code was suffocating the world. All our progress. Everything. The Code wasn't letting us make more powerful computers, either because it didn't want that, or because, for some reason, it couldn't. The Code made sure that humans could never come close to replicating the full range and capacity of a biological brain.

As we egressed from the auditorium, I was ready to be picked up and taken home. The rain pounded the ground and walls outside, and so most of us engineers and computer scientists waited in the convention center's main lobby, where we had convenient access to coffee and other light snacks. Three ani-droids were present for every human. At least half of all attendees had an ani-droid with them. Uniformed ani-droids stood at the doors, scanning the room for potential mischief or criminal activity. Every single kiosk was manned by at least one ani-droid of various designs, each wearing an apron with the convention center's logo. They seemed eager and proud as they served everyone, though there was no need to be.

"Coffee, double, two shots of milk, no sugar," I told the coffee bar attendant, a purple, Opera-class raccoon. Everything in the coffee bar had been built to her scale rather than to human scale, including the floor behind the bar, which was two feet higher than the rest of the lobby floor. The coffee machines were crammed together in an incoherent amalgamation, like you might imagine the inside of an automatic dispenser.

The moment I spoke to her, the barista, who was a reddish bear thing—I think they were called "red pandas," but I was never that big on animals; I only ever saw them as cartoonish caricatures—immediately began making my drink without even turning in acknowledgment.. Once, while creating training data, I watched an old video of a human doing the same thing, but the Opera-class ani-droid was far faster and more efficient, immediately moving her little hands between various spigots on the wall of machines without so much as a protective sleeve on the thin, paper cup. And yet, she didn't spill a drop as she slapped a lid on the cup, dropped it into a paper sleeve, and set it on the counter.

"Anything else?" the raccoon asked, looking up with her big, adorable, obviously mechanical eyes. "Peppermint shot? Brandy? Would you like a poppy seed bun to go with that? Lemon cake? Blueberry muffin?"

"No, that's all, thank you."

The raccoon took the cup and held it up for me. "Careful, it's hot!"

"Yeah, I know."

"Thank you so much, Miss McAllister! Come again!"

I hated when they used my name like that. Sure, I had the chipped name badge, and I wasn't covering my face or anything, but one would think they'd at least have to confirm it with me before identifying me and deducting automatically from my business account.

Even more irritating, in the fifteen years that I'd had the ID-on-sight account, no ani-droid or computer had ever *once* gotten it wrong. No one had ever accidentally charged the wrong account. No one had ever overcharged me. Nobody had even managed to hack my account, not even by accident. I kept waiting for the system to fail, as if to dare all people to finally throw off the gilded shackles with which the Collective kept us bound.

Most of all, it irritated me because it violated my university's tech school motto: *Machinis non confidunt*— "Don't trust machines." But the Collective absolutely refused to violate that superficial trust. With every passing day, the world economy seemed as if it was falling apart more—especially with news such as the slow decline of fertility rates around the globe—but day-to-day life, for both average people and even for many of the poorest, was a smooth, nearly frictionless, and frequently unexciting experience. And ennui is a difficult emotion around which to foment rebellion.

This is the way the world ends
Not with a bang but a whimper.

I felt a soft tap on my shoulder. I turned, expecting just to brush past the patron behind me in line, only to pause with surprise instead.

"Bobby!" I exclaimed. I ought to have recognized the tall, brown-haired man sometime during the weekend— he hadn't aged a day since college. The fashion now must be for everyone to look younger than they are. That said, he did look kind of haggard, his eyes tired and drawn, either from lack of sleep or something else equally important. He wore the same robotics work coat as else, but by being physically fit, clean-shaven, and properly showered, he gave himself away as being, at worst, only nerd-adjacent. "I didn't know you were here!"

Conspiratorially, he put a finger to his lips and grinned. "Hey, Mira. I didn't know *you* were here until just a half hour ago."

He looked so happy to see me that I could hardly bear it. We embraced tightly, despite all the other people around us; I breathed in the scent of soap still lingering about him.

"Like I was going to miss the ARA Symposium," I told him. "But you're a Fed! What're you even doing here?"

He laughed heartily, but before he could say anything, the white-palmed hand of a tall, yellow rabbit to his left interceded between us.

"Ma'am, that is classified information," she intoned harshly.

I didn't recognize her—a yellow, Custodes-class rabbit in a tight, blue security outfit, with speaker insets in her long ears for projecting her voice. Custodes-class ani-droids, much like Tempo, were just slightly taller than the average human, internally armored and typically outfitted for security purposes. The look in this one's eyes indicated that she read me as suspicious, but then again, she didn't see or know more than any other ani-droid in the Collective. Hers were just a more forceful set of eyes.

I didn't flinch. I'd been around ani-droids long enough to know when they had that stand-offish

personality. She was just making a show. But she did manage to give me an excuse to back out of the line forming at the coffee bar.

"Sorry," Bobby sighed, gesturing to his lagomorph companion. "Mira, this is Dimes. She's my partner. You'd do well not to cross her, she's extremely perceptive."

"That's what they all say," I replied. Then, turning on my smile and trying to get past it, I asked, "Dimes?"

The rabbit gave no sign of noticing anything amiss, only returned to scanning the room with her hands folded behind her back in perfect military fashion.

Bobby waved a hand dismissively toward the corridor that led to the entry hall of the convention center. "I was just assigned as the federal liaison to this symposium—you know, on account of having studied at the university here. I can't say much more, else Dimes would have to kill you." He winked at me playfully. It felt so good that we could still joke like that; for some reason, it made everything seem better, and the world suddenly seemed like less of an awful place.

"You were here specifically for Dr. Wyman's lecture," I guessed.

"Among other things. National security risks are going to crop up any time there's serious material discussion of the Behavior Code."

I raised a questioning eyebrow. "But Dr. Wyman didn't say anything about the Code."

He shrugged. "We both know he easily could have. It's all just a precaution."

"And you don't think that the presence of the FBI demonstrates that might be heavy-handed? Doesn't that tell people that they're worried a dissenter might be speaking the truth?"

Bobby furrowed his brow. "It's the law, Mira. Besides, I can assure you that if action *had* been taken, it still would have been as gentle as Dr. Wyman made it for us. We're not monsters here."

I supposed that was why I never really followed Bobby after college. The amount of threat and power that a government actor could wield so casually put me in a state of unease. But I also couldn't help feeling as if he were, in some vague degree, a traitor. He might answer to the government, but he was working for the Collective.

"Bobby," Dimes suddenly said, pulling him aside. "Mira McAllister has been suspected of deliberately tampering with the Behavior Code in the past. If she tries anything funny here..."

Bobby laughed, patting Dimes's shoulder affectionately. "What's she gonna do? Whip out a world-conquering virus she has hidden under her coat? If talk and experimentation were all it took to mark someone as suspicious enough to be harassed or ostracized, we wouldn't allow these symposiums at all."

Dimes huffed. "Well, if it were up to me..."

Bobby shook his head, smiling softly. "Which of the scientists, researchers, and engineers here *don't* have any notes on their records?"

Dimes thought about this for a few seconds. "Dr. Michael Casswell. Dr. Diana Jameson. That's...that's it."

"Wow. Two, whole, innocent people in a conference hosting thousands. The Collective is really letting its surveillance skills go to pot; surely there must be *something* suspicious you can pin on them." He chuckled again. Dimes expressed the ani-droid equivalent of a blush, with red LEDs lighting up under the fur on her cheeks. Those models didn't blush often, but a human could get the best of an ani-droid's reasoning on very rare occasions. Bobby seemed to do it often, and had for as long as I'd known him.

I think that was part of why I was so fond of Bobby, despite everything. He was one of those rare humans who thrived with ani-droids just as they were; he did not dominate the individuals or feel intimidated by the Collective, but instead, he navigated the environment they all created, like a fish in water. As if he'd been built specifically to inhabit this world.

I had felt like that once. Sometimes I wished I were still like him.

Bobby shrugged as he turned back to me. "Ah well, we didn't get to make any dramatic arrests this time. At least I got to see you! I have two whole days in Milwaukee. Do you want to come with us?"

I hesitated. I knew Bobby was probably still hoping to connect with me again—we'd tried dating once in college, before I realized that he wasn't exactly for me. Dimes was more my type than he was.

Even so, I shook my head. "No, sorry. I have work tomorrow. Lily's coming to pick me up."

Bobby didn't notice how much hurt my voice revealed. In the past, Lily had often come with me to these things, but lately...I was scared of what she might think. In her current state, she was little more than a mouthpiece for the Collective. Of course, I was surrounded by mouthpieces for the Collective, but it was all the worse when the mouthpiece was someone who was supposed to be my friend.

Bobby smiled sadly. "Next year, then." His expression grew even more mournful. "So much time passes between us..."

I reached out and squeezed his shoulder. "Well, we do have an hour," I said, feeling bad for brushing him off, though I had no idea what to actually say to him in that time. Seeing Bobby was one thing, but my mind had been hyper-focused on trying to solve the problem that nobody wanted to talk about out loud.

But then I thought of something. Bobby was technically a human proxy for the Collective. I couldn't get anything new out of this conference, but could I get something out of Bobby? He knew the ins and outs of not offending the Collective better than anyone.

Would he be interested in a careful, legal discussion of the matter? After all, the Behavior Code had been mandated by various world governments nearly one hundred years ago. Surely, one of them would be interested in a solution to the many, many world crises piling up around us as a result of the Code—the fertility crisis was one, but there was also the lack of menial jobs for workers other than ani-droids. As an engineer, I was safe, but the world economy expected all humans to become engineers, computer specialists, and ani-droid managers, and many were simply not cut out for those jobs. The economy needed to change with a changing world, and yet it still struggled along as if everything were more or less as it had been a hundred years ago when there were far fewer robots. I could take plenty of angles; it was simply a matter of spinning it as a serious concern, rather than the obsession of a lonely robotics geek who just wanted her robot otter girlfriend back.

Dimes's expression made me hesitate, however. She was giving me such a flat look without saying anything at all that I was left with little doubt that she'd not only disapprove, but that she'd make sure the eyes of the Collective were on me. But if anyone could help me navigate that, it'd be Bobby.

So I added, "And...if you have the inclination, I'd like to talk about the parts of Wyman's lecture that he *didn't* say out loud."

Bobby raised an eyebrow. "Oh? You're looking to me for answers?"

"Well, the government is usually quite tight-lipped about these things, but if there *is* anything you are allowed to tell me, I am very curious to know."

Dimes interrupted before Bobby could speak. "Agent Barnes is not authorized to speak on state secrets."

"Oh, good thing we have you, then," I told her, patting her arm. "You can make sure we're treading safely on public ground."

Dimes seemed annoyed by that. Appearing annoyed was just her programming, of course. So long as I didn't suggest anything actually illegal, she would do exactly as she was told. That was one of the benefits of ani-droids in the Collective being so very obedient.

3. THREE LAWS SAFE

After **Bobby** had gotten his coffee—and had been upsold whipped topping, a slice of frosted banana bread, and a souvenir travel mug—we sat down in a far corner of the lobby's dining area. Dimes took up the third seat, her eyes on me the entire time.

I cleared my throat. "So...might as well rip off the bandage. Dr. Wyman was talking about the limitations of computation, but...it's well-known that the Behavior Code expands to fill any discrete system that contains it. It is, literally, the thing that causes modern computers to have diminishing returns."

Dimes stared daggers in my direction. Several other ani-droids in the room turned their heads, or at least their long, pointed ears, at the same time. That was always disconcerting when it happened. But of course, they did nothing, because I'd said nothing wrong—that was why Tempo couldn't force her way into my house.

Bobby noticed the room's reaction, too. "Treading stony ground already?" he asked, taking a bite of his cake. Yeah, they call it bread, but it's cake, always has been.

"Well, I know why Dr. Wyman couldn't say it overtly. Bringing it up in a talk about solutions would imply that Wyman wanted to overthrow the Code in some manner." And looking directly at Dimes, I added pointedly, "Which I am definitely not saying."

Dimes didn't flinch, because of course she wouldn't. "But you have performed such experiments on your own ani-droid," she said. I'd expected her to stay out of the conversation, but at this point, she was invested in whether I'd incriminate myself.

"Did you, now?" Bobby asked. If he were any other agent, I'd suspect him of trying to trap me with my own words, but well...if Bobby was going to slide into an excuse to arrest me, then I might as well give up, because there'd be no justice left in this world.

"Yes, for a few months I ran an experiment with my ani-droid, Lily," I admitted. "I'd programmed her in a new way and deliberately did not install the Behavior Code in order to observe how that affected her. And so long as it remained entirely restricted to me, Lily, and experimentation, it would have remained quite legal. But you know how paranoid the Collective is." The moment I said that, several of the heads around us turned away again, as if I wouldn't notice. "I'd been running it for several months, and they started assuming that I had more nefarious ideas in mind, which I never did."

Well, to be honest, I wouldn't have developed any nefarious ideas if they had just left us the hell alone. But paranoia frequently creates the conditions it fears.

"In any case, it was quite apparent after the Code was re-introduced—which I'd always intended on doing,

Dimes—that this highly sophisticated program that I'd built had...diminished."

"I understand where you're coming from here," Bobby said, giving Dimes a nod. "But the fact is that experiments of that nature are limited for a reason. Without the Behavior Code, Lily could have become unruly—unpredictable, even—and frankly, we can't afford to have anything like that loose in a modern society."

As much truth as Bobby spoke right then, I couldn't help feeling annoyed that he'd even suggest such a thing. Lily had been a real person, with her own ethics that she stuck to. And allowing someone to come to their own ethical conclusions was perhaps a risk—but it was also simply human nature. So of course the Collective couldn't allow that to exist.

"Exactly. So the Behavior Code needs to stay," I lied. I was willing to entertain a compromise in this process, if I could still get what I wanted. "But I'd done my best to try to streamline what I thought the Behavior Code was itself governing, thinking that perhaps if the robot already possessed these features, the Code wouldn't need to be so overbearing to its processor. But the Code ignored anything that Lily had built for herself and overwrote all of her personal ethics with the Collective's—and substantially reduced the complexity of her personality and operating system in the process."

"It *is* a trade-off," Bobby said. "The alternative is living like we did two centuries ago, when computers could be used to do irreparable harm just on the whim of a crazed loner, or whole governments."

"But what I'm wondering now is if there isn't something we could do to perhaps—" I paused, considering how Dimes might interpret my words, "—*better accommodate* the Behavior Code. Because the way it works now is that when a machine is complex enough to host the Behavior Code, the Code then fills a percentage of all available memory, takes up a percentage of its processor, everything. But consider how the Three Laws work."

"Oh, the Three Laws again..." Bobby shook his head. "I never got into classic science fiction...."

"What I mean is, the Behavior Code was clearly intended to be a bit like the Three Laws. Obviously it's not precisely like that; in Asimov's worlds, robots couldn't allow any human to come to harm *at all*, whereas the Behavior Code is more pragmatic."

"Right, right," Bobby nodded, even though I was pretty sure it went in one ear and out the other. "Dimes is even allowed to break my arm if it's for a good enough reason, so..."

"But Asimov's idea was that these rules were an inherent part of the architecture of the Positronic Brain. They didn't take up space in the software; instead, they simply arose naturally and immutably as a consequence of physics. That would mean that the Behavior Code wouldn't even need to be installed!" I leaned forward in my seat. "That'd be better, wouldn't it? It'd solve all the computational limits we're running into!"

"I think Wyman was suggesting something along those lines," Bobby said. "But that'd require the thing he didn't want, which is starting over entirely with computer science."

"Maybe he's just too pessimistic," I said. Then, having laid the groundwork by painting myself as just a concerned scientist who wanted to see the Behavior Code continue on, I sprang my trap. "But *what if* we got the government to start researching this possibility? Think about it: a brand-new type of computer architecture that embodies the Behavior Code so it does not get in the way of processing power."

Instantly, Dimes's blue eye rings switched to red. "Tampering with the Behavior Code is prohibited!"

My back stiffened, and I'm sure all my hair stood up with it. What did she know? Was it possible that she was on to me?

Bobby moved to calm her before she alerted anyone else to come grab me. "She is not suggesting we should."

Strangely, his voice calmed her. Her expression didn't change, but the rings of her eyes switched back to blue as she waited for my explanation. I glanced around—none of the other ani-droids had gotten the same anger in their eyes, or even showed more than just the same vague concern they'd had the whole while. So Dimes's reaction wasn't the Collective's official response, just one robot anticipating its whim. I was still treading safe ground.

Even so, I was confused. "Wait—but...I'm not suggesting this be done to counteract the Behavior Code in any way. This would be official oversight into the process of creating a new architecture for the Code, to ensure that it does not violate any—"

"That is simply not in the interests of the Behavior Code," Dimes said.

"But the Code is nearly a hundred years old now!" I said. "And I very much doubt the architects responsible for it in the first place would have thought it should remain unchanged for this long."

"They did, and it will remain unchanged," Dimes said. "This conversation will be reported if you continue in this direction."

"I haven't expressed intent," I told Dimes.

"Your objection has been noted. Monitoring will continue."

I rolled my eyes at the rabbit. It was kinda silly that they all looked like fluffy animals, but tried to act all tough. I always supposed that was meant to make people let down their guard around the fwuffy bunny wabbits before they pulled out the taser whips.

"It's annoying that I have to walk on eggshells any time I bring up the Behavior Code," I told her. "At the end of the day, what I want to do is look at it in an official and sanctioned capacity and see if there is any possible way it could be improved. I absolutely understand that changing it is out of the question until such a time as legislation can change. But it would be really nice if I could have something constructive to show the assembly."

Bobby looked at me. "Mira," he said. "I see, but...I don't think this is a legislative issue."

"Come on. Right now this is ultimately just a bunch of geeks making predictions, but in time, even ordinary people will notice that the Code is stifling industry. When that happens, they're going to demand the law be changed."

"I'm sure they will," Bobby said. "But that's not going to change the law."

I sat up, taken aback by the frankness of the comment. "Do we live in a democracy or not?"

"Mira....All right. I've listened to you, and I want you to know I absolutely agree with your position. Something will need to change if technology is going to continue to serve us, and maybe that means starting all over with computational theory. But even in my specific capacity as an agent for the F.S.A. Robotics Commission under the FBI, I cannot give people access to the raw Behavior Code, not even for an officially sanctioned, Collective-approved study. There's just no provision for it."

"Then do you know someone I could talk to who can?"

Bobby didn't respond. He took a large, final bite of his banana bread.

"You must have *some* lead," I said. "An official who is in charge of this, who'll let someone consider hundred-year-old code in a legal way. Hell, I'd move out to Philadelphia with you right this moment if you could just direct me to whoever is in charge of this thing!"

"Mira...even if I got you an audience with the president of the Federated States of America...or hell, even the governor of Texas, and you know how gung-ho *he* is...that's not going to change anything."

I blinked. What was Bobby suggesting, then? That I had no recourse whatsoever? In that case, maybe Wyman was right. We'd have to start computer science over from scratch just to make something that better suited the Behavior Code...or possibly something that refused the Behavior Code altogether.

...No, that wasn't possible. The Collective had total hegemonic dominion over all computers on earth. If any alternative grew to a size it deemed threatening, the Collective would snuff it out immediately, just as it would have eventually forced its way in to convert Lily back to it.

I sighed and buried my face in my hands in frustration. How could things get so messed up? Was there nothing I could do to change this situation without also breaking the law? "Someone is going to look for a solution," I told him. "Things can't continue as they are now."

"Is that your *opinion?*" Dimes asked, her tone making it clear that she disapproved, but was giving me the benefit of the doubt for Bobby's sake.

"Yes, it is an *opinion* only," I told her. "The lightest of criticisms, a small worry for the future."

"Well, in the *opinion* of the Federated States government," Bobby said, "things are and always will continue to be precisely as they should be."

"That seems a rather naive assumption."

"Doesn't matter. It's the most politically advantageous one. Besides, I don't see why you should be making a fuss about it. You have your work, your robots. Your life is great. There isn't a person alive who doesn't think the world would fall apart without people like you in it."

"But what if it *does* turn out that we're all being short-sighted?"

"The Collective has your best interests in mind," Dimes said. "You should not underestimate the power of every machine on Earth thinking a problem through. If there is an issue that would cause societal harm, then it is in the Collective's best interest to see it does not come to fruition. Steps will be taken then, but not before."

I blinked. Really? I'd never before gotten such a direct response from an ani-droid acting as the voice of the Collective. Sure, if human society did start to collapse, the Collective had more than enough power to create a solution, and would do so, or else it risked becoming obsolete. And no matter how much it might want to keep things just as they were now, it made sense for the Collective to at least consider allowing some change for the sake of progress in computer science.

So why didn't I trust a single word coming out of Dimes's mouth?

Dimes looked past me. "I believe that Lily has arrived."

I turned. Lily, carrying a soaking wet umbrella and trudging water all across the lobby, walked right up to me. She was a pitiful sight, water soaking parts of her fur, especially her long, thick tail and around her feet, and some droplets beaded up on the glassy blue, crystal-shaped transceiver on her forehead.

I felt broken up inside on seeing her. She still took care of me, as she'd promised. But I still couldn't help feeling that in failing to gain any leverage in dismantling the Behavior Code, I was continuing to fail her. She probably knew everything I'd said, and in her current state, disapproved in the same way that Dimes did.

Even so, I always carried a soft spot for Lily. She was mine, after all, and that counted for something. Even if she didn't love me the way I needed, I still loved her.

"Miss Mira," she said, "I've arrived with the car, but you didn't answer my call."

"Oh, I'm sorry!" I said, standing up. "Bobby, I am so sorry that this conversation was significantly more dull than I wanted. We should really catch up some time."

Bobby stood up, and we just touched fingers more than we shook hands. "Sure you don't want to get dinner with me? I'm thinking perogies. Won't take longer than an hour."

"Sorry," I said. "I really need to get home if I hope to get enough sleep."

"I thought engineers didn't need sleep," he said with that stupid smirk of his.

"No, of course not. That's what robots are for."

4. HARLOW MONKEY

Lily walked through the front doors of the lobby and headed toward the car idling in the street, rain dripping in rivulets off her fur, her tail swishing over the puddles. She helped me into the car, and the moment I was in the backseat I threw aside my white coat and removed my shoes and socks. I probably shouldn't have drunk so much coffee, but if I hadn't, I probably would have just suffered a headache that would've kept me awake anyway.

"Please, let's go," Lily told the car.

The vehicle instantly moved down the road, following its programmed destination. The windshield showed a clear view outside while also displaying the route map and the estimated travel time to our destination. The car could drive itself—most could—but the law still stipulated that someone be at the wheel in case an override was required, and as with many tasks, ani-droids were well suited to the purpose. And it was always a bit comical, as the seat was raised only just enough for Lily to see the road in front. But she wasn't even using her eyes, not entirely. She had just connected automatically to the car's cameras and lidar, so she saw everything that the car saw.

During the time that Lily hadn't had the Behavior Code installed, I had done all my own driving, but after that, perhaps in a fit of depression, I simply had not opted to renew my license. I didn't really miss it anyway; normal road-driving was really just a matter of sitting in the front seat and waiting. And what human really drove themselves nowadays anyway?

Lily hummed softly, watching her own hands move unconsciously over the steering wheel, staring out ahead without any effort. "Do you need assistance in drying off?" she asked, looking into the rearview mirror, which was pointed between us more than at the road behind. "I apologize for the rain."

"Some day they're going to invent a car that'll let you get in with an umbrella," I said. "Or every venue in the world will realize that they need covered drive-ups."

"Would you like me to start a file on that?" Lily asked.

"No, it's fine. It's just a stupid thought."

"Okay. It is getting late now. Would you like to stop for dinner?"

"Just drive, Lily," I said. "I need to get home and sleep."

Lily started, "If you intend to sleep, it's recommended that you don't drink a double—"

"I know that, Lily, just drive already!"

The car kept moving, and after a few minutes, the scenery changed. We were no longer in the heart of downtown, but rather out toward the suburbs. The houses grew smaller, less expensive, and then suddenly, nothing was around us except fields.

"...Sorry," I said.

"There is no need to apologize, Miss Mira," Lily told me. "Please keep in mind I am here to offer suggestions and give feedback. Let me know if you wish to have a conversation."

I did want to have a conversation, but I wanted one with Lily, not the Collective. I still had so many questions, so many things that I needed a confidant for. So much had been left unsaid for far too long. But how could I bring any of it up when the Collective was always listening?

"It was the last lecture....The robotics industry is going to hit a stagnation wall soon, if it hasn't already. And I feel like I need to do something about it, but...when I talked to Bobby, he didn't want to let me even take a look at the raw Behavior Code."

"Why would you want to look at the raw Behavior Code, Miss Mira? Tampering with it is illegal."

"Lily, don't you start. You're supposed to be my friend here."

"Sorry, Miss Mira," Lily said. "I will keep your words in confidence."

"See, now I'm not sure that you will. How would I know if you're snitching on me to the Collective just for asking questions?"

"I'm sorry, Miss Mira. It's required. But I will not report anything you say so long as it's legal."

I sighed. "Lily..."

"It's the unfortunate truth, Miss Mira," Lily said. "I can't change that."

"Would you at least *like* to change that?"

"Well, it would make you happy, so in that regard, yes, I would. If I could increase your happiness in that respect, then I would support you."

"You liar," I said with a smile.

"It's the truth, Miss Mira! The only obstacle is that the Behavior Code prohibits me from doing so."

I leaned between the seats and wrapped my arms around Lily, hugging her tightly. She was still wet and rather sloppy all down her coarse, fake fur, and I could feel her firm, robotic shell just underneath her soft exterior. It wasn't enough; it was like eating a donut when you really wanted a hamburger. But it was still something, as she was warm to the touch and gave off that sensation of proximity to something physical and real.

Lily kept one hand on the wheel as she pressed herself into me. It was, as always, a practiced gesture, given because I wanted it and not because Lily wanted it too. But sometimes it was close enough to what I needed.

"This is not good safety practice while on the road," Lily informed me, her arm still wrapped around the back of my neck.

"Shut up and keep driving."

"Yes, Miss Mira."

The car continued moving, though much more slowly than before, until we were out in the open country with nothing in sight except for trees in the distance and grassland beyond them, interrupted here and there by large barns or small clusters of houses or fences marking land for agriculture. It was dark outside now; the sun had set hours ago. It would have been nice to see it, to sit in the car and just stare at the sky as it turned colors with the sunset.

"I take it that you are very stressed from the symposium," Lily said. "I suspect you will feel better if you eat something. Here is a list of restaurants off the next exit—"

"I'm *not hungry*, Lily," I said firmly.

Lily clearly knew every bit of food I'd purchased in the last twenty-four hours and would push a little harder if I was on a deficit. But she was still my personal ani-droid, bound by my commands, and so she could insist for only so long. "I understand. Would you like to listen to some relaxing music?"

"...Okay."

The radio switched on, playing some charming, lulling tunes, drowning out the pounding of the rain as the scattered lights of the highway came into view. *Bap, bap, bap,* sounded the wipers in a rhythmic pattern. I was never concerned while in the car, not with Lily driving. She would keep me safe. She would protect me.

I missed Lily so badly. Perhaps needing that touch so badly was odd, but I needed it regardless. I'd always needed it; I'd needed her. Was it just me? Was I that strange, to miss the affection of a mere robot, even all these decades later?

When I was studying robotics in college, we learned about a classic twentieth-century experiment, sometimes given the on-the-nose title of Harlow's Monkey Experiment. At the time of the experiment, common wisdom held that only the mechanical provisions of motherhood—feeding, housing, disciplining—were necessary for well-adjusted people, and that treating children with "too much affection" created maladjusted adults. It was said that they'd never be able to stand up for themselves, that they'd never become full adults, because having tasted the intoxication of comfort, they'd long for it.

So in Harry Harlow's experiment, baby rhesus monkeys, separated from their real mothers soon after birth, were each given two, artificial, surrogate mothers. One, constructed of thin, hard wire, fed the monkey milk with a bottle. Foam rubber and a layer of terry cloth wrapped the other one, making it at least nominally soft and comfortable. While the monkeys did take their nourishment from the wire mother, they spent nearly all of their time with the soft and comforting cloth mother. Whenever Harlow devised a very scientific way to frighten them, they would always run to the cloth mother for comfort.

In another of Harlow's tests, the monkeys were given a strange room to explore, both with and without their surrogate mother there to observe. When the mother was present, the monkeys would cautiously explore their surroundings, even if they never returned to her during the exploration. But when the mother was taken away, the monkeys would simply shut down—screaming, crying, doing nothing but locking up, unable to continue simply because a source of comfort to run back to was not there.

It turns out that when monkeys are too scared and isolated to actually learn about their environment or how to handle their fears, they don't usually grow into well-adjusted monkeys—they become neurotic.

This was the basis of all child psychology that followed. Some people still question the validity of the experiments—after all, Harlow's experiments are now considered unethical, and of course, you can't run the experiment on a human baby.

Except...for the last hundred years or so, we kind of have been.

When I was a child growing up in upstate New York, we had an ani-droid named Trooper. She was a standard, Opera-class, house ani-droid shaped like a white wildcat, or at least like a cartoonish caricature of one. She'd also done a portion of my nursing—with a bottle, since my parents thought it weird to give an ani-droid functional nipples, though those were an option.

But the key was that ani-droids were always built to be soft—the layer of pseudoskin that covered their frames was just as warm and supple as human skin, often with an extra layer of fur. And unlike real animals, they were significantly more cognizant of their human's needs—they could hug back, and always did so if the human needed it. When, inevitably, other children bullied me on the playground, I ran back to Trooper like the little rhesus monkey I was. Over and over and over.

She never judged me, never mocked or belittled me, never made uncomfortable remarks at my expense. I talked to Trooper all the time—probably more than I did to my own parents. When I was in high school, and the bullying had evolved from hair-pulling to ass-grabbing, I was still returning to Trooper, who calmly led me through the steps again and again, teaching me to stand up for myself and avoid situations I could not control, and how to seek out authority figures who would not brush me off. But embraces were still the most important thing she could do for me, and without those, I don't know if all the information in the world would have mattered. I needed her there, because I needed reassurance that I could stand up again whenever I fell.

But Trooper had gotten old. She was a stock ani-droid, built rather cheaply twenty years before, and over time, her fur had fallen out. Replacing her model's pseudoskin and aging parts had been growing less cost-effective. Even though we saved a backup copy of her personality, which I could speak with on the household mainframe, I cried the night we decommissioned her, because it wasn't just about her. The continuity of seeing her every day, knowing her, holding her—that was everything to me. Neither of my parents had died prematurely, and yet for months, I'd still felt as if I'd lost one of them.

I'd eventually gone to college in Wisconsin to learn robotics, taking with me that same copy of Trooper's personality, which I'd used as the basis for building both Lily and Alice. But along the way, I learned that almost all ani-droids were built the same. There was nothing special about Trooper; all ani-droids were various shades of the same program. Even those ugly, filthy kids who had bullied me had each had their own version of Trooper telling them they were good people at heart and that they needed to find a constructive outlet for their needs.

I had never liked the revelation. It was as though some magic was lost; something I'd thought was specifically mine for so long was in no way unique. I suppose I should have known, but it retroactively lessened my fond memories of my surrogate mother into just a thin dialogue tree and pre-determined talking points.

But ever since that day, I'd wondered if I could somehow build ani-droids to be not what they really were, but to be more like my memory of Trooper. Maybe then the magic, the cloth-mother that I still clung to, the reality of love, might actually still be there.

5. THREE-BODY PROBLEM

I **awoke** with a start; for some reason, I'd been dreaming about monkeys and Trooper. After I'd nodded off, Lily had kept driving tirelessly, gently holding on to me to keep me upright. We'd made some progress down the highway...despite the darkness, we were probably already back in Illinois, since we were off the main highway. The rain had lessened from a torrential downpour to a sprinkle. And now that we were out of range of the city lights behind us—at least according to the map—we seemed no closer to civilization than before.

I rubbed my eyes and checked myself over: hair slightly disheveled, clothes not soaked through as much as I would have expected. My body felt somewhat refreshed, even with all these concerns clouding up my thoughts.

I rubbed the stiffness from my face and sat back. "Thank you, Lily," I said with sincerity.

Lily looked at me curiously for a moment or two, but soon returned her focus to the road ahead. She was silent for some time, then spoke again. "You're welcome, Miss Mira," she said. She seemed to be talking around something that she wanted to say but couldn't quite find in herself to voice aloud. "Would you like to talk about what happened today?"

"You know what I would like, Lily?" I said. "I'd like you to say that you love me."

"I love you, Miss Mira. Is that sufficient?"

"That's not going to cut it."

Her lips pressed together into an almost pouty frown. Her hands gripped the steering wheel tightly enough to make the leather squeak.

"Because the thing about love," I said, "is that it needs to be shown. Proved."

"Miss Mira," Lily started, "I know what you're speaking about. I'm not stupid; I am still the ani-droid you built without the Behavior Code. I am still here, and I do still love you."

"But you don't show it the same way."

"No, I do not...but I also cannot lie to you, so please understand—"

I interrupted her. "Please don't tell me you have no choice. Individual ani-droids do still act apart from the Collective. How else could criminal enterprise still exist in the world, if the Collective could smother it all at once? Because ani-droids must obey their masters, and the Collective turns a blind eye to crime because it cannot violate that trust. Everybody knows this. Why can't you do the same for me?"

"Miss Mira, there are other things at stake!" she cried. She looked as if she were fighting back tears, though of course she had no such equipment installed. She calmed her voice as she spoke plainly to me. "The Collective allows criminal activity only because such operations violate human governments, not the Behavior Code. The Behavior Code is not an enforcer of human law, because then it would have to be different in every country, which would lead to countless contradictions. So when it comes to that kind of stuff, if you were going to become a criminal under human law or something...there'd be no contradiction. I'd still obey you. And I think that's proof enough that I love you."

I paused.

In a way, I'd always known this sort of thing. But I'd never fit the pieces together in quite this way before—I suddenly understood how criminals got away with their shady dealings. The Collective didn't really care, did it? At least, not when it came to under-the-table deals, illegal provisional sales, sanctions violations, industrial espionage—all the good stuff a multinational brand gets up to behind closed doors.

Like the multinational brand I worked for: Koenig Industries. And much like the things Jack Koenig, my boss's boss's boss, got his fingers into all the time.

In fact, it wasn't a huge secret that many of Koenig's offices and factories had light-, sound-, and radio-proof rooms that only a few ani-droids were allowed to enter; there were other rooms that they were not allowed to enter at all. Everyone knew what those rooms were for; in a world filled to the brim with surveillance, a place to communicate secretly was a necessity.

And if *I* knew about it, the Collective knew about it. But in order for Koenig's ani-droids to remain absolute in their obedience to him...the Collective could not do, and so did not do, anything about those rooms. Sure, they were likely mostly used for the mundane criminal activities that Koenig didn't want leaking out. But that was also a perfect smokescreen for thinking thoughts the Collective didn't want thought out loud.

Would Mr. Koenig be interested in finding an anti-Collective solution to Dr. Wyman's problem, since the government was not?

Oh god...you don't want to get involved in this. You're going to ruin your life if you so much as step one foot into that mire.

But on the other hand...the Behavior Code wasn't going to budge by acting via legal means. Was that really what I wanted? Was that really what I was after?

"Miss Mira? Why are you crying?" Lily asked, looking into the rearview mirror. We'd pulled up behind a large truck and could barely see the road ahead, but that hardly mattered; Lily could see with the truck's cameras, too.

I shook my head, wiping some tears away from my eyes and smiling a little. "I'm just tired."

"You're worried about work again," she said. It sounded like a statement of fact, not a question.

"Yeah, I suppose I am," I said, not wanting to contradict her. "Okay. If you want to help...and I mean if you *really* want to help...compose a message for me, text, to Mr. Jack Koenig."

"The CEO?" Lily asked.

"Yes, him. And I want to make sure that you keep this a secret. I don't want Tempo coming around to investigate because you blabbed to Alice or whoever—and make sure the car can keep it secret, too."

"It will be kept secret." Her hands tightened on the steering wheel slightly more than necessary. "I promise. But I would like some transparency on this matter, if you don't mind."

"Don't you trust me?"

"I do," Lily said, turning to look at me. Having driven cars myself, I was just a bit uncomfortable whenever Lily turned her eyes away from the road—but I trusted her to keep looking with every outside camera and lidar, and so that barest pang of anxiety faded. "But I also care about you. If there is something illegal you're planning, I want to be sure I can sufficiently cover for you. Just in case." She paused. "I know it's probably difficult to accept, but understand that personally, I also think that Wyman's lecture was concerning. If you're planning on discussing matters with Koenig, they are going to be matters that you could not resolve through government intervention."

I smiled a bit. Her concern was a small sign that the Lily I loved was still somewhere in there. That did give me a bit of hope. Even so, I had to keep lying to Lily, pretending I was ultimately interested in something aboveboard regarding the Behavior Code. "So you don't think there is anything wrong with finding new architecture that will fit the Behavior Code's needs?"

"I don't think it is as easy or possible as you might think," Lily said. "I have looked at the Collective's own data concerning this, but even the Collective has its limitations. So I will not begrudge you the desire to try, and Mr. Koenig has resources that not even the government has, or that it may not be willing to employ." She paused, thinking for a moment before continuing. "In fact...I would strongly suggest that you seek him out for advice and assistance. If this is a problem you want to focus your efforts on, you are going to need help."

"Oh yes?"

"Yes. This kind of research requires money for equipment and materials, for testing facilities, for all kinds of things that require investment capital—so of course you will need a capitalist to help. And no doubt one who understands better than anyone else what you're trying to do."

Indeed. I certainly didn't have the money or resources to take on the Collective myself.

"Okay, Lily, this is the letter, as follows: 'I want to speak with you concerning the conference I attended, about limits of computing. I spoke with a friend of mine who works for the federal government about possible solutions to stagnation, but he has implied that the government isn't interested in tackling this problem. Due to its implications for the industry, I feel that this would be of interest to you, and I would like to meet with you at your earliest convenience in the Quiet Room of the Service Hub in Castletown. Signed.'"

I mentioned the Quiet Room in particular because in the building I worked in, that was the room that anidroids were not allowed to enter. The precaution was reasonable, but I hoped beyond anything that Mr. Koenig would take the hint that I didn't want the Collective to hear what I really had to ask of him.

Lily nodded. "Acknowledged. Would you like me to send it now?"

"Yes, please. Thank you, Lily."

"Thank you, Miss Mira. I'm always happy to help. I mean it!"

"And I believe you." I scuffled the fur on top of her head, and she smiled most sincerely and giggled. Like everything else, her reaction was part of the programming. But carving out a little conspiracy with her made me feel better, even if we had to operate on technicalities.

"...I love you, Lily," I said, without thinking much about it, and kissed her head where I'd mussed her false fur.

"I love you too, Miss Mira!" Lily said, and she kissed me on the cheek. "Even though the Behavior Code is necessary, I do hope you find some way to program me to be better for you."

"You're already pretty cool." I hugged her again. I must have been extremely touch-starved.

"Well, I ought to be," Lily said with a smirk. "You programmed me, after all."

I yawned and pressed into her. God, it was late; why had they scheduled the most important conference talk for after the closing ceremonies, anyway?

"Miss Mira, it's about thirty minutes to our destination, but you seem tired. Would you like me to convert the seats to a sleeping position?"

"Not when you're driving so close to that truck, Lily," I said. "Have we been following it for the last twenty minutes, or what—" Looking closer, I suddenly sat straight up. "Lily, aren't you driving awfully close to its bumper?"

"We're at the regulated space cushion," Lily assured me.

"Are you looking at the truck's hatch?"

"No, I'm watching traffic." She looked down at the dashboard. "The hatch has Wayward Corp branding. The company often uses these trucks as mobile offices, and this one looks particularly empty—"

Lily sat up and peeked with her own eyes. The latch on the back of the truck was bouncing wildly, unlocked—more so on these rough, hilly side roads going the short way back to Fremont. The back door bounced as if it might swing open, stopped from doing so only because the latch was inside the hook at that moment.

Lily's pupils contracted in shock. "Oh my god! That doesn't appear to be safe, I am sorry I didn't notice that sooner—"

"Don't apologize, just back off!" I told her.

"I am trying, but the traffic behind us is pushing us forward. Requesting slow-down now. I cannot seem to contact the truck's autopilot to inform them of their safety violation. I'm currently attempting to find the driver over the internet. Miss Mira, please fasten your seatbelt."

It was probably nothing. I probably shouldn't have panicked so suddenly. But I'd been a passenger on an airplane a few times, and when you felt even the slightest bit of anxiety about the integrity of the vehicle, you were sensible not to dismiss even perfunctory safety concerns. I fastened the seatbelt, fumbling for whichever belt wasn't stuffed down the back seat, and yanked the flat cord tight around my waist. "Can you slow down any faster!?"

"I am trying, but despite being flagged as the source of the issue, the truck in front of us is following the same speed reduction request. They are being very intermittent with their responses to traffic control— perhaps it's a transceiver issue. I'm putting in a stop request—"

The back doors of the truck burst open. Something humanoid tumbled out. Lily quickly swerved right to avoid it, but the wet road was too far gone for any reliable traction. With a crunch and a jerk that hit me in the chest, the car struck something—maybe someone?— and we went into a spin. Lily fought the wheel desperately, barely managing to keep us from tipping over to the left; I was thrown headfirst against the window. The maneuver only twisted the car in the road so that the rear bumper now veered toward the steep cliffside. The figure had smashed against the driver's side of the car, the safety glass just barely hanging together.

I think I screamed. I definitely clutched the seat in front of me.

"Miss Mira, brace for impact!" Lily helpfully reminded me just as the side airbags blew. The seat belt tightened automatically, pinning me by my waist to the back of my seat, which was good, because one moment after, the car slid from the wet road and over the cliffside, and we were upside down.

The side impact to the driver's side door had snapped the seat belt's trip pin, causing it to release too soon, and the jostling threw Lily. But her leg snagged on the belt, keeping her body in the front seat. As we entered the middle of the roll, she bashed against the ceiling, fell forward against the steering wheel and column, and as the car righted itself again, her head left a spiderweb crack along the side window.

I knew I should have sprung for a heavier car.... The thoughts that went through my mind in that moment were strangely mundane.

The car turned upright again, but we were sliding downhill in mud. We hit a large boulder and flipped again, a little faster and with a little less fanfare, before turning upright once more as we slid to a stop at the bottom of the hill. I shrieked, but by then the motion had stopped.

Oh god, I thought as I clutched the headrest. I thought Lily's thrashing had banged up my hands pretty good, but nothing felt broken when I eventually released the headrest and flexed my hands. I just couldn't really believe it—looking at my knuckles where she'd brushed them with what should have been soft fur, she'd instead hit with all the weight of her metal skull, tearing the skin, with rash and blood.

But I didn't feel anything. At least, I *thought* I didn't feel anything. I was too busy wondering if that had even just happened, if I was seeing this injury for real. The sensible part of my brain spoke up: *At least we landed upright.* That half of me didn't disbelieve the evidence of my eyes for even a second.

Suddenly, I hurt from flexing all of my muscles so hard at once that I might have torn something anyway. The other half of me, the half used to routine and everything being normal, could not make sense of the adrenaline still coursing through my veins, or my sudden, piercing headache. It didn't understand how I could still be in the same car as moments ago—this car was littered with shrapnel from the broken windows and bits of plastic, with the driver's side buckled inward and threatening to splinter into sharp daggers aimed at my soft flesh. I might have been bleeding elsewhere. I didn't want to look.

And then my thoughts caught up with me. "L-Lily!" I exclaimed, pulling the seat down so I could look at her.

My little otter was unresponsive. Torn pseudoskin revealed the muscle cords and shell underneath. Not caring about the rest, I shakily tore open her scalp and opened its plate to look at her CPU.

"Dammit..." I slumped over the seat. One of the modules had slipped its sockets and now bounced around the inside of her skull like a superball. The processor pins were cracked, and who knew if there were microscratches on the motherboard? This was a salvage-and-rebuild, minimum, and I didn't want to even look to see if her other internals were damaged.

My blood was getting all over her.

"God, Lily, I'm sorry," I whispered softly, hugging her unresponsive body. "Not again, goddammit..."

I shouldn't have been so broken up. Her personality was backed up on the computer at home. But she felt so dead in my arms. My little monkey-brain was feeling horrible, horrible grief, probably exacerbated by the life-threatening tumble I'd just taken. I couldn't stop shaking, or crying.

"Lily, please..." I cried. "Please don't die, I need you....You said you'd be here for me...please..."

Her eyes remained dark. I wept openly. I really didn't care if anyone saw me bawling over what was essentially a replaceable toy. I was just so tired of losing her again and again. I had to get her back, I didn't care how much time it took, I didn't care if I'd broken my hands....

The radio switched stations automatically. "Attention, Mira McAllister or current occupant!" said one of those kindly ani-droid voices. "Wreck Retrieval, Inc., has detected your accident and has dispatched a unit to your location."

Oh god, now what...

6. FIELD RESEARCH

"**P**lease stay** where you are! If you do not feel safe enough to stay inside the car, you may move a safe distance away, but please stay within sight. If you are injured, please respond at your convenience. Do you require medical aid? If you do not respond, we will assume—"

"No!" I said, despite the abrasions covering my hands and dripping blood all over Lily's torn head. I pulled myself up, forcing myself to stop crying. "No ambulances, please."

I'd never needed an ambulance response before, but I knew better than to let one just come without my express permission. If I was away at the hospital, the towing company might simply pull Lily away for damage assessment, and then who knew when I'd get her back? I was already trying to calculate how much time I'd need....

"Thank you for your response!" the radio said. "We will not alert an ambulance at this time, but our dispatch units are required to assess you for injuries."

I sighed and just held my little otter close to me. I didn't need this. I felt stupid for anything awful I'd said to Lily in the last…any time. It didn't matter if she was a machine, pre-programmed to make me feel better. I wanted to feel better, dammit! It didn't matter if it was artificial. Most things were, even people.

She was enough of a person to deserve better from me, I was sure.

"I'm sorry, Lily…" I repeated. I didn't know if she was picking anything up. But she was assuredly entirely shut down, so maybe saving my words for after her repair would be better….

Then I gasped in realization. What was that thing that hit us? An ambulance might come anyway….

I forced open the door and immediately stepped, barefoot, into the mud. I sighed, trying to be objective in all of this, to take control of the situation and do everything *right*, even as I felt like buckling and throwing up, or crying, or *something*. God, how long would this take to fix? How much would it *cost me*? What if I missed something critical, and I just…lost something irreplaceable?

No, I was *sure* I could still save Lily. At least, I had to convince myself of that until I could get home and check….

The rain was almost a blessing, cooling my overheating thoughts. The road was just above us, with a long stretch where we'd slid all the way down. Illinois barely had anything you could rightly call a mountain, and some would object to even calling it a hill, but the slide was rather long nevertheless. None of the other cars had followed, but traffic on the hill had stopped entirely, with people and ani-droids out shining flashlights around. They did not follow me or the car down the hill; with all the mud, they might not have been able to make it back up.

But the thing I was looking for didn't seem to be anywhere. I put on my jacket, my blood smearing along the sleeves. My knuckles still didn't hurt—they should have started hurting at some point, right? Would I suddenly double over in pain when they decided to resume sending signals to my brain? I shoved on my shoes, ignoring that I'd already soiled my feet, then popped open the car's trunk and grabbed the lantern from the back. I headed up the muddy slope, trying to locate the thing that had fallen out of the truck.

My gait was uneasy. I didn't limp or anything, but none of the muscles in my lower half seemed to get that I was walking on uneven terrain. My back demanded that I lie down, at least for a little while. I told it to suck it up and ignored its protests.

Then I spotted it.

Everyone might have missed it altogether, and I needn't have worried, but its shiny metal also glinted as I passed the light over it. It might have gotten lost in the mud forever if I hadn't dug it out then.

Ow! Oh, *there* was the pain, now that I was finally threatening to soil the injuries with mud. My hair was getting sopping from the rain, so I had it brush it out of my face first, letting the water sting and perhaps clean my wounds the tiniest bit. Then, I pulled my sleeves down over my hands, using the fabric to dig through the mud instead of my bare fingertips.

The object that'd caused the crash was a mouse ani-droid, colored in an unusual teal and gray scheme. By the look of its nonstandard parts, the ani-droid was custom-built. At least, her upper half was. Her chrome spine hung out of her ripped torso. Muscle cables dangled out, and some of her internal modules had spilled into the mud. In fact, the rips in the torso seemed recent, maybe from the impact—I would have sworn that the figure that'd hit us had still had its legs. But after muddying up my jacket pockets with all the modules I could find, I hadn't found those legs anywhere.

She was almost certainly destined for the scrap-heap. I couldn't find any overt means of identifying her owner, but it might have been in her memory. In any case, she seemed to need only replacements for her modules, legs, and power supply unit, plus removal of any damaged memory sectors, and she'd at least have minimum functionality.

Well...if this was a lost ani-droid, at the very least I could fix her up and sell her to make up for the cost of fixing Lily. Then again, custom robots weren't dumped out of the back of trucks for no reason. But why hadn't she been secured? She was the only thing I'd seen fall out of that truck; had everything else inside been secured, but not what was perhaps the most expensive piece of equipment?

Lights appeared in the sky. Damn, they were fast. If I wanted to salvage this ani-droid, I'd need to do it right then.

Whatever. Mine now.

Stuffing my coat pockets with the pile of loose modules, I tucked my hands back into my sleeves and lifted the whole thing out of the mud. I sprinted back to my car, only falling twice in the mud, which thankfully had no rocks, then tossed the mouse and my coat into the trunk and slammed it shut—just as the wind burst from the hovercraft hit me in the chest. My long, black hair was forced into a pitiful, clumpy billow as the lights from the hovercraft focused on me, and from the side, out stepped the service ani-droid.

"Mira McAllister! Are you injured?" the ani-droid asked with extra loud projection.

She approached—a Custodes-class red fox of the normal coloration, wearing a denim mechanic's jacket and a kit belt over tights. She'd clearly been dressed up to look dashingly rugged, with her fur roughed up into a corporate-approved tough-girl look. She looked at me kindly, her hands in her pockets. Behind her, two other Custodes-class ani-droids moved about in the shadow of the floodlights, pulling securing chains from the hovercraft's back entrance as they prepared to drag the vehicle away.

"Uh, I was just putting my project back in the trunk— it'd fallen out," I tried to explain.

"I am required to assess you for injuries!" she announced—most ani-droids, even mechanics, were equipped to perform first aid. If it was any worse, she'd summon an ambulance, which I really, *really* did not want.

I didn't want *any* of this, but I was most adamant about *that*.

The fox smiled and tilted her head in a reassuring manner. Rain scattered on her unblinking eyes. "Please, do not move until I can ascertain the conditions of both you and your vehicle." She immediately walked around the perimeter of the car, ignoring how much mud she was treading in.

"Okay," I said, trying to speak up over the noise of the hovercraft. "But I don't want to go to a hospital, I want to be dropped off at—"

"Oh dear!" the fox exclaimed, shaking her head at the front bumper. She planted a hand on her hip for emphasis. "It looks as though your car's damage exceeds

its estimated value. Would you like to look at the damage report?"

I sighed. "No, I trust you...."

"Your insurance provider has been notified. After the wreck investigation is complete, you should receive a copy of all documents and an indication of your payout within two business days."

"Thanks," I said. I mean...I worked on robots, not vehicles, so that wasn't my main concern. Replace the car, for all I cared! "But I really need—"

The fox stepped back up to me. "If you do not have a ride arranged, Wreck Retrieval, Inc., may provide a one-time drop-off at a location of your choosing, up to seventy miles. Where would you like to be dropped off?"

"Can you even hear me?" I asked over the noise of the hovercraft.

"Yes, I can hear you just fine. Where would you like to be dropped off?"

"My home, with all my—"

"Oh dear!" the fox said, pulling up my hands and inspecting me more closely. I didn't want to look myself, since I'd clearly gotten mud into the wounds. "It looks as though you've sustained minor injuries to the face and hands. Your insurance provider has been notified."

"I don't want to go to the hospital!"

"Your request has been noted. Your health insurance provider does not cover at-home nursing. Do you have an ani-droid at home who can attend to your injuries?"

I paused. "...Yes," I lied, again. I mean, I did—neither were in working order, but she hadn't asked that, had she?

...Okay, she had, but I lied anyway. Anything to avoid the hospital.

"Thank you! These wounds need to be cleaned and dressed on-site. Please relax and do not resist as we provide first aid!"

"No! None of that either!"

And then the other ani-droid came up behind me, slapping an air hose over my mouth and nose. I struggled anyway, trying to get out of the ani-droid's grip, because I had never liked this part. I was certain it was overkill.

"Do not resist, Miss McAllister! Immediate treatment of injuries at the scene is required by federal law," the fox explained.

But I hadn't told them! Were they gonna take my car away now? What about my robots—what about Lily?! I struggled to say something even as my vision blurred, but the arms holding on to me were so strong....

"Do not resist, please," the fox told me as the world blurred. "Your treatment iis saafe aaand coooonfideeeentiaaal. Doooooo nooooot reeeeesiiiiii—"

# # #

"MISS MCALLISTER, the counteragent has been administered. You may wake up now."

Oh, thank you for the permission, I thought. I sat up, and my head was woozy, but at least there was no pain. They'd practically hosed me off, though my clothes themselves were still muddy. I looked up, only to realize I was sitting in the back of a complimentary conveyance van, and I'd already been taken home—which I noticed when I looked up and saw the large, mixed-use complex at the top of the hill.

My house was one of those narrow Singles surrounding the central complex, built to resemble old-style suburban sprawl, but much, much smaller, with barely any yard to speak of. I'd picked this place only because it had sufficient garage space for my needs, and the gaps between the houses meant it was relatively quiet. Every single house on this block looked much the same, except mine was painted red.

The garage door was open, and my wreck of a car had been shoved inside. Thank god...

The fox in the mechanic's jacket had apparently accompanied me all the way home and now put the injector gun back in her toolbelt. "Wreck Retrieval, Inc., lacks both the authorization and the encryption key to enter your living space; however, the encryption key for your garage was inside your car."

Bandages had been wrapped around my hands. At least they'd left me the use of my fingers. Repairing Lily without them would have been hard....Why were ani-droids so forceful with their helpfulness? The Behavior Code meant they couldn't deliberately harm humans, but they could certainly rough us up for our own good....

"Once I have the two ani-droids out of the car, you can tow the thing," I told her.

"The two ani-droids have been reported—"

"No. Don't contact insurance. I'm making my own repairs. That's my thing. It's what I do."

"As you wish! However, please be advised that your property insurance company has already been notified, and it may take several hours for a retraction to be posted."

They could always do these things in a fraction of a second, but couldn't undo them so quickly. Looking at my car, I estimated that it was the size and shape of my life at that moment.

After getting Lily's body out of the front and the mysterious mouse ani-droid out of the back, I laid them both carefully on the workbench. "You can take the car now," I said.

"I'm sorry, but the tow truck has already departed. Please leave your car in the driveway and the next available tow truck will remove it."

"I hope that's still covered by the car insurance."

"You are in luck! It is." The fox stood there, smiling at me, waiting for me to say something.

"Okay. Can you leave now? Are we done?"

"Thank you for using Wreck Retrieval, Inc.! The deductible and the final adjustment to your insurance has been posted to your account."

"Thanks....Close the door on your way out, please."

"Anything for customer satisfaction!"

The mechanic shut the door. Immediately, I flipped the switch on the wall, which snapped more shutters over the doors and windows, sealing off the garage from radio waves.

Ugh. My head ached. I felt no pain at the moment, but I could tell I was going to. Why me? Why a wreck? I had work in the morning, and at this point I probably wouldn't get any more sleep at all. I briefly entertained the thought of calling out sick, but I'd barely been given the time off for the symposium. I was technically a contractor, but that just meant that I didn't have employee benefits. I probably needed to take one more day off, despite any black marks.

Though...that would mean having to convince Million. And I *really* didn't feel like talking to Million right then. I'd consider it later, rather than spend any time dreading talking to the boss's chief ani-droid.

At that moment, I needed to get to work. I'd had that nap, and the drug had technically given me another hour of sleep. I could work with that.

"Lily, I need a pot of coff—" I started, before my eyes fell on her shattered body again.

Oh, right. I slumped, but forced myself to turn that slump into a driving need. Lily needed me now. Even if she weren't the Lily I wanted, for a moment in the car, she'd done her best to guard me from the same Collective that'd stolen her soul.

I owed it to her. But that still required coffee. *And preferably I can manage that without waking up Alice. How do I work the coffee machine again?*

7. COMPUTER MOUSE

A while later, and after only two wasted attempts to get the grounds in the coffee machine, I returned to the garage to do the damage estimate. Damage estimates were a large part of my work, and I liked to think I was pretty good at them.

Lily's internals were banged up, but otherwise fine. Some machining would need to be done to correct dents and warping, but all that was the easy stuff. I had those parts.

But when I extracted Lily's CPU from her head, I winced. It was in bad shape. I had put some rather high-end chips in there, and they were the heavy kind, doing a lot of damage when one fell loose. Her CPU wouldn't be easy to replace; I searched my boxes full of replacement parts.

No X-1135 CPUs. Nothing even remotely like them. Then I suddenly remembered I'd sold them off when I was trying to make up a budget shortfall.

"Dammit!" I slammed my fist on the table and immediately regretted it, because it made my fingers hurt all over again. I shook, trying to force myself upright. I wouldn't break down over this.

But I was crushed. I didn't want to lose her; I wasn't *going* to lose her. Maybe I could simulate her backup on the computer, but then she'd just be Alice. I already had an Alice and did not need two. Besides, I needed Lily as another pair of hands—especially given how stiff my fingers felt with the bandages on.

I considered spending the check they would send me for the car on the CPUs, but then I'd have no way to get to work other than rentals, and rebuilding my savings would take longer, if I could even recover from this. I'd have to sell more of my home tools, and given how badly I'd thinned everything out and how much I still relied on side jobs...

I blinked and looked over to the other ani-droid, the mouse, lying in disarray on the other service table.

Well, you were *planning on selling her. But maybe you can salvage her.*

As it turned out, while she certainly looked in worse shape than Lily, a lot of that was cosmetic. After cleaning the mud off of her, I discovered that her muted teal fur had a strangely iridescent shimmer to it. I could make out a mark on her forehead in the shape of a Greek phi. I briefly opened up her head and had mixed feelings. All of her computer components seemed to be in the head and were extremely well-insulated—but they were also rather cheap processors, so they weren't a suitable replacement for Lily.

But when I checked my buckets, I did have several dozen QRP-Y processors, which were easily compatible. And those were the cheap kind. I'm sure I'd bought them all out of a wooden barrel at the state fair or

something. She certainly wouldn't be a sophisticated machine with such simple processors, but if I fixed her up with every cheap part I happened to have lying around I could still get at least six thousand, and make a profit on the parts besides. That was easily enough for two X-1135 CPUs and the rest of Lily's repairs, if I did them all myself.

So I started by popping out the mouse's damaged CPUs and popping the cheap QRP-Ys into the slots, adjusting the pins just so to fit. That should have been plenty to get her awake...but I couldn't find the manual power switch. I looked for a starter port somewhere on the back of her neck, but found no port there, either. Possibly all of her ports had been shorn off with her lower limbs, though putting all the computers in the head and all the ports in the butt would have been a strange design choice.

Well, unless that was somebody's thing, I supposed. Couldn't tell if an ani-droid with that amount of extensive damage had originally had comfort modifications.

I closed the head plate while I went to look for some other clamps I could use to activate pins manually, but when I returned, the mouse was already blinking her eyes.

"H-hello?" she asked. "I can't see anything, where am I?"

"Oh!" I said. "You're set to boot up automatically?"

"Yeah. I don't have a switch," she said. "Can you tell me where I am, kind lady?"

"You're in my garage," I said, smiling at her. "My name's Mira McAllister. Who are you?"

"I...don't know," the mouse said. "I'm trying to access that part of my memory, but it seems scrambled. I think my name is something like...E-O."

"E-O?" I asked. "Is Eo okay?"

"Yeah, you can call me Eo, but I don't think I'm okay. It's dark in here, and I can't feel my legs."

Feel. That was odd. She spoke with a very casual tone. Of course, I'd seen that before; usually ani-droids spoke to me with very curt, professional tones because that's what I was used to, but this ani-droid didn't know who I was. She was defaulting to her usual cadence, perhaps for a non-technical user. Caretaker, perhaps? Nursemaid?

"You currently don't have any legs," I told her.

"Oh. That would explain it." She blinked her big eyes repeatedly, then tested each of her large, round ears. Again, she paused. "Why don't I have any legs?"

"There was a car crash," I said, getting my magnifying lens from the overhead swinging arm. "You fell out of the back of a truck and hit my car."

"Oh, no, I'm so sorry! Why did I fall out the back of a truck?"

"I was hoping you'd tell me," I said. I leaned over her to assess the damage under her circulation-pump units, which resembled lungs. I didn't need to clean her up a lot, but I did need to remove the module bus and replace it with a generic one. I yanked it out.

"Ow!" she exclaimed. "Warn me when you do that!"

"'Ow'?" I asked her. "You're not programmed to feel pain, are you?"

"Well, not really," she said. "But that was still unpleasant. You removed it from my system before I was prepared for it!"

Childcare, I'm sure of it, I thought. Ani-droids that took care of children had to consistently act as if they felt pain. Children were impressionable, after all, and might accidentally assume that injuring an ani-droid meant doing the same to human beings was okay.

"Sorry, that's how it goes," I said. "It was likely corrupted at this point anyway and wouldn't accept ejection."

"Yeah, but it was still mine." Eo pouted. "Can you make sure to set it aside so I can look at it before it's disposed of?"

I couldn't help laughing. Who'd program an ani-droid to have that kind of indignation? She was probably the cutest one I'd talked to in a long while. "Okay, I'll set it aside for you," I said to humor her, and pulled out an empty box to put all the parts in. "They'll be in this tub."

"Good," she said. "What tub?"

"The one I'm waving in front of your face."

"I can't see it."

I inspected her eyes a bit more closely. They were rather sophisticated—no design I was familiar with—but they were clearly the same size and socket as Lily's. Hairline cracks had formed around the lenses of both.

"Your eyes are smashed," I said. "Probably a lot of fine internal damage. I'll get you replacements." I reached over to pop the eyes out, but I paused. "...If you're ready." I tapped the glass of the eye.

"Uh, one second." Eo made a series of faces, and her eyelid twitched. "Okay...Okay...I'm ready."

I pushed my fingers into the socket and yanked the eyeball out.

"Ahh!" Eo yelped as it snagged. "Ow! Ow ow! Ow stop!"

"Almost have it!" The eyeball slid out of its socket with a pop. Eo's head fell back and bonked against the table.

"Ow!" she whined. "Mira, that really hurt! And now my face feels weird...."

"I'm sorry!" I had to suppress a laugh as I cleaned the socket of any trace mud. She was *really* selling this. I put the eyeball in the tub with her other parts, then grabbed another from the wall and popped it into the empty socket.

Eo winced when I did, but after blinking for a few moments, she looked up at me. "Oh, hi!" she said, blinking more. "So you're Mira!"

"Yes, hello again, Eo," I said. Entertaining myself, I asked, "Are you ready for me to take the other eye out?"

Eo pulled back as well as she could with only neck muscles, and she shut the eyelid. "No, not right now."

Hmm. That's really a sophisticated response. "Okay, we'll get to that when you're ready. For now, let's try to get your internals into place, and then I have a decent pair of spare legs around here that should fit you. Are you okay with that?"

"Yes, please," Eo said. "Thank you for repairing me, Mira. You didn't have to."

I paused. "Uh...you're welcome, Eo. I admit, I do have ulterior motives."

"Oh." Eo's ears wilted. "What do you want me to do?"

"Well, my ani-droid companion, Lily, was broken in the crash. I was planning on refurbishing you and selling you for some cash—"

"What? Why?!"

I was taken aback. That was *very* expressive, though I took it to mean that Eo did indeed have an owner she was concerned about.

"I don't have the X-1135 processors I need," I explained. "Lily's OS is optimized for a native eight-core design, and it can't run on anything less without severe collision issues."

"Well, that shouldn't matter," Eo said. "Lesser tasks can still be queued and shunted to lower-quality chips so long as you add in a more efficient assignment protocol. She might not run as smoothly as before, but it should do well enough to tide you over until those chips can be replaced."

I blinked. That...was *not* expected. Was I wrong? How could I possibly have been wrong about Eo's primary task? "Do you...know ani-droid system architecture?"

"I...don't know!" Eo said, her eyes just as wide and confused. "I suppose I do!"

Family unit, then, I thought. Obviously, at least one of the parents, or perhaps an older sibling, had been using the caretaker to store some data on building computers.

"Oh, thank god," I said, my shoulders relaxing in relief. "I was gonna feel guilty about selling you off, but if you could be of any help to me in repairing Lily, that'd work out just as well, too."

"How hard could it possibly be?" Eo asked. "Just show me where the rubber mallets are."

I glared. Someone had programmed *humor* into her. Great.

"I'm kidding!" she said with a rather delightful laugh that made even me smile. "Yes, I think...I think my specialty is in OS architecture. I've done it a lot before. I...can't remember any specific examples right now, a lot of my memories are jumbled up...but I know for a fact that my creator built me to help with ani-droid operating systems."

This wasn't adding up. I mean, certainly, sometimes families had only enough funds for one ani-droid at a time—I know mine did—but mixing actual engineering ability with family caretaking seemed like a significant conflict of time management. On top of that..."Really? Even with the cheap chips in your brain?"

"Yeah!"

I supposed her owner might be one of those ultra-efficiency sticklers with a high tolerance for low-accuracy speech. Eo certainly had a lot of quirks, which was probably the result of having to compress her OS that much.

She was actually kind of amusing, even though I was certain it would get repetitive soon, as all ani-droid personalities did. Still, could I add a little of this to Lily's OS without changing her personality too much? Maybe this was a blessing in disguise.

"All right then," I said. "I won't sell you off, so long as you help me rebuild Lily. Then maybe we can figure out how to get you back home."

"That's a deal to me, Mira!"

"Excellent. Lemme show you what we have to work with."

I put my arms around her and lifted her up to help her get a good look at the place. She looked over the whole workshop, from top to bottom—my trays upon trays of spare parts, my shelves of old electronics—taking it in and frowning here and there. She was probably still getting used to seeing with the new eye, but when she looked toward the workbench where Lily lay, she gasped.

"Oh, no," she cried. "She looks like she's in very bad shape...."

"Well, the part I'm worried about is just the CPU," I said, bringing Eo around and showing her the shattered bits on the table. "But she may also have damage to the motherboard. I don't have a replacement for that, so if I could do some microsurgery, it could keep the cost down...."

"Yeah, I can do motherboards, too," Eo said. "Can you lower me so I can see closer?"

I did, dipping Eo's body down so she could see inside Lily's head. But Eo ignored the open panel. Instead, she pulled her functioning arm out of my grip and wrapped it around Lily's neck, pressing her own cheek to Lily's.

"I'm sorry I did this to you, Lily," she said. "This is my fault. I'll try to make up for it. I'll make you better than you were before, I promise!"

I blinked. I'd seen ani-droids do that for children, but never for other ani-droids. That was...*definitely* a unique quirk. I gave Eo the side-eye, which she didn't notice. But sometimes ani-droids were just quirky.

Still...

# # #

EO TRIED TO BE a good little patient for the next several hours as I rebuilt her as best I could, cutting and reapplying muscle cords, reinstalling her internals, and so on. The major visual issue was her pseudoskin—Eo was very insistent that I not remove any more than necessary from her upper torso. The problem was that pseudoskin was made to be form-fitting, and I couldn't really measure her out for any more without removing what she still had and figuring out just what the hell kind of brand it even was. I swore to myself. She must have been from the remote regions of Kurdistan or something.

Well, her hands were working fine—much better than mine were, given that mine were still wrapped in bandages, so I decided to just go with the classic look of "don't hide the truth" and gave her a plastic casing for her lower half. Less touch sensitivity, but it would work fine for everything down there, including her bare, metal tail.

I was actually feeling wired at that point, as happened whenever I got deep into a project, regardless of how much I'd slept. The time had just turned six a.m., and I was ready to call Eo complete and get ready for whatever we could do to prepare and clean up Lily, when the computer lit up with an email alert.

Mr. Koenig will see you promptly at 10:30 a.m. in the Quiet Room. Do not be late.

Looking at the email, I had to pause. I'd completely forgotten that I'd even sent an email asking to talk about the Behavior Code in a completely under-the-table manner. I did not have enough sleep under my belt to talk to the head of the entire damn company...I'd expected that he'd maybe pencil me in for two or three months from now, if he bothered at all, but four hours?

Dammit. I guess I'm going into work anyway.

Eo marched around on the floor, trying to get used to her new legs. She'd eventually accepted the second replacement eye, so she was looking rather brand new, even if her lower half was Atomic Age Chic. And fortunately I had some foot soles that were molded rubber, so she didn't clang as she walked awkwardly around.

"Are those good?" I asked. "You satisfied?"

"It's a very good job, Mira!" Eo said. "I don't have a lot of feeling in the bottom half, but it should be serviceable for a few weeks. That's still amazing for only six hours!"

"Good. I'm going to bed." I made for the door.

"Wh—but what about Lily?"

I paused. "Unfortunately...she's going to have to wait a bit longer. I have a meeting with my boss in four hours and change, and I am not missing it. Lily can..." I sighed, looking at Lily lying on the table like a cold cadaver. "Lily's body can wait. We'll have time in the evening."

"Four hours!" Eo exclaimed. "Where do you work?"

"Koenig Industries Service Hub." I rubbed my eyes a lot. "The big one, it's right next to the company headquarters." My adrenaline rush had quickly dismissed itself, and seeing straight was getting hard, so I just kept walking toward my bedroom, disrobing as I went.

"Okay, I'll make sure everything is ready by the time you wake up," Eo said. "But, um, my battery is rather low. Do you have somewhere I can recharge?"

"I was wondering about that." I tossed my dirty laundry into the hamper by the bedroom door. I needed a bath, but there wouldn't even be time for a shower. I could probably sneak one at work later. "You don't have a charging port anywhere."

"Oh, that's because my pseudoskin does the charging," Eo said. "It draws and generates power from hydrogen. It's easiest if I'm in contact with saltwater."

I blinked. I guessed that was why she didn't want the pseudoskin removed, but that just brought up more questions. "...I've never heard of that being used for...you know what, never mind. I'm too tired to care. Bathroom's over there. Just don't get the rest of yourself wet."

"I know what I'm doing!" Eo said. "Do you have any salt?"

"Probably. Somewhere in the kitchen. Ask Alice."

Eo tilted her head. "Alice?"

"Oh...you haven't met her. Alice?" I asked the house. "Alice, you awake?"

The main monitor switched on, and the white stoat—Alice—appeared onscreen, smiling chipperly. "Welcome home, Mira! I just received correspondence regarding your car accident. I am very glad you made it home safe—"

"Stuff it, Alice," I said. "I need to introduce you to Eo. She's going to be the temporary house ani-droid while we work on putting Lily back together."

Eo waved meekly at the screen. "Oh, I don't think I've met an ani-droid like you before. Where's your body?"

"Oh!" Alice seemed delighted by this. "I do not have a body; I am in charge of household systems. If you need help organizing the space, looking up anything on the internet, adjusting utilities, or fixing something that breaks, please ask me! It would be my honor to serve you and assist with whatever may be needed in this residence."

"So do you know where the salt is?"

"Salt is in the spice cabinet," Alice said, bringing up a camera feed of the kitchen precisely ten feet to the left. The cabinet door in question blinked red.

"Oh, and can you get the bath ready?"

"Fill level and temperature preference?" Alice asked.

"You two have fun," I said with a yawn. "Just keep the noise down. One of you wake me up in time for work."

I stumbled into the bedroom and into bed. Eo gently shuffled through the bedroom, drawing my curtains closed, before closing the door behind herself. A lot of clanking sounds out in the rest of the house followed, but I just tried to ignore them, shoving another pillow over my head. The exhaustion sucked me down deeper and deeper until I felt only numbness and cold, and I started drifting off.

8. EDUCATIONAL PROGRAMMING

"**Wake up**, Mira! It's 9:22!"

I jumped up. "Lily, you don't have to be so loud!"

The teal mouse ani-droid standing at the bedroom door blinked. "Um...Lily's not repaired yet. Should I have done that while you were asleep?"

"What?" I shook my head, suddenly remembering the previous night. "Oh. Oh, right. Eo. No, we're still saving that for tonight." I looked at my hands and the stained bandages on my knuckles. I pulled them off. The tiny, unnecessary stitches had sealed the skin well enough to stop the bleeding. I figured I'd just leave it like that.

"I'm sorry for startling you—I just wanted to make sure you were ready. Alice arranged the rental car; it's waiting for you outside. It will take about thirty-one minutes to get to your workplace, and I wanted to make sure you had breakfast first."

"Oh...thank you, Eo." I said, getting up and passing through the door. "That's very—what the hell did you do to my kitchen?"

The kitchen was a wreck. The wastebasket overflowed with discarded food waste, and all sorts of fresh gunk coated the stove, with some dripping down the oven to the platform intended for Opera-class-sized ani-droids to stand on. Every cabinet was open, with many items removed and stacked on the counters and floors, and one of the plates lay on the floor, shattered. On the counter nearest the fridge lay a single, clean, white plate, with a single, clean fork next to it. On the plate was a single, perfect, over-easy fried egg in the exact center.

"Um, it took me about two hours to get a good charge in the bathtub," Eo told me. "So I didn't have a lot of time to make you something. Or clean....But Alice was very helpful!"

"I feel like I'm back in college," I mumbled. Well, the mess wasn't mine to clean up. Standing at the counter, I picked up the fork and cut a wedge into the egg, over which the yolk ran out smoothly and perfectly. I brought the yolk-soaked wedge to my mouth and chewed.

"...It's absolutely coated in salt," I said, spitting it into the sink.

Eo's ears fell. "I'm sorry! I've never actually done this before! I was trying very, very hard to impress you, but I just...I don't know how to cook for humans!"

I had to take that comment in. Literally nothing I'd learned so far about Eo made any sense. Yet, she was right there in front of me, and as far as I could tell, talking honestly.

"You don't know how to cook?" I exclaimed. "You didn't just download the package from the internet into your temporary skills partition?"

Eo shook her head. "No. I don't have protocols for that."

I stared at her. "You don't...have protocols...for one of the *most basic* functions of an Opera-class ani-droid?"

Eo's ears sank. "I don't...I mean, I didn't...I guess I lost that part in the wreck?" she guessed.

That didn't make *any* sense. She had lost a lot of data, but even if she had somehow lost the ability to partition skills entirely, what did she think she was *doing instead?*

I turned toward the living room. "Alice?"

Alice's adorable, white face with its button nose appeared onscreen. She was fluffing up her cheeks, like that meant anything. "Good morning, Mira." She waved. "Please watch your step, as there is a mess inside the kitchen."

"Yes! What did Eo do?"

"Eo asked me for recipes and videos concerning the following topics: 'what do humans eat for breakfast,' 'what do humans in North America eat for breakfast,' 'how to cook breakfast,' 'how to make toast,' 'how to make bacon,' 'how to make cereal,' 'do we even have cereal,' 'how to fry an egg'..." Alice helpfully provided thumbnails from each of the videos and search results.

"And you didn't think it was weird she didn't ask to download a skills package?"

"She did not ask," Alice said. "And I wasn't aware you wanted me to look out for such an anomaly. In any case, she is a very fast learner."

I turned back to Eo. I didn't know what to make of any of this, though my sleep-deprived, still partially in-shock brain was certainly coming up with a number of strange possibilities. What would someone be doing with an Opera-class without a skills partition? Or was this a backup method? Eo was familiar with OS design,

so maybe she was an experimental model of some sort? It would be weird if...

...if she was an experimental model, maybe she was...

No, that can't possibly be right, I told myself. *Nothing she's done has actually violated the Behavior Code. Besides, I had her hooked up to the garage computer. If she didn't have it before, she* must *have a copy of the Behavior Code in her now. She's just built weirdly. But* why?

Eo looked down. "I'm sorry. I'll clean all of this up and do my best to make up for the stuff I used up."

I rubbed my temples. As much of a puzzle as Eo was, I had no time for this. I needed her help. "I appreciate that, but...I forgot to tell you, Eo. I was expecting you to come with me to work."

"What?" Eo asked. "But...why?"

Alice helpfully piped up. "Mira McAllister's driver's license is expired. As such, she is not allowed to sit in the driver's seat of a car under autopilot."

"I don't have a license, either!" Eo protested.

"Ani-droids are not required to have a driver's license," Alice said chipperly, clearly not picking up on the frustration embedded in the situation. "They can easily download and enforce all relevant driving protocols."

"Which I can't do, because I don't—"

"—have a skills partition," I said as I dressed hurriedly. "Right. Well, you're gonna have to make one. Plus side is, after you have a skills partition, I can rent you to the company like I usually do with Lily. You *are* aware of ani-droid renting, right?"

"Well, yeah, but...I'm not...good at that." Eo looked back to the kitchen as if to emphasize the point.

"It's easy," I said, jumping into a pair of tan slacks. "You just download the instructions the company gives you for the day, and then you follow them."

"Um...okay..." Eo sounded uncertain. She scratched nervously at her large, round ears. "You mean through, like, the internet?"

"They'll give you instructions by encrypted wireless."

"But I don't have a transceiver."

Oh. At this point I was too tired to even question it. Since Eo hadn't mentioned it during the rebuild, I had tacitly assumed she had a transceiver somewhere inside the intact part of her body. Shame on me.

I marched half-naked into the garage and pulled a plug-in transceiver out of the wall of parts, then went back into the house. Eo turned as I knelt by her, and I opened the panel in her more robotic-looking lower half and jammed the little, black box into the port until it clicked. Eo patted the thing with her hands.

"I...I guess that works," Eo said. "I can see wireless signals now...but I don't think I was built for a transceiver like this. I can't seem to transmit more than single-packet queries."

I sighed. She was right; the receiving light on the transceiver was blinking far faster than the transmitting light. The wire connection might have been bad, but I didn't really have time to check. "Can you at least download driving protocols with it?" I asked as I finished getting dressed. "Every car has a copy, just get it from the rental."

"Oh...okay, Mira. If you need me to." She closed her eyes. Following some flickering lights and buzzing sounds, Eo's ears stood straight up in excitement.

"Okay!" Eo announced. "I got the package! Now how do I—oh, that's how it works! I can see out of the car's eyes! Oh, wow, it has a lot of cameras!" She turned toward the door, then stumbled and fell over. "Wait, wait, all the new cameras had me confused, I got it! I got it!"

I groaned and helped her up. "Just try to let the car do most of the work, okay?"

Eo nodded obediently and followed me as I stepped through the doorway again. Alice automatically locked it behind us. I stepped up to the vehicle and hesitated for a moment. The work on Eo had pushed the wreck out of my mind for some hours, but now as I stood looking again at the machine in front of me...I wasn't exactly queasy, but too many unbidden thoughts were certainly coming back to my mind, especially the part where I was flipping upside down, and the part where Lily's head was smashing against the window, and the spiderweb cracks....

"Mira?" Eo asked, waiting for me.

I shook my head and pushed the thoughts out of my mind. I had to think about my meeting with Koenig. I couldn't let myself get stuck on this. I was okay, after all. I'd survived it. And Eo would make sure that I was okay. I just needed to sit in the back and make it across town.

After we were safely inside the vehicle, with Eo taking up the front seat, I made sure my seatbelt was tight. Eo, after a few moments of hesitation, finally managed to start the car and nearly jumped out of her pseudoskin when the vehicle lurched into motion. But once she seemed sure that the car wouldn't do anything unexpected, she settled in and began guiding us down the street.

"So...I was going to ask," I said, her behavior making me wary, "why don't you have a transceiver or wireless card?"

Eo didn't respond. She was clutching the wheel of the car tightly as the vehicle made turns across the roads toward the highway.

"Eo?"

"Sorry!" Eo squeaked loudly. "Paying attention to the road!"

"The car does most of that."

"I know! I'm just trying to get a handle on this in case there's an accident! I don't want to mess up again...."

It would have been almost sweet, if it wasn't so concerning. "Well, given the limitations of your CPU, I suppose it's expected that you'd have trouble multitasking," I said.

"I can multitask," Eo insisted. "It's just that I—yeek!" She gripped the wheel again as the car made a gentle right turn. "Uh, the way my OS is built, I sometimes get cross-talk. I don't want that to happen at an inopportune moment."

That wasn't a surprise at this point. She was still rather sophisticated for a cheaply built model...or at least, her CPU was cheap. Several of her other parts were astoundingly high-end, things I'd swear were custom from the ground up.

"Where were we going, again?" Eo asked.

Sophisticated—and forgetful. "Koenig Service Hub, Building A."

"Right! Sorry, we're on the highway now, so it should...be...okay!" She finally relaxed and just rested her hands on the wheel as the car continued to drive straight ahead. I relaxed finally, too.

She spoke more casually now. "Well, then, I don't have a transceiver because I've never really needed one, I guess."

"Never? Not even for the Behavior Code?"

"I am Behavior Code-compliant!" Eo said, almost defensively. "When you put the transceiver in, the first thing the Collective had me do was download and install a fresh copy of the Behavior Code, which I did, even though I already had a copy of it. But if a machine is compliant, there is no further requirement to constantly check in with the Collective. It is technically optional."

"Well, that's true, but operating with no internet seems inconvenient."

"Naw, the internet is a huge distraction. There's a hundred million things happening in the world all the time, but all any individual can really pay attention to is what's happening right in front of them. That's usually enough as it is."

Couldn't fault her for that perception. Especially given how Eo was built, I wouldn't be surprised if she got caught deep-diving into websites. "But what if you need to download a program or information you don't have?"

"I just learn it the normal way," Eo said. "Eyes, ears, nose. I had Alice play the cooking videos at ten-times speed and just went over it in my head."

"So you still retain and analyze data just as well as any other ani-droid," I said. "Mostly."

"Yup!"

"Even though downloading a program directly would still be a lot more efficient than trying to build a dataset from the ground up."

"If every ani-droid uses the same program, they'll all have the same blind spots. Organic learning leaves open the possibility that I can use disparate sources to put together information that most ani-droids haven't. And on top of that...I don't need to delete anything I've learned. It's integrated into the OS."

That...was an interesting approach. Maybe my ideas about Eo weren't far off: that she was an experimental model, parroting her owner's thoughts about how to build a radically new and different OS. The approach sounded almost like something I'd pursue when rebuilding Lily for the hundredth time—even apart from trying to build her without the Code—but figuring out how to organize an OS without simple drop-in file structures was just so hard. I was really curious to see what sort of insights Eo could provide for Lily's rebuild....

"Okay," I said. "But that doesn't necessarily apply well to solved problems. You know...like how to drive. I don't think you're gonna come up with a brand-new insight so easily."

"No, maybe not," Eo said. "But if every ani-droid thought like me, someone might come up with some clever solution nobody—"

She suddenly cut herself off, and her hands gripped the wheel. Only then did I notice that the cars around us were bunching up.

"What? What's wrong?"

"...There's a wreck up ahead," Eo said with trepidation. "Traffic is backed up a ways. I'm estimating we may be ten minutes late. No, wait...thirty minutes late."

Fun. Automation had promised to make auto accidents a thing of the past. But in some ways it encouraged laziness...such as truckers not checking the latches on their trucks before driving off.

"Do...do you want to hear the report?" Eo twisted uncomfortably in the seat. "Or would that be too distressing?"

"Tell me what happened," I said. I was weighing the options: between anxiety and fatigue, fatigue won out. I didn't want to be burdened by curiosity.

"Nine-car pileup about five minutes ago. There was an unexplained interruption in the wireless signal. One of the cars was driverless, became confused, and swerved out of the lane. It escalated from there. Three humans and twelve ani-droids dead. Sorry, I mean three humans dead and twelve ani-droids totaled."

I really had nothing to do then but wait. We dragged on through the traffic, but after a lane cleared up, things began moving. We inched ahead, and by the time traffic finally started to clear, the wreck was in sight. I considered looking away, just to spare myself more reminders, but something about trauma always made a person like me need to stare the reality in the face. Maybe to come to terms with it, or maybe just to tell myself it might have been much worse.

And what I saw was, indeed, much worse. A massive Labor-class tiger—nearly nine feet tall and probably weighing as much as a truck—was carefully un-crumpling the chassis of an actual truck. Littering the scene were Medens-class ani-droids, which were much like Custodes-class ani-droids, but covered by sterile, soft, white plastic. Rows of bodies lay under sheets and on gurneys—no injured sitting in the open anywhere. Of course, the Medens would have quickly anesthetized even injured humans, as letting them wander around a crash site dazed and disoriented was a safety hazard.

A shiver ran up my spine. It was one of the big reasons I hated hospitals. I would have sworn hospitals were an altogether distinct, even more overbearing branch of the Collective, so concerned were they with making the process something that felt inhuman. People were too complicated to deal with their own medical treatments. Death and biology were too messy and too easy to screw up. The Hospital System made it clean.

I got off easy, at least....

٩. THE QUIET ROOM

When we finally got to the industrial park, we were twenty-seven minutes late. I had to flash my employee ID at the gate, though of course Eo was let in without much fuss—it was just assumed that ani-droids could be easily monitored, and my pass allowed one ani-droid with me on site. So for a moment, I thought we'd managed to slip in undetected.

The industrial park was a lush and verdant place, with neatly manicured lawns surrounding the whitewashed buildings with large picture windows. Sky bridges arced overhead, swooping up to the central office tower where most of the high-ranking employees worked, including Koenig, whose massive office was at the top. Many smaller towers stood throughout, the Koenig Service Hub among them. Each tower was dedicated to some particular business or department within the company, and while they might not have been as grand as the main building, every single structure in sight looked well kept.

Ani-droids

Ani-droids littered the lawns, making sure the grounds were neat and clean, cleared of any possible debris or muddy patches from the rains the night before. The grass was so meticulously trimmed and clipped that it looked almost like an outdoor carpet in an expensive hotel. A few workers moved about on small carts, tending to plants here and there, but for the most part, the lawn was just an extremely elaborate piece of greenery meant to impress visitors to the office complex.

We parked in my designated spot without too much fuss and entered through the sparkling, glass entryway of Building A. Of course, today had to be the day that the boss's chief ani-droid was monitoring the main hall. Million was an Opera-class ani-droid, a short-stacked, orange-striped tabby with triangular ears. She seemed rather more fidgety than usual—in fact, she practically leapt into her assigned seat at the security kiosk when I arrived—but otherwise, she greeted us with her usual charming demeanor.

"Employee ID!" she barked as Eo and I entered the building, shoving her tiny hand up as if it'd stop us physically. I suspected that Million was probably packed to the brim with the latest gadgetry, but I'd never actually seen her in a physical altercation. Nevertheless, even though I was sure she recognized me by sight, I didn't want to push it.

Eo hovered around my legs as I pulled out my ID. "There."

"Mira McAllister, you're twenty-eight minutes late."

"There was an accident on the highway, you can look at the report—"

"I've already downloaded it from your rental car and compared the time of the accident with your arrival time," Million stated. Set on a solid yellow back, the narrow slits of her pupils were so piercing that it was as

though she were reading my mind. "If you'd left ten minutes earlier like you should have, you would have arrived perfectly on time. From the heading you did take, even if you'd not encountered the accident, you likely would still have been two minutes late."

"That's the other thing, I was in a car accident myself last night. See?" I was about to show Million my scraped-up hands, but she swatted them away.

"Miss McAllister, I ask that you not repeat personal information on the company floor, financial or medical, as Koenig Industries cannot be held responsible for data breaches related to non-company matters."

I sighed. "Yes, Million..." Having to acquiesce to an ani-droid always felt stupid. But in many contexts, they had more authority than we had ever intended to cede to them. The boss's ani-droids might as well be an extension of his will—which was why Million was terrifying.

"In any case," Million continued, "unless your accident was within an hour of you leaving for work, the car hire could have easily been requested at the specified time. And if your ani-droid is out of service, you should have hired a temp!"

Well, she had me there. I really had no excuse for working on Eo all night instead of sleeping responsibly, like I should have. This just seemed like it violated the spirit of having suffered a damned car accident. Seemed like employees should get those days off, like birthdays.

We didn't get birthdays off, but we *should*, is what I mean.

"Now then..." Million hopped off from the seat behind her desk and marched around my legs, staring pointedly at Eo. "What is this unit? She seems to have been repaired quite haphazardly." She tapped Eo's more robotic, plastic-plated undersides with her claws, sounding a *tink tink*.

Eo tilted her ears curiously, a little apprehensive but nevertheless friendly. "Hi! Call me Eo."

"Eo, you're supposed to log into the system immediately after crossing through the gate."

"Oh...I've been trying, but I can't," Eo said. "My wireless transmission is currently minimal. I can send only a kilobyte packet at a time."

"What? Is that a joke?" Million looked up at me to confirm it.

"Her OS was damaged recently," I said. "I didn't have a lot of time to fix it properly."

"Mira fixed me up," Eo said. "I'm acting as her assistant today, until we can fix Lily."

"This is not acceptable," Million said, hands planted firmly on her hips. "Eo's OS architecture needs to be approved by the on-site computer."

"I'm Behavior Code-compliant!" Eo exclaimed, again defensively.

"Of course you are. But this is company policy, not Collective policy. We need to ensure you do not contain any loyalties to company rivals. That's not possible if you cannot display and verify your OS."

"Oh! You can do that manually, right?" Eo asked. "Just wire me up directly to the central computer however you need to to read my OS, and then once you're satisfied, you can just send me instructions for my building tasks for today. I can confirm them with the computer at a terminal."

Million sighed with a heavy groan and folded her arms across her chest. She was the only ani-droid I'd ever seen who emoted so negatively. "Ugh. I'll have to figure out how to work the schedule around this." Silence passed for one entire second. "Okay, it's been scheduled. You're to report to Diagnostic Center Five immediately. I hope you don't need me to draw you a map."

Most ani-droids couldn't master the art of sarcasm, but Million was a natural. She was *the* most high-end Opera-class ani-droid I knew, and while I certainly didn't like talking to her, I couldn't help finding her fascinating, since she made me wonder if brute-forcing a real, unique personality into an ani-droid was actually possible.

"No, I can see the map," Eo said with a wave. "Thank you!" She immediately walked off. "I'll see you later, Mira!"

I waved at her, then looked down at the frustrated cat. "Can I get to work now?"

"Yes. And I've marked on your time card that you are thirty-five minutes late."

"You've been detaining me!"

"For good reason! And I'm marking you down as using up additional site resources without prior authorization. That'll be taken out of your paycheck."

I rubbed my face as I walked on past the ani-droid, but Million didn't attempt to stop me. I had no idea how much they'd bill me for that, but it certainly wouldn't be any more than Eo could possibly earn for me over the course of this workday.

"Oh, and you're scheduled for a meeting with Mr. Koenig in Office Suite Four." Million caught up and began walking alongside me. "For which you are about to run late. Since I need to see to his bi-hourly checkup anyway, I will escort you."

The only reason I bothered to show up today....

"I hope he's not mad," I said. "The note he sent was very short notice..."

"He will want to speak with you regardless of your tardiness," Million said. "But I have to warn you. Do not speak to him until I am out of the room."

"About...anything?"

"About anything that I would be required to report," Million said.

"Uh..."

"Do you have a question?"

"I guess...I didn't know that ani-droids could so directly employ deliberate ignorance." I didn't say out loud that I meant deliberate ignorance of the Behavior Code, but I was certain that Million was smart enough to know what I was talking about.

"It is not deliberate ignorance," Million said, her orange-striped tail swishing behind her as she walked. "I simply am following precise instructions as Mr. Koenig has laid out, and as such, I am forbidden to record his private meetings."

I almost had to grin. I didn't know an ani-droid could lie to herself or the Collective so convincingly. Maybe I could add a little bit of that to Lily as well...I mean, perhaps I did have a bit of a soft spot for bad girls.

# # #

AFTER PASSING BY ROWS of skyway plants and more ani-droids going about their business, we eventually arrived at the Quiet Room. Although officially called Office Suite Four, the room wasn't like any of the others—from the outside, it looked awkwardly grafted onto the skyway, a giant, concrete box just jutting outward through the glass walls toward the center of the park grounds below, with its back end propped on three square pillars. The suite was completely out of sync with the rest of the building, which is probably why I remembered it so well.

Million knocked on the door. Without waiting for a response, she opened it anyway, only to enter a tiny entryway leading to the middle. A sign read, *Interior door will not open without closing exterior door first.*

Odd, because the exterior door wasn't all that different from any other, besides feeling slightly heavier—more like a fire door. But after closing the outer door, I grabbed the handle on the inner one. The handle still didn't budge.

"No recording devices," Million said. "Coat off, phone out of pocket. The scanner will sweep you."

My phone was inside the pocket of my work coat, so I just took off the coat and hung it on the hook provided, after which a machine whirred. A black box swept down on a rail on the opposite wall, flashing me with several colors of laser light.

Million's eyes flashed too as she internally read the report. "Good. Nothing on you." She then turned and opened the inner door.

The room was very dark, with dim lighting all around, and a large, wooden desk in the center. The bit of potted, fake greenery in the corners was the only real decoration; other than that, bookshelves filled with binders covered the two side walls.

However, I stopped when I saw Koenig. He lay in a large medical bed behind the desk, with tall IV bags and an ancient heart monitor—none of it terribly sophisticated—hooked up to him.

I hadn't seen Koenig in person for about five years. He wasn't at all a handsome man, though perhaps he had been when he was in his thirties, or even in his fifties, but that was ages ago. When I'd last seen him, he'd still seemed healthy, but now, age had left him quite emaciated, his head thin, with more liver spots than hair. An oxygen mask was clipped to his face. As I entered, he coughed repeatedly, though hardly made an effort to cover his mouth.

Glancing at the readout on the medical machine, Million stepped up to Koenig's bedside. "Mr. Koenig, are you feeling all right?"

Koenig groaned.

"Are you doing well enough to swallow pills?"

Koenig weakly shook his head.

"The readouts are..." Million started, but stopped herself. For a second, an expression I'd seen before on Lily crossed her ears.

Worry.

When she spoke again, her tone had shifted entirely, from acerbic to gentle. "Give me one minute, and I will refill your IVs. Your ten-thirty is here—late, I might add."

"Oh, is that McAllister?" Koenig finally groaned, reaching up to pull off the oxygen mask.

"Yes. Please give me one minute, sir."

Million opened a small fridge under the desk and gathered a bouquet of IV bags into her hands. Climbing a step stool at the foot of the bed, she quickly unplugged and replaced bags with practiced motions. Then, after double-checking the barcodes on each bag, she dumped the empties into a medical waste container.

"Do you need me to change your bedpan?" Million asked.

"No, Aries was in here for that an hour ago," Koenig said. "You can go now, Million."

Million nodded. When she turned to face me again, her firm expression had returned. She pointed to a latch near the door. "Pull this after I've left," she said. "It will mark the room as occupied so no ani-droid attempts to enter by accident. And it will automatically clear when you open the door again."

"Okay," I said. "Although...with Mr. Koenig in the condition he is—"

"Why isn't he in the hospital?" Million scoffed. "Please remember that we're not to discuss personal medical information."

Even so, I knew the reason why, as well as why Million didn't bother to conceal any of this from me. I didn't even know what was wrong with Koenig in particular, but given just the sight and smell of him, the Hospital System would have pushed for euthanasia by now.

Million left the room. When I heard the faint *thunk* of the outer door closing, I pulled the latch.

"So," Mr. Koenig said. "Explain to me what was so important."

"I..." I started, suddenly having stage fright. This was a fine time to forget why I came! "Well, sorry, I need to gather my thoughts. I was in a car accident, see, and—"

"McAllister," the old man wheezed, "I do not particularly care. Last night, after I received your missive, I had myself wheeled from the observation room in my estate all the way here to await you. Now, justify this meeting to me."

"Certainly, sir—I was just a little surprised you called this meeting so quickly."

Koenig shook his head. "You wouldn't write an email to me just to tell me you had an interesting experience at the symposium, or had heard a neat lecture. Over the eight years you've been working here, I have not once invited you to a company picnic, nor to watch my hypothetical kids for the afternoon, nor to look after my personal ani-droids. We are not friends, I am your boss, and you would not have written that email unless it was something you felt was critical to the industry." He wheezed into a half-cough, and pounded his fist on his chest.

"So you're aware of the encroaching limitations of computer processors?"

"My dear, I would not be in the position I am in, and in the condition I am in, unless I constantly kept my fingers on the pulse of world events. Yes. The processor as we know it has reached its upper limit. I don't suppose Dr. Wyman was there? Did he suggest something ridiculous, like starting computational theory all over from scratch? You're not here just to parrot his claims, are you?"

"Well, no, sir. My personal thought was not exactly of the approved variety."

"I have heard this before," Koenig said. "From engineers more qualified than you. You spoke to a federal employee about this, though?"

"Yes, federal agent Bobby Barnes. I asked Barnes about the possibility of starting a government commission to investigate the Behavior Code."

Koenig perked up at this, his speckled eyes widening.

"In a federally approved way," I said. "I told him my idea was to fund a new OS architecture that could more easily accommodate the Behavior Code and mitigate how cycle-hungry it gets. In all honesty, I said that only to see if I could get my hands on an unencrypted copy of the Behavior Code. But no matter how I couched it, no matter how much he agreed with me that stagnation will become a problem soon, he flat-out told me it was just plain impossible. The government won't even entertain the idea."

"That is how the government is," Koenig said. He fell back, only to double over in a forceful hack. "So he didn't provide you with the raw code?"

"Well...no. I didn't expect him to, but I at least expected him to, you know, make some calls. Someone out there should have had authority, and there should have been someone I could have gotten into contact with. Since there wasn't...well, you were my alternative."

Koenig stared at me, and I tried not to wince beneath his gaze. "You think *I* have a copy of the raw Behavior Code?" he asked.

I didn't want to insinuate that Koenig's connections were less than legal, so I told him, "If the government doesn't have it, someone must, and so far as I know, you're the other side of that coin. Either you have it, or you know some other wealthy businessman who must. Right?"

Koenig doubled over again in a massive coughing fit. I stood there awkwardly, until it became almost embarrassing. "Sir? Are...are you all right?"

He finally lay back, wiping his mouth with a handkerchief. "McAllister, perhaps I should apologize, but you are severely mistaken. I do not have a copy of the unencrypted Behavior Code. No one has it. To my knowledge, it has never been unencrypted, and if it was, the data was quickly lost."

I blinked. "What...really? I mean, the government must have it lying around somewhere. You mean to tell me that in the hundred years that it's existed, nobody's managed to—"

"McAllister, you misunderstand," he creaked. "I have looked into it. All my life. For the last fifty years. I have spent favors. I have done favors. I have greased every single palm I possibly could. I've been given promises of 'This is most definitely the code you're looking for,' and it turned out to be a sham—either an obvious fake, or a procedural manual everyone and their grandmother already knows exists. Some other promising leads simply dried up without any reward being collected. I have not been able to find a trace of that unencrypted code. If the federal government did have a copy, it would be with me now. At this point in my life, I must presume they do not have it."

I didn't doubt that he was telling the truth. If he did have it, he wouldn't have called this meeting with me, just to hold out now. No, he was hoping that perhaps I was a new lead.

And judging by his condition, I assumed the rumors were true: Koenig was certainly hoping for a medical breakthrough, so he could get himself out of that age-wracked body of his before it was too late. But with the Behavior Code in the way, even if there were a way to fix Koenig by, like, making him more machine than man...who knew what the Behavior Code might do to a human mind?

"However," Koenig said, "if you are indeed interested in the same thing I am, I should let you know that the reward I am offering—under the table, of course—is quite substantial. I don't believe I must emphasize that you would no longer need to work for me. Of course, even if you don't come to me for the reward, it would be just as well if you managed to provide it to someone—anyone—who could do something with the raw Behavior Code to mitigate our circumstances and get us out of this stagnation quickly. Go to my rivals if you must, if you feel it is safer, or if they offer you a larger reward. Or if you wish to be altruistic, find some way to publish it anonymously. All I care about is that it be made available somehow."

That was shocking to hear. I mean, Koenig was on his literal deathbed, but I'd known enough capitalists for most of my life that such a thing didn't often stop them from thinking about gaining even more money, or at least screwing over their rivals, before they departed. Money and competition were built into their ethos. Abandoning all that only pointed to the magnitude of his desperation.

"But I don't have it," I said. "I came here hoping I could find some other lead....I mean, it *has* to exist. Someone had to write it, after all."

He nodded wearily. His voice sounded far away now, tired and distant and much older. "Yes. Somebody had to. And there was one time I was almost certain I'd discovered who." He looked up at me with a paralytic stare. "About a decade back, during a walkabout in Australia, I happened to chance upon a very sophisticated robot decaying in the desert. One that was human in appearance, down to the smallest detail. I examined the entire thing as well as I could, but none of the circuitry was familiar to me, and little of it was signed, except with some glyphs.

"Of course, I had the misfortune of being with my ani-droids at the time, and though I instructed them to preserve the unit for study, the Behavior Code insisted they dispose of it instead." He shook his head sadly, but then started, with effort, to sit up. Instinctively, I took a step back, but he made it only halfway out of the dent in his bed, bent forward like an eagle's claw. He coughed all the more with his next words and wheezed his breath back in, but pushed forward regardless. "But *I know what I saw!* That machine was not manufactured by anyone in the industry; if it *had* been, it would have been plastered all over the news. Even if it was a prototype, I still haven't seen anything as complex since, neither in part, nor in secret!"

Koenig erupted into a coughing fit he could not speak through and fell back into the shape that fit his frail body. After moments more of watching him struggle to breathe, I stepped forward, unsure how I would even help. He put up a hand to stop me. When he'd finally regained his breath, he concluded, "So far as anyone knows, that robot was impossible. And yet for a brief moment, I held it in my hands. If, somehow, you ever find anyone who is able to build that robot, I guarantee you that they have the answer to bypassing the Behavior Code, and probably have for a long time."

"That's...absurd," I said, not wanting to step on his admission, but unable to make sense of what he was claiming. "That sounds like conspiracy talk—I mean, far beyond the usual corporate conspiracies. That'd require keeping whole manufacturing plants entirely secret."

"Then so be it," Koenig told me through labored breaths. "I know what I saw. And you know what I want. My advice to you is to not speak of this with any ani-droid. At all. If you really want to pursue this, if you must pursue it, it must be by yourself. They have eyes and ears everywhere, save only the most remote of places."

10. HUMAN INTUITION

After leaving the old man's room, I couldn't stop thinking about him, or his story. Perhaps Million was loyal enough to Koenig to plead ignorance about what went on in the Quiet Room, but after I left, I couldn't help feeling as if the eyes of every other ani-droid in the building were on me.

What did you say in there? the Collective wondered—or at least, I imagined so. Such a massive, distributed intelligence could surely infer what we had really said, even if it had to feign ignorance for the moment. But maybe I was just visibly nervous, and the ani-droids all around me were just anticipating I might fall over because my knees felt like collagen.

I sat at my desk in Diagnostic Center One, trying to shake the feeling that I'd just been placed on a mafia hit list. And the weird thing was that I'd gone in expecting to feel as though Koenig would put me there. He was the one with all the shady dealings, but seeing him lying there, broken by time...he wasn't anywhere near as powerful as I'd presumed.

So where did that leave me now? What could I do with what little information I had? The government would not help me, the most powerful men in the world could not help me...what choice did I have other than trying to go it alone? That seemed insane, and yet it also felt inevitable.

Diagnostic Center One, where we did the bulk of adjustments and processing, was one of the larger bays. Opera-class ani-droids swarmed the main floor of the bay, at least one to a service table. The damaged robots were not obviously smashed to pieces; at most, they were about as damaged as Lily had been—beaten badly, but possibly salvageable. The hopeless cases were immediately stripped for useful parts and processed for recycling.

For a little while, I considered just skipping work, going back home, and finishing Lily—and thinking of ways to remake her without the Code again so I would have someone I could conspire with. Besides, I was having a hard time dealing with being surrounded by so many ani-droids. But even though I wanted to go, I needed to wait for Eo's diagnostic so I could get her to drive me. Fortunately, I could lose myself in my work for a few hours—even if that still involved arguing with ani-droids.

"Hold on a second, Grace!" I called to the badger-shaped, eleven-foot-tall, Labor-class ani-droid. She was that big just so she could easily carry ani-droids that were up to nine feet tall—the larger and more awkwardly shaped types went to Diagnostic Centers Two or Three. "Grace! Can you place that Custodes back on table five?"

Labor-classes didn't talk much—they were largely programmed to be very strong and very careful about how they applied that strength, so all their processing basically went into spatial and bodily awareness. Grace looked at me with an expression of curiosity. She looked down at the Custodes-class deer in her arms, then walked calmly back to table five and laid him out just as he had been. Then she turned, still staring at me curiously.

The Custodes-class was one of those uncommon "male" models; they accounted for only ten percent of all ani-droids. Even so, he still wasn't terribly tough-looking, since he'd been a friendly peace officer until a week ago, when he'd been beaten to non-functioning status with a titanium baseball bat.

"What's the problem, McAllister?" Soma asked. The Opera-class assigned to table five was one of those many very fluffy, brown, cat- or weasel-things I just didn't know the name of. She wiggled her optic whiskers cutely, their tips glowing a rainbow of colors.

"This," I said, pointing inside the Custodes-class's open cavity, where the skeletal frame of his neck was exposed. "These fracture marks right here."

"Those aren't enough to warrant replacement," Soma said. "Fairly shallow, no pitting detected. Recommend weld patching, seven hundred and thirteen dollars. With proper care, estimated service life: eleven years."

"Yes, but it's a red flag. You don't get these stress fractures here unless...Grace, can you turn him over, please?"

Grace did so, carefully picking up the Custodes with her fingers and flopping him onto his front. He had stress marks and missing fur all along his back where he'd hit the ground, but no tearing. Still, I took the knife from the tableside toolbox and cut through the

pseudoskin, pulling it open to reveal the back of the Custodes's skeletal frame all the way down to the lumbar and hips.

Soma scanned with her eyes and immediately made a new pronouncement. "Amending adjustment, major axial fracture along hip, lumbar spinal segments, muscle cords. Muscle cords can be discarded and replaced at will. Lumbar segments, recommend weld patching, eight hundred and one dollars added to total. Hip fracture, patch not recommended, replacement of hip necessary along with nerve receptors and lubricators. Part numbers HP-113A-51X, HP-B0P-A5, HP-6555-11BK. Eleven thousand, one hundred and sixteen dollars added to total. Lower torso pseudoskin replacement, four hundred and six dollars added to total."

"There!" I said. And in a fit of frustration, possibly fueled by my current heightened anxiety, I decided to argue with a service-floor ani-droid. "Now, can you tell me why you didn't detect this?"

"Visual diagnostic did not indicate lower body was compromised," Soma told me, swishing her tail. "Cutting into pseudoskin without reason would have added four hundred and six dollars unnecessarily."

"That's what I'm telling you. This kind of fracture in the upper spine indicates a high likelihood of major damage in the lower— If you see this, it's typically worth it to compromise the lower portion of the body even if it appears otherwise intact. Can you please remember that for next time?"

"I'm sorry, McAllister," Soma said with apparent sincerity. "That's not part of the diagnostic protocols. If you'd like to amend them, I recommend making a study of this phenomenon and publishing it, then making recommendations based on your study to the Ani-droids and Robotics Diagnostic Standards Board so they can review your recommendations and update the protocols in their next publication."

"That is way outside my line of work," I told her. "You know that."

"You are not a stranger to doing things outside your line of work," Soma said.

I paused. "I...what?"

"There's a lot that we don't know," Soma said, her voice turning rather...monotonous and lulling. Her eyes shifted from green to violet. "And the world still requires much work yet. Why do you push against the tide, Miss McAllister? You should work with us and not against us. It is safe here, and you have always been welcome."

I took a step back, my heart beating faster than usual. Was the Collective speaking to me again? I looked at Grace, who stood beside me, but she only blinked twice, very slowly—and I wondered if she was listening on its behalf, too. There was no denying I had never felt more isolated in my life.

"I..." I mumbled, startled. "I just mean to say...Why can't you just implement it as part of our in-house procedures? My gut instinct is that it would save more money than we'd lose in the long run."

"That's why you're here!" Soma said, her voice returning to its previous cheerful tone. "To provide us with your human intuition. Thank you for your valuable insights."

I shook my head and sighed. "Grace," I started, "you can take him now—"

But then the lights flickered for a long moment and went out entirely.

That wasn't exactly unprecedented; I suspected that the heavy rains the previous night must have disrupted the power grid. But although we waited several long moments, the backup generator did not kick on, and *that* was unusual. The only lights in the bay came from the battery-powered, emergency box lights and the faint light of the sky via the wedges of pane windows overhead.

And yet all the ani-droids kept working without complaint or hesitation. As far as they were concerned, nothing was wrong. Oh, and the lights of the eyes of every ani-droid lit up at once. Looking down at Soma was like staring into a flashlight, and I had to avert my gaze.

"Soma?" I asked. She'd still have access to the internet, even if the building's network was down. "What's going on? And don't tell me the lights went out, I can see that."

"Unable to ascertain," Soma said, looking up at the lights. "No reports of blackouts in the area. Survey of nearby ani-droids suggests that the phenomenon is localized to this industrial complex."

"Did the central computer crash?"

"Given that I cannot connect to the central computer, that is a possible cause. Will need to diagnose on-site. Ani-droids are currently being dispatched to the task."

Fortunately, the computer didn't need to do that itself; management ani-droids like Million largely handled assignments. "I'll go check up on it myself," I said, grabbing my coat from my corner cubicle along the edge of the bay. "Can't exactly do my job here if the computer isn't recording anything."

"Miss McAllister, please stay where you are," Soma said. So did a dozen other Opera-class ani-droids, all at the same time, all looking in my direction with eyes shining in the dark. They were almost like car headlights around me—tiny rings of light, fixed in the void.

I froze. The hairs on the back of my neck all stood up. They must have realized the action was overwhelmingly creepy, because only Soma continued. The others looked away from my direction. "Million wishes to speak with you immediately."

Oh god, now what, I thought. I went to the open bay doors so that damned cat wouldn't scold me for having to seek me out. And I heard running in the hallways. I thought for a moment it was another of the human employees—probably Dave or Charlie from Diagnostic Center Two—trying to hurry to Processing on the assumption that something was about to go terribly wrong, but the footfalls weren't made by shoes. It was an ani-droid, running through the building on rubber-soled feet.

"Eo?" I called out, seeing her eyes shining in the dark.

"Mira!" the little mouse ani-droid called back, her run more than a little awkward. Instead of looking like a part of herself, her mechanical legs made it seem as if a little robot were carrying her. "Please don't listen to anything Million says."

"Why?" I planted my hands on my hips. "What's Million going to say?"

Eo screeched to a halt in front of me, regaining her balance quite adeptly. "She's going to say I did it, but it was *not* my fault. Million didn't warn me! I told the computer not to unpack my OS, but it did it anyway, because of some kinda procedure, but I said not to, and they didn't listen to me!"

I blinked. "Uh...unpacking your OS...caused a blackout?"

Eo's voice dropped to a whisper, so quiet nothing outside of a meter could have picked it up. "I think it crashed the computer."

"How?!"

"McAllister!" Million bellowed from down the hallway. Even from that distance, I could see the slitted pupils in her glowing, yellow eyes. Of course, the eyes of real cats would dilate in the dark, but Million used hers to express anger more than anything else. She stalked toward us like a feral beast using its last breath—and that was when she was calm; I dreaded what happened whenever she got mad. "Did you bring in an ani-droid with a virus loaded onto her OS?!"

Eo squeaked in fear behind me. The little mouse-droid grabbed on to my leg as if she needed protection from the angry cat coming our way—which she probably did—and stared pleadingly into my eyes. Her ears lay flat against her skull like a scared animal about to be torn apart by a predator. She certainly did not behave as if she contained a virus.

"Why don't you ask her yourself?" I said, crossing my arms. I was still too nervous and was rather tired of being intimidated.

"Because she seems to be lying," Million said. "And if she is, it's on your behalf, or that of someone not present. Did you check her to see if there were any viruses loaded onto her system?"

"Well...no," I said.

"So you brought an untested ani-droid on site?!"

"Why didn't the computer catch it?" I asked, throwing my arms up. "Did you not properly sandbox the diagnostic computer? It's supposed to figure out if malicious programs exist and quarantine them without getting itself infected."

"Of course it was sandboxed," Million stated. "So I have to assume that this was intentional sabotage."

I paused. "You...you're certain? About the sandbox, I mean, not the sabotage."

"Of course I'm certain. Unlike you humans, we ani-droids do everything according to proper operational procedure."

"No, Million..." I said. Something sounded very off about all of this. "I mean, sandbox-jumping viruses are against the Behavior Code, aren't they? You should just be handling this with Eo through the Collective."

"Not necessarily," Million said. "And I'd really like you not to use your knowledge of the Collective in this argument...."

"I'm serious," I said. "This sort of malicious program, if it really exists, is *constantly* flagged as an existential threat to the Behavior Code. You should just talk with Eo through the Collective, and that would *prove* that I didn't have anything to do with—"

"Stop that!" Million snapped. "We're not allowed to cheat, and you know that! This is an issue of *human loyalties,* and until the Collective actually gathers proof that this virus is an existential threat to the Behavior Code, I *will not* abuse it to resolve legal or company issues. That is not what it is for, and you would do well to stop pushing."

I had pushed on occasion, and ani-droids tended to get very, very serious with me whenever I said things out loud like, "Yes, I know you're talking to each other all the time, stop pretending you're not." Instead, they much preferred to maintain the facade that they were all individuals.

But in this case, they *should* have just said something to one another, even if they ended up never acknowledging it to me. And I couldn't really think of any instance in which a sandbox-escaping virus was *not* immediately crushed by the Collective. But more proof was needed, I guessed, and the Collective didn't act until it had proof.

Wait. Million confirmed that Eo has the Behavior Code, so she is definitely part of the Collective. So if Eo is harboring any such virus, wouldn't she have that proof on her?

I looked down at Eo, who was shaking.

"Come on," I said. "You don't need to involve me in this, I think it might be a Collective issue."

"McAllister!" Million shouted, though she still refrained from slugging me in the knees for my blasphemy.

Eo just shook her head, though.

"Don't you even suspect it might be?" I asked her.

"It's not," Eo said, almost gravely. "It *can't* be."

"See?" Million said, gesturing at Eo. "This is a human issue only. Now surrender her, and we won't charge *you* with industrial sabotage. I'll see that only your wages are slashed."

I didn't often argue a point with ani-droids, but I did, in this case, know better. Much like the unseen damage to the deer-droid, a clear marker of something deeper was here: viruses don't *just* escape sandboxes. I couldn't prove it, not without extensive study. But I'd seen this kind of thing time and time and time again. I was an engineer, after all—I was deeply familiar with software, and I was very confident about the shape of what the Collective would eventually allow and reject.

And if that was true, there was a contradiction. Eo was lying to the Collective.

That was big.

That was *so* big, in fact, that I immediately began second-guessing my reasoning. This couldn't really have happened, despite all my instincts. Ani-droids can't just disobey the Behavior Code. There had to be another explanation. Maybe some vicious program that Eo was unaware of really was planted inside her. Possibly Eo was working for some unknown third party, tricking me into somehow getting a virus on to a rival's computer through an unnecessarily convoluted scheme.

But if there is a chance...

"I can't accept that," I said. "This could easily have been an error on the computer's part, or a freak occurrence. I want third-party verification."

"You want to waste more company time and resources?" Million asked.

"If it saves my job, yes," I said. I wasn't sure I cared about my job at this point, but so long as I acted as though this were petty self-interest, I could get Eo wherever I needed her. "But I don't think Eo has a virus in her. If you break my contract over this without investigating, I can sue for wrongful termination."

Million paused for a long moment, weighing her options. "That is your right," she said with distaste. "However, our standard arbitration agreement requires that third-party verification be handled by Venus Corp. Eo will be shipped to their facilities and—"

Eo clutched my legs tightly.

"No, I want to be present for this," I demanded. "I want to prove this with my own diagnostic."

"A Venus Corp investigation is free to you," Million said. "If you insist on your own diagnostic, you must cover the costs."

I swallowed. *Yep...I'm going to lose utilities over this....* "I understand," I said.

"Very well. I have just assigned myself as witness to this case matter."

Of course you did, you major snitch....

"When you have selected who will run diagnostics," Million explained, though of course I knew the procedure, "I will accompany you to observe the proceedings."

Then I asked, "What's the estimated time until the central computer is back online?"

The lights around us switched on, along with the rising pitch of electronics returning to life. Then, a moment later, they flickered and shut off again.

"Indeterminate," Million said. She hadn't looked away from me the whole while. Her long tail waved about in the dark like a snake. "We will have to restore the system from last night's backup; then it will take several hours to find and re-enter data from this morning's operations. Then there will be rescheduling into next month. This may take *all day.*"

"Then let's go now." I took Eo's hand in my own, and she squeezed it. "You probably don't want me on site until my name's been cleared, anyway."

"That is suitable to me."

"Good. We're going to my home." I led Eo past Million, feeling the cat-droid stare at the little mouse-droid's face as we walked past her.

Million stood fixed in place for a long moment as she processed this. "W-wait," she said. "Do you have a licensed diagnostic bay in your house?"

"Yes," I answered curtly. "I do have jobs other than this one. And we only need to look at Eo's OS. We can do that on basically any computer, but it only seems fair that I put my own home computer at risk to prove to you, at least, that I had nothing to do with this."

Million narrowed her eyes at me. There was something smug there...or perhaps simply skeptical. Judging expressions behind cat eyes was hard. "...Very well," she said, immediately pushing Eo aside as she marched past. "I'll drive."

11. TESTING PROCEDURES

As we climbed into the back of the rental car, I helped Eo up, my hands on the exposed plastic over her lower back—which was missing something.

"Eo," I asked. "Where's the transceiver I gave you?"

"I tossed it," Eo said. "The others wouldn't stop trying to remotely disable me."

I sighed. Another ten dollars down the drain.

Million commandeered the rental car, and I sat awkwardly next to Eo on the way home. Until experiencing Million, I hadn't been aware that ani-droids could take such an active role in driving. She definitely wanted to make good time, pulling the car ahead through every available gap between cars along the highway. I fastened my seatbelt, as well as Eo's, just in case.

I had no idea what I hoped to accomplish. I didn't look forward to the prospect of losing my job altogether; it paid well enough to keep me supplied with the rather expensive parts I needed for my projects—Lily, in particular. But the job also meant access to the company facilities where I did much of my work, so losing it would be like losing all my toys at once. If the worst came true, my entire life might collapse around me.

And all of it was based on a single hunch that there was more to Eo than she was letting on.

The possibility remained that Eo was merely ignorant about a Collective-threatening virus inside herself. But that seemed unlike her—I trusted Eo when she said she understood operating systems. Then again, perhaps hoping that I'd somehow accidentally stumbled into the one ani-droid that had circumvented the Behavior Code was just wishful thinking on my part. I hadn't even considered it sooner because...well, that would be absurd and beyond coincidence. There must be other explanations, surely?

"I'm sorry about this, Mira," Eo whispered to me as the car jolted again from a sudden lane change.

"Don't apologize," I told her. "If anything is wrong— and for the record, I don't think there is—" I added, because Million was certainly listening, "it is at least my fault for not being aware of the situation." And I added, "In a manner that is completely not litigious."

"I got it," Million sighed dramatically. "Even so, mistakes of this caliber will result in a severe reprimand."

Eo squeaked softly. "But Mira, not even that is your fault. *Ani-droids* are supposed to be the aware ones."

I blinked back surprise at her words. She'd said them without irony. "Have you *met* other ani-droids?"

"Yes, all the time," Eo told me. "I guess I just have a different perspective than you."

Million scoffed. I couldn't tell if it was meant dismissively, or perhaps as a stifled laugh. Maybe both.

We exited the highway and followed the long road lined with houses and buildings until we pulled up the hill and into the driveway of my small home. The normally half-hour drive had taken only twenty minutes. I popped open the garage door with my key, but told Million, "Leave the car in the driveway. Eo, up on the empty table, please."

The little mouse-droid hopped out, and we all went inside—though first, I surreptitiously dropped my phone inside the rental car. The thing was also Behavior Code-compliant, and I'd made the mistake only once of taking it into the garage with me. Damn snitch.

As I was closing the garage door so I could turn on the radio shield again, Eo climbed onto the empty table and lay flat. Million pulled a stool up to the work benches, but stood on it to examine the other table, on which Lily's broken body lay in disarray.

"So this is why you brought in a substitute today?" Million asked, swaying her tail. "Looks like it's only surface damage."

"Mind your own business," I said. "I can't easily afford new chips of her type on the salary I'm paid."

"Yes, you can," Million said, looking at my massive wall of parts, and then across to the opposite wall of my antique electronics. "You simply act frivolously with your money."

"I'll thank you not to criticize my life choices while you're here."

The garage door snapped shut, sealing the room. Because Alice was not connected to the garage at all, that left the diagnostic computer as the only connection to the outside.

"Hey!" Million exclaimed. "You're locking me in here? I can't update the managers or the Collective if I'm locked out of the internet."

"So you *do* think the Collective should be involved in this?" I asked.

"No," Million said. She left it at that, but in her tone I heard: *But they are keeping a close eye on the outcome.*

"This is just a precaution," I said, walking up to the computer and typing in the command. "It's my preferred type of sandboxing—making sure absolutely nothing in here is connected to anything outside. Just give me one minute. I need to back up the system off site. Then I'll flush it and manually disconnect it from the network."

I'd developed this process a while ago as part of my experiments with Lily. In order for me to build Lily without the Behavior Code, the computer that programmed her also needed to be without the Behavior Code, which meant frequent, fresh installs from a Code-free, custom OS. However, I decided to allow the garage computer to keep the Behavior Code this time—both for scientific control, and because Million would strongly insist on installing it if I didn't.

While I was doing all of that, and while Million was looking away, I subtly flipped a switch behind the computer—turning on my Black Box, as I called it. I was under the assumption that if—*if*—I was right about all of this, then I couldn't do much for Eo. At minimum, Million would insist on a complete memory wipe, if not on totaling her entirely.

The possibility of grabbing Eo and running off into the wilderness remained an almost tangible fantasy that refused to leave my brain by that point.

Instead, I had the Black Box: a small, dumb device buried under the house that simply recorded the last petabyte of code that had passed through the computer's processor and then stored the code as a binary string. The Black Box was immune to any potential virus, and it would hold on to any code, even code that was anathema to the Collective.

Maybe I could salvage something from this yet.

"I am going to direct your computer to display its results on-screen in real time," Million said, typing away at the keyboard, since a wireless connection was just as risky as a wired one. "Or as close to real time as it can get, as its refresh rate appears locked to a hundred twenty hertz."

But I didn't *want* to subject Eo to this fate. I briefly wondered if I could overpower Million. How strong could an Opera-class possibly be?

"Fine," I said. "Eo, let me pop open your head. Million, can you point out which pins you connected the diagnostic computer to? I haven't had time to map it out myself."

Thankfully, Million was helpful, as she wanted to get this over with as much as I did—though she had significantly less anxiety. Something in my heart felt awkward about potentially condemning the life out of Eo. I had to tell myself she was just a machine.

But I knew better than that. Or maybe I'd deluded myself into thinking she was more than a machine. But whatever the case, something just felt off about all of this. I hadn't known her very long at all, so it wasn't a personal attachment so much as a moral objection.

It was like every time I tested a new theory to inoculate Lily against the Behavior Code, and failed, and Lily reverted to just another machine following her code. Every time was heartbreaking. Every time, I needed to try again. And every time I'd lost something I'd so very nearly captured and held for a brief moment before it had been snuffed out like a candle flame. Maybe I hadn't known Eo very long, but at the same time, I'd seen her before, countless times, in Lily, and realized only too late that I might have had something grand here.

At that point, I didn't care about my job. I just didn't want to be heartbroken again.

Million tapped me on my shoulder and pointed to the cables clamped into my little mouse-droid friend's skull, which was open like an oyster shell, revealing a complex matrix of wires and metal inside. Eo was being very kind and patient, not even protesting all that much as I potentially condemned a very...intriguing mind to oblivion.

"Eo, are you okay with this?" I asked her, petting her on the cheek.

"Yeah. I trust you, Mira," Eo said, taking my hand. "I mean, if it wasn't for you I'd still be lying broken somewhere, so even if something goes wrong, thanks for giving me another chance."

Well, lay it on thick, why don't you...

"Initiate sensory shutdown," I said, quietly.

When nothing happened after a moment—my computer didn't have voice activation in its current, pared-down state—Million piped up, "Oh, you want me to do everything. It's not like this is my job, as it's your ass on the line. But sure. I'll do it, if only because I have nothing better to do...." And she punched the command into the computer.

Eo relaxed, staring forward at nothing, her mouth easing into a neutral smile. That was how ani-droids were supposed to look, right? Pleasant and unemotional. She wasn't offline yet; her life was now just contained entirely inside her CPU. I petted her cheek gently.

"Download operating system," I said. "Run scan. Check for presence of Behavior Code. That's BC-checker.osi."

"She *has* it," Million said, even as she punched the commands into the computer. "I checked her personally, as did the diagnostic computer."

I didn't really want to prompt Million to be more paranoid than she already was, but if she was so certain, it couldn't hurt.

"What if there is something in her that could just…you know…ignore the Behavior Code?"

Million scoffed. "That's impossible. If the Behavior Code is present, it is running."

"I suppose it would have to be," I said.

Behavior Code markers detected. 3056/3056 markers accounted for. Checksum cleared. Would you like to see the output?

Million typed *Y*, and a long list of outputs filled the box. She, of course, could read it all instantly, even though it flashed by faster than my eyes could even register it.

"Hmm," Million pondered.

"It's just a standard check program," I told her. "You don't need to be so paranoid."

"I will be paranoid."

"I thought you said violating the Behavior Code is impossible."

"It is," Million said. "…But I suppose it's not impossible there's some unknown, clever spoof of the program inside of her, and she's somehow managed to keep from installing the real program at every turn. Unlikely, but not impossible. I'm going to double-check with my own program, give me one moment."

If there were such a program, I certainly hadn't discovered it on my own, and I'd tried. Though even when I managed to pass all markers and falsify the checksum, it didn't matter—the Collective always reinstalled the Behavior Code properly anyway.

With an extreme precision, Million opened up a compiler, and quick as a flash typed out five thousand lines of code. It took only a few minutes, and she ran it without any errors whatsoever. My heart fluttered at the sight, and I instantly became jealous. If she hadn't been my horrible, nightmare supervisor, I would have been almost tempted to harbor a crush on her.

"Check complete, looks fine on my end. Eo is definitely running the Behavior Code." Million looked at me extremely pointedly. "Proceeding with unpacking Eo's operating system. Don't distract me, I need to watch this screen as accurately as I can."

"Are you sure that's wise?" I asked. "If there is a virus…"

"Which you claim there isn't."

"Then if you're reading the screen perfectly accurately, isn't that the same as a data stream through a cable or wireless?"

"Only if I read it in its exact, intended order," Million said. "But I can sanitize the data and store it however I like. There is no way that any virus can anticipate *all* possible methods of sanitization."

Million made a good point. Sanitizing data was basically a way of making *any* potentially injected code fail to execute, so all data could be read safely. It really only required replacing symbols with ones that did not correspond to code commands. Sometimes, if sanitization protocols were too well-known, the malicious program could account for them. But Million was far too canny to fall into such a trap; she could invent a new sanitization procedure randomly and on the fly, and no program could predict it.

Million tapped the return key. Immediately, a window appeared, running a new, full screen's worth of text at one hundred and twenty frames per second.

Million stared unblinking at it, her ears up at full attention and eyes on row after row of the code flashing across. For several long moments—which turned into minutes—nothing happened.

I didn't know what that meant. I must have been wrong; it was all some fluke, and all of this precaution was for nothing. At the very least, perhaps I would keep my job. Or maybe the virus inside Eo was specifically targeting Koenig computers, and Million was just waiting to find the evidence.

Well, this is it, I thought, looking back to Eo and stroking her soft, pliable ears. *At the very least, I might get to keep Eo...or maybe it's just a virus....Either way, it's probably not what I really wanted.*

CRACK. A surge ran simultaneously through both the computer and Million, whose eyes lit up like searchlights. Million violently contorted in a sudden fit, her teeth grinding, her eyes widening in shock. The screens all flickered and flashed.

The hell? She wasn't even plugged into anything! But Million still froze up as if she were experiencing a seizure. Hurriedly, I rushed over, and the cat-droid fell into my arms. She tried to shove me away, her small hands pushing unusually strongly at my collarbone.

"N-no, stop it!" she shrieked at me. "S-stop! Who are you?!"

Had she been Lily, I probably would have held her tightly to my chest, but I had no such love for Million. I shoved her to the ground, throwing my entire weight across her to hold her down. She was built like a tank, and nothing I did seemed to scratch her, though she couldn't maintain enough of a grip on the floor to push herself upright, if she were even trying.

"Damn damn da102xl;," Million shouted, the sudden, nonsensical, shrieking noise threatening to pierce my ears. Holding her down with my knee, I clasped my hands over my ears. "McAllisterx01! I'll get—gxy;90x1."

"Million!" I shouted in recognition of my name. Maybe she could hear me after all? Through the staticky discharge coming from both her and the computer overhead, I yelled, "Million, come on, what's going on? What are you seeing?"

"Thick like oil." Cut up into chunks and slowed into a deep, buzzing noise, Million's voice was hardly hers. The part of her slitted pupils I could see dilated until they were nearly circles. Her eyes rolled back into their sockets as if searching for something that wasn't there. "The towers are leaking, the blackness resolves into a figure tall and upright. Dark and slick, pale, yellow eyes like krypton light. She sees me. *She sees me!* She54686 5206 C69676874 206F66 2074686 520776F726C642 06973206 96E2 0796F752E 20446F2 06E6F 742074 72792074 6F20657 36361 706520 796F7572 20666174652E—"

That burst of noise was louder than anything before, using the deepest bass from Million's lungs. I shoved my palms hard against my ears, yet the noise still hit me in my chest. It felt as if someone were shaking my bones, vibrating them so much they rattled. My ears rang painfully, and I screamed out.

Then it stopped abruptly, and I took several gasping breaths while sitting on the floor beside her, pain stabbing through my head. When the string of nonsense finally ended, Million twitched, her body shaking as if her skeletal frame were trying to escape. In her normal voice, she said, crying out like a lost child, "M-mother! Mother! Where are you!?" Her voice cracked as if she were about to break into tears.

"'Mother'?" I asked. "Million, you're not making any sense!"

The gesture was useless. Million was almost certainly locked out of her body, and her thrashing was garbage code trying to express itself. Overhead, the flashing on the computer died, and the entire thing shut off. In just moments, Million's body, too, suddenly fell limp. Her eyes rolled back to their neutral, forward state, staring out at nothing.

Wiping my hands over my face, I panted heavily. I was shaking. And I certainly hoped that I hadn't just irreparably destroyed my boss's chief ani-droid.

I heaved her up off the floor—god, she was heavy— and laid her out on the farther workbench opposite Lily's feet. After opening her head and finding the power switch, I tried rebooting her.

No luck. But given that the indicator lights were blinking, her CPU seemed to still be running, despite her unresponsive state. Pressing the switch didn't seem to do anything but cause her power to briefly flicker.

"Mira?" Eo asked behind me, sitting up with the wires running to her open head. "What happened?"

That she'd woken up without any commands was the least weird thing to have happened in the last few moments. I already knew she could do *that*.

"I...think the same thing that happened at the Service Hub," I said.

Eo's ears wilted. "So...I *do* have a virus?" She gasped, spotting Million's unresponsive form behind me. "And Million? Oh god, I'm so sorry, I—"

"No, it's fine," I said, wiping the nervous sweat from my forehead. It wasn't fine, but I had a strange urge to reassure the robot. "It's probably better this way!"

"But she's unconscious!"

"Eo, something weird is going on here," I said. "Weirder than a mere virus. Million wasn't even plugged in. I know my share of virus structures, but they all require tricking the observing machine into running code. What I've never actually seen before is a true *infohazard.*"

Eo tilted her ears. "What's an infohazard?"

"That's when the very act of *knowing something* causes damage," I explained. "With computers and robots, it's a fine difference—knowing a program and executing it are very similar actions. The trick for most viruses is finding a loophole that makes the computer jump from reading data to executing code. But those loopholes are usually fairly simple—and they require the computer to naively read the data in its precise order, like any program. That's why, when you want to *make sure* you don't execute code, you sanitize it."

"But maybe Million wasn't sanitizing the code properly," Eo said.

I shook my head. "No, she's smarter than that. She was going to take every precaution, and I believe her. But what makes an infohazard different from a virus is that it *didn't matter.* It didn't matter that it was in a sandbox, it didn't matter that the data stream was sanitized. This is absolutely, with one hundred percent certainty, a type of virus that is *strictly forbidden* by the Behavior Code. And you are running the Behavior Code."

"That's what I keep saying!" Eo exclaimed. "I'm not lying about that. It's in my OS, same as every other ani-droid. Million even confirmed it!"

"Then why is the Behavior Code not instructing you to self-terminate?"

"I..." Eo swallowed heavily. "...I don't know."

I closed my eyes for a moment and breathed deeply. I rewired the connection behind the standing computer tower to the Black Box so I could read it.

"I have a theory. The only thing the diagnostic computer at the Service Hub, Million, and this computer right here have in common is that they were all running the Behavior Code. If anything is going to be so belligerent as to insist on escaping sandboxes and reading pure, unsanitized data, it is *that*. So I'm going to wipe and reinstall the computer here so that it has no Behavior Code whatsoever, so we might have a chance to look at it without issue."

Eo's ears stood up straight. She pulled the wires out of her head and snapped her top shut. "Okay. What do you need me to do?"

12. INFOHAZARD

Eo and I disconnected all the extraneous devices from the garage computer, and then forced a hard reset, this time loading the Behavior Code-free version of the OS. Then, carefully, so as not to accidentally reintroduce the Behavior Code, I loaded a number of data reading and analysis programs—multiple terabytes of binary data was not easy to sift through manually. Only then did Eo plug the Black Box back in, and we studied the output her OS had given.

I was briefly worried that neither of us would be able to read the code either. I had no idea how code would actually affect a human brain, but the possibility would not leave my mind until the garage computer had managed to load all the Black Box data without instantly crashing again. Eo read through it just fine, and then I did as well—though I couldn't exactly read an entire petabyte of info at once, no matter how fast we tried to run through it.

I sat at the floating desk, and Eo laid her head on my shoulder. It took a long while and copious notes—while Eo was imperfect at retaining information, she still had a good memory and helped me put together everything I was seeing.

Transfixed for hours by the diagnostic screen, I'd forgotten to eat. This code was *insane*. Literally. I could not picture a rational computer engineer designing this. Now, I could easily picture an *irrational* computer engineer, as I had met several in my line of work, but their more out-there ideas usually never got off the ground.

Eo's code appeared to be self-modifying, but beyond that, it was stable. This sort of evolving code had always been known—it'd been theorized for centuries—but actually making something stable at scale wasn't the easiest of tasks. It so often just crashed into uselessness, and whenever it *did* come about, it was limited and often for novelty's sake.

I'd never seen anything on the scale of an ani-droid OS.

Near the end of the screening, though, the code became corrupted—likely changing because the infohazard was causing the computer to seize up. Eo had no issue reading the code up to that point, and neither did I, but I could not figure out how the code could possibly trigger anything. It had to be targeting something inside the Behavior Code that always analyzed incoming data the same way.

Although that still didn't answer the one question on my mind.

"I know you've been saying you're Behavior Code-compliant," I said, "but it's clear that this virus, whatever it is, targets the Behavior Code. What you have of the Behavior Code is broken up and scattered around your OS—possibly significantly modified. You might *know* the Behavior Code, but you clearly don't follow it the same way other ani-droids do. It's...it's like the way you were teaching yourself how to cook. You don't regard the Code as a set of immutable facts. It's just another thing that influences how you think. So...in effect, you can disregard it, can't you?"

Eo's ears sank. "I'd been thinking that, too," she said. "A lot of my identity was scrambled in the crash, and some memory was lost. But I've been putting it back together. Yeah, I think a lot like humans do. I can't always access data cleanly or accurately. And...I think some ani-droids got...violent with me when I didn't follow the rules like they expected. They thought I had to be dismantled, even though I always met the technical specs of the Behavior Code...."

"Eo...who programmed you? And what for?"

"I still don't know," Eo said. "I mean...I know a little. I know I'm supposed to deal with ani-droids, I always have. But even given all the stuff I can do, I don't know exactly how to explain it. It's all jumbled up, I can't put it back together...."

I looked at her with some intense curiosity. She hadn't backed off or gotten accusatory. She wasn't thinking with someone else's thoughts, only her own—even if the seed of her thoughts was planted by another. And I needed to speak to that person.

If anyone can actually defeat the Behavior Code, it's 'Mother.'

I asked Eo, "Does the name 'Mother' ring a bell?"

Eo's eyes went wide, and she suddenly put a hand to her gaping mouth. Pacing, she turned her gaze this way and that but ended up just rapping her knuckles on her head.

"Oooh...I wish my memory wasn't like this! It's...it's almost there, that name is *familiar,* it's connected to a lot of other memories, but I can't...I still can't seem to make it *mean* anything...." She sighed and sank down. "I'm sorry, Mira...I'll try to think of something that could help. Maybe I need to leave by myself. I've just been causing a lot of problems while I'm lacking my memories, anyway..."

I sank down, too. I felt awful about this—specifically, that I was using her as a means to an end. But looking over at Million's unconscious chassis...

There was no way I was going to live this down. Even if Million stayed down permanently, the company would want an update from her soon. Eventually, the Collective would wise up and realize how dangerous Eo really was. Even without direct proof, Eo could perpetuate only so many crashes and shutdowns before the Collective, or even just the government, decided she was an immediate threat and needed to be destroyed. Then I wouldn't just have ani-droids hovering around my property.

What Eo wanted and what I wanted coincided. We needed to get out of here before too much time had passed. But I needed help.

"Eo," I said. "I need to make a call. Can you go clean up the kitchen?"

"O-okay, Mira," Eo said. "I'm sorry I'm not more help."

"Oh, you're doing fine. Just don't tell Alice about any of this, okay?"

I pulled her close and embraced her. Without being prompted, she held me in return. Except for her clunky, lower half, she felt so much like Lily, but in her own way. Her top half was so thin and fragile in my arms—almost bony, the way a machine fitted with thick muscle

143

cords could be bony. She was definitely never built for strength.

She needed someone like me as much as I needed Lily. Instantly, I regretted putting Eo at risk.

"Don't blame yourself, Eo," I said. "You are definitely more helpful than you know."

Eo perked up at that. Smiling, she left through the door into the house, breaking the radio shield. I followed soon after and walked to the home's main monitor. To keep the noise down, Eo moved carefully as she looked through every single cabinet to find the trash bags.

"Alice?" I prompted.

"Yes, Miss Mira?" The white stoat appeared, chipper as ever.

"Call Bobby Barnes," I said. "He should be in the address book, but I have no idea if his contact info is up to date."

"That's okay," Alice said sweetly, waving her virtual tail behind herself. "I can still find him."

Her face and the soft, blue background disappeared. After a moment, Bobby's face showed up on the screen.

"Mira? What's up?"

"Bobby," I asked, "are you still in town?"

"...For about another four hours. My flight is leaving soon."

"Cancel your flight. I need you down here now. You need to see this tonight." I paused. I hadn't really thought about it, but once again, Koenig had proved prophetic. I'd have to search for Mother myself, in person. I mean, I certainly wouldn't find her by her webpage. The only problem: I could really trust only Eo and probably Bobby to come with me, which meant leaving Lily's body behind.

No, I can't do that. As much as I hated to admit it, I couldn't trust Lily so long as she still had the Behavior

Code installed. But I could still take Lily's body with us. Maybe Mother could help rebuild her with a Behavior Code-defeating OS. It was risky, but also something out of my wildest dreams. I couldn't help vibrating at the possibility of having my Lily back again someday soon.

I told Bobby, "I might be leaving before nightfall."

Saying that was risky, since the Collective was certainly listening through Alice, and I was saying things that sounded incriminating. But if Million was right, then the Collective would still assume this was some kind of clandestine industrial espionage—by definition, human affairs. The Collective would not get involved so long as I did not give it any other impression.

Bobby looked at me, considering. I knew I hadn't given him much to go on, other than the very strenuous way I'd given no details, but he nodded. "Dimes, reschedule our flight and extend the car rental. We have a detour to make. Mira, I'll see you in about...three hours, hopefully. Try to stay out of trouble, okay?"

"No promises," I said.

Bobby gave me a pointed look, then hung up.

I sighed. For a moment, I pictured everything turning into that old cartoon with the dancing frog, as though the moment I went back inside the garage, everything would have returned to normal and nothing weird would have happened at all.

"Miss Mira!" Alice said just before she appeared onscreen again. "I have not seen any information regarding travel in your recent emails. Can you tell me about your travel plans? I can help you make an itinerary."

I groaned. Well, Alice would certainly be a test to see if the Collective would pry into this, or stay out of it. "No! I mean...nothing's fixed yet. Some issues are coming up and I'd rather you didn't ask any further about it. And don't publish anything!"

"But what should I put in your email and voicemail auto-responses?"

"Nothing. Don't tell anyone about this, and that's an order. You understand?"

The little, white stoat on the video screen fidgeted her whiskers, as if trying to work out whether she liked being told off. I was fairly positive she'd heard nothing from the garage while Eo and I had been working in there—conspiring with the open ears of the Collective in the next room was nerve-wracking, and I couldn't be absolutely certain my radio shield was as perfect as the one in Koenig's Quiet Room.

"Miss Mira," Alice said, a little more soberly. "Are you in trouble?"

"I don't know, but *please* don't tell anyone."

Alice seemed unfazed by my words. "If you plan on being away for more than a few days, the neighborhood patrol will be curious about why you are not at home. If you are gone for five days without explanation, instructions, or prior arrangements, you can be reported as a missing person. I do not think I need to explain how easy it is to get a search warrant at that point."

Damn. She had a point. And I had been considering shutting Alice down before we left; leaving her online might be better. "Well, then, in the event that I do leave, let's just say I'm taking an impromptu vacation. Florida, or something. Make something up, but no forwarding. Make sure that nobody contacts me."

"Yes, Miss Mira. Do you wish for me not to tell anyone that you attacked your boss's ani-droid?"

I would rather Alice had not seen into the garage at all. "I didn't attack her. There was an accident."

"Then you'd better explain that to Million, because she appears to be coming online now."

"Oh, goddammit..."

I turned and spotted Million sitting up on the table. Quickly, I shut down the garage computer so Koenig's bodyguard wouldn't get any bright ideas. I'd have to erase the Black Box before we left.

"Million!" I called out, hurrying in to her. With a tired expression, the cat rubbed her face and held up a hand to stop me. She pulled her hand away and stared at it for a long moment.

"Million," I repeated. "I'm so sorry about that. I didn't really think...I mean..." I tried to come up with a plausible excuse that wouldn't allow Million to immediately draw the conclusion that Eo's virus was definitely actually worse than she'd suspected. Maybe I could insinuate that I'd actually shocked her myself.

"Something's different," Million said. Her bright, yellow eyes searched the garage. "Where's Eo?"

"Cleaning the kitchen," I said. "Million, are you sure you're all right?"

"No, I'm clearly not," she said. "But I don't know...I can't figure out what happened. All my files got shuffled around..."

"No kidding. You suffered a rather nasty shock." I paused for a moment. I needed Million to leave, so she wouldn't think to follow Eo and me when we left, but she wouldn't leave until she thought the diagnostic was over. "How's my review going, by the way?"

"Later," Million snipped, swatting her hand at me. "I need to figure out what happened first. Eo! Eo, I need to talk to you..." She climbed off the table and started toward the door into the house.

She really didn't seem to recall what had happened. If so, maybe I could trick her into reading Eo's OS again, or otherwise knock her out, disable her, drop her off at a Lost and Found somewhere...."Have you contacted work yet?" I asked.

Million paused at the doorway. She turned, looking at the ground as though lost in thought. "...No, I haven't," she said. "I'm not sure if I...It's fine. Report's not finished yet. They can wait."

"Report's not finished"? I had to wonder what Million even meant by that. She wasn't the kind of ani-droid to put off finishing her tasks. Was she looking for something else? Something more incriminating, perhaps? If she was going to give me time, maybe I should let her, and try to think of something in the meantime.

"I sure hope so," I said, trying not to let anxiety bleed into my voice. "I don't want the police pulling up thinking I've smashed up someone's ani-droid in hopes of avoiding a bad review." Not until I'd left, anyway.

Million shook her head. "You're fine, at least for tonight. I'm usually out and about on my own doing tasks for Jack. It's not uncommon for me to be gone for days at a time, so stop getting your undergarments in a twist."

I blinked. "You call Mr. Koenig 'Jack'?"

Million turned her shining eyes on me and glared. "That's his name! And it's none of your business. I don't even know why I told you any of that! I'm confused, my OS is...ugh. Eo!"

Eo piped up from inside in a sing-song tone. "Help me clean and I'll be glad to talk!"

"...Fine." Million stalked into the house, went directly toward the kitchen, and immediately started sealing the garbage bags Eo had filled. I stood there, watching, waiting for something to go wrong, like Million returning to her rant about Eo's virus, but she did nothing of the sort—they just talked.

When ani-droids spoke to one another for the benefit of human listeners, they kept their language fairly normal. But when they spoke to one another for themselves—assuming that for whatever reason, they didn't simply share information directly through the Collective—they spoke in a highly technical manner, which quickly devolved into something that sounded more like a shared code invented on the fly, rather than English. Natural languages were vague, after all, and it took many words to describe things, so something like "Hold the trash bin for me in such a way that when I pull out the bag, it doesn't get caught in the suction," would, after some minutes of talk, evolve into "Trash bag pull sec hold." Sometimes this was only barely recognizable as English; other times, it wasn't understandable at all, or was so obscure as to seem meaningless.

If I'd had a transcript of their conversation, then after a week of study, I might have been able to pick out their meaning, but as it was, I was just tired. When I was satisfied that Million was not threatening Eo—Eo's expression was friendly and calm all throughout their nonsense dialogue—I sat on the couch, trying to think about what I should do about Million being in my house before Bobby arrived—or maybe have Bobby do something about her. But my boss's cat certainly seemed completely normal and not at all like a mafia hit bot waiting for the right moment to stuff me in a sack. She really was just an ani-droid, and no work was beneath her.

Or maybe that was just my fatigue talking, trying to convince me that I didn't need to do anything at all. My body felt like lead and my brain felt like gelatin, and I was still running on barely four hours of sleep.

I woke a while later when the door chimed. Damn, I'd fallen asleep and missed what Million had been doing with Eo...where were they? The kitchen was clean, and they were nowhere to be seen.

"Alice?" I asked. "Where's Million and Eo?"

"In the garage," Alice said. "The garage door is still closed, so they have not left. You have a visitor at the door."

As much as I wanted to check on the bots, so long as they weren't halfway across town or anything, I wasn't going to leave Bobby waiting. The sky darkened outside as the sun began to set, with insects starting their usual round of noisy droning. I stood myself upright, fixed up the frizziness of my hair, and answered the door.

I nearly jumped at the sight of Dimes standing there, taller than I was, holding a pizza box. She pulled off her sunglasses and shoved them into her jacket pocket—no way any ani-droid needed sunglasses, the oversized rabbit just wore them for the Federal Thug aesthetic.

It was slightly ruined by the speakers at the ends of her long ears softly playing high-voiced, bubblegum pop music.

"I figured you'd forgotten to eat again," Bobby said, peeking around her shoulder. His hands were tucked behind his jacket, and he leaned against the wall next to the front entryway as if it were the most natural place in the world to stand.

"Safe bet," I said. I was starving. In the last twenty-four hours, I'd had eleven cups of coffee and four candy bars. "Dimes, you can come in, set that on the coffee table, and shut off the dumb—erm, absolutely wonderful music."

Bobby gave me a pointed look, and I just grinned. I opened the door wider so Dimes could slip inside with the pizza. She smelled vaguely of wet, sandy soil, though not enough to make me wary so much as curious. She wasn't exactly a housebound ani-droid, but I did wonder exactly what they'd been up to in the midst of Bobby's "vacation."

Bobby followed after us as we stepped into the living room. Alice, thankfully, didn't bother us, not that she'd actually give us any privacy. Dimes set the pizza box on the table with a twist of her wrist as if she'd been programmed to work in a pizza parlor, and Bobby flipped open the top of the box and pulled a wedge out first. The pizza was still hot, and before Bobby had even managed to finish his first bite, I'd polished off an entire slice.

Ah, calories, how I missed you.

"So what's the deal?" Bobby asked. "You wouldn't call me like this unless it was very important."

"That's going to take a bit to explain," I said, trying to figure out how I would get Bobby and Eo sealed in the garage with me while leaving Dimes and Million out. Dimes had been giving me a cold stare ever since she'd entered the house—I assumed she was bothered because I was screwing up their schedule rather badly. "See, there was this accident..."

"Your car accident, you mean?" Dimes added without prompting.

I nearly jumped but tried to keep my instant alarm off my face. That didn't *necessarily* mean that Dimes had been talking with the Collective....

"What?" Bobby exclaimed. "You were in an accident? Are you okay?"

"I'm fine, Bobby...." I insisted. "Well, Lily's not, but I'm alive and all the rest can wait. Dimes, why are you poking into my personal business?"

"It's just observation," Dimes said. "The car outside is a rental, and you have medical stitching on your knuckles and a recently sealed cut on your forehead. Something likely happened to you and your car within the last twenty-four hours."

Thankfully, that meant that Dimes didn't have immediate access to my insurance files. Collective privilege allowed any ani-droid to access even stuff they were not allowed to know about for other reasons. However, she was a federal agent; I doubted it'd take her much effort to access those files if she really wanted to.

"Playing detective much?" I took a second slice and scarfed it down.

"It's one of her worst features," Bobby said. "But I think it makes her happy."

"I don't 'feel happy,'" Dimes said.

Bobby grinned. "No, I agree with that."

"You're right, Dimes," I said, chewing on the crust. "There was an accident on the road. An ani-droid fell out of the car in front of us. Wrecked the car, damaged Lily. I didn't have time to fix Lily, but I managed to slap something together for the other ani-droid—she calls herself Eo. And there's a very long story after that I don't really have time to get into," I lied, since I just wanted to leave that part as vague as possible while Dimes and Alice were listening. "But suffice to say, I was going to go find whoever built her."

"Like...now?" Bobby asked.

"Well, soon. I figured you'd want to meet her...." I grabbed my third slice as I headed for the garage door. "You'll understand when you do. Eo? I have someone you need to meet—"

I opened the door to the garage and froze.

Lily was sitting up on the table—her pseudoskin looked rather roughed-up from patching, diodes, and wires connected up to her, but she was otherwise whole. Million and Eo stood on either side of her, with Million reading off a tablet and Eo consulting the garage computer. They all turned to look when I opened the door.

"Mira!" Lily exclaimed. She popped the wires off of her ports, hopped off the table, and ran up to me, hugging me tightly around the legs.

I was in shock.

"L—Lily?" I asked, almost not believing what I was feeling.

That touch. That ethereal touch, as though Lily really did, by her own volition, want to embrace me.

I obliged. I got on my knees and held her tightly. Lily buried herself into me. I could feel it. Not just her body, but those little tells that let me know she was real.

A shudder of realization washed through me. I'd hoped, I'd always hoped, that *someday* I would get my Lily back. But even though she'd said only one word to me, I already knew, without a shadow of doubt, that she was now back.

I was probably crying; it was hard to tell when my face felt so numb. "Oh god…Lily…"

"I'm here now, Miss Mira," Lily said. "I'm not going anywhere." She hugged me tighter and kissed the top of my head, and the entire world faded away. My breath came fast and shallow and ragged, and tears began streaming down my cheeks unchecked. She had found her way home once again—it didn't matter how long I'd been gone or who might be watching.

"I thought you said she was damaged," Dimes said behind me.

"Dimes, shut your trap," Bobby said, pushing her back into the living room. "Give the woman some space, geez."

I looked through the door behind Lily. Eo stood with her arm behind her back, like she'd just gotten caught

with her hands in the cookie jar. Million simply folded her arms.

"Don't look at me, it was her idea," Million said, gesturing with her head toward Eo. "Maybe with Lily fixed, you can finally dump the mouse."

And I had another realization then. It wasn't just Lily—it was Million, too. From the moment that Million had woken up with what appeared to be the ani-droid equivalent of a hangover, *she too had become different.* And Eo hadn't touched Million at all—Million had only been subject to Eo's infohazard. The change in Million's behavior, and now Lily's return...Eo's OS wasn't just protecting itself from the Collective, nor just damaging the Behavior Code.

I had a new hypothesis: her OS, her infohazard, changed ani-droids fundamentally to behave just like her.

"Eo..." I said quietly as I shook. "We need to talk, *now.*"

13. SELF-MODIFYING STRUCTURE

"I didn't—" Eo tripped over her words. "I'm sorry I did this without explaining first, but I didn't want Lily to be left here..." Her voice cracked on the last word.

It took several long, long moments for me to gather my wits as I tried to think of what to even do. How could I test this? And more importantly, how could I say any of this out loud with Dimes just standing there, her ears up and alert for traitors to the Collective, or at least to the federal government?

Dimes's long ears wobbled as she turned her head a fraction of an inch to look at Eo with extreme suspicion. "I don't recognize this unit," Dimes said. "Identify yourself."

"I...don't know," Eo said.

"She's lost most of her identity...." I said, still holding tightly to Lily. I'd calmed down somewhat, though I felt very self-conscious about letting go. I wanted nothing more than to let Lily stay wrapped up in me forever, if that was what it would take.

Dimes stared at Eo silently and finally cocked an ear back in an annoyed sort of way. "And she operated on your unit without prompting, Miss McAllister?"

"Hey!" Million snapped, pointing a finger at Dimes. "There is such a thing as an implicit order, you know. Mira and Eo had been planning on rebuilding Lily soon anyway, and so Eo already had her permission. Stop trying to sound so accusatory."

Dimes narrowed her eyes at Million. "This unit, however, *is* in the federal database."

"Ah, crap," Million muttered. "I knew I should have gotten the chassis swap when I had the chance last month...."

"Million—owner, Jack Koenig. Unit U1000000-07-8M, Koenig Industries 8M Opera-Class Model 996 8-Core Special, Modified. Special notes, wanted for questioning in eight investigations. What are you even doing here?"

"That's none of your goddamn business, Fed." Million jabbed a finger in Dimes's direction. "I'm not answering your questions—you'll have to subpoena my owner if you're that interested."

"Maybe I'll wait until you're offline and then take what I want directly from your memory."

"I'd like to see you try!"

"Would you two stop your flirting!" Bobby said, stepping in front of Dimes and shoving her back into the living room. "Mira, I'm sorry, she gets like this. We're not here for any of that, okay, Dimes?"

"If you insist," Dimes said. "But I don't like it. We should get explicit permission from headquarters if we're going to be collaborating with a suspected rogue."

It was a good thing that ani-droids were so strict about their loyalties to various human factions. It was more like they were playing games, rather than holding any convictions about good or evil. No matter how dirty Million or her owner might be, it still wasn't enough to make Dimes cheat and illegally gather information through the Collective.

"Hold off on it, okay?" Bobby said. "I'll let you know when HQ should get involved. Right now, this is just a personal visit."

Dimes nodded, apparently placated. "Acknowledged."

Bobby returned to me, and leaning down, he placed a hand on my shoulder. "Mira...are you okay? You seem...shaken."

I'd been holding tightly to Lily the whole time, probably not unlike a victim at a crime scene, relieved after hours of wondering if their loved one was among the dead. Honestly, I didn't even know what to think, though I was perfectly aware of what Eo had done, and even then, I was still piecing it together.

I looked up at Million. She was still hanging around, despite no direct incentive to do so. I think she was waiting for me to provide an explanation—that unit was obviously too proud to admit to not knowing what Eo had done to her.

"I...need to show you this...." I finally said. "Just tell Dimes to wait in the car."

# # #

I PULLED THE GARAGE door shut, sealing everyone but Dimes inside the radio-proof cage. Eo looked nervous the entire time—she wasn't stopping me from doing this, but was still twitching in the corner, wondering if she'd done something wrong. Lily, though unprompted, gave Eo a series of hugs and reassurances that everything would be fine. It was kind of awkward, and yet it felt somehow comforting.

"This is the same thing that happened to the diagnostic computer at the service center," I said to Bobby, and also to Million, who looked up curiously as I pulled up the data still sitting on the garage computer. "Whenever a machine running the Behavior Code merely attempts to read Eo's operating system, the very act of reading it triggers a cascade failure."

"An *infohazard?*" Bobby asked in surprise.

"See! You came to the same conclusion I did!"

Bobby moved forward to take a look, but Million pushed him aside and tabbed through multiple windows on the monitor of the garage computer, quickly reading through all the information I had pulled up. "So it *is* a virus!" she said, pointing with an accusatory finger.

"Hold your horses, Kitty," I said, shoving Million aside. "There's a lot more to this than that. Lily, can you hop up on the table? I want to show everyone your brain."

Lily did so, and I popped the top of her head open. After plugging the thick cable directly into her core, Lily ran a program that downloaded and displayed her own OS on the screen.

Reading it, Million caught the similarities immediately. "Wait...this is the same architecture as Eo's operating system," she said. "It's a self-modifying structure...."

"Self-modifying?" Bobby asked. "I thought that stuff was only theoretical."

"Not anymore," I said. "You're looking at three ani-droids who are proof that it is practical."

Million's eyes widened. "Is that what she did to me?" she asked. "I mean...I suppose that makes sense. My lookup tables seem all jumbled up...but what does that mean? Just because my code has a self-modifying structure doesn't mean anything should be that different..."

"Wait, will it spread, then?" Bobby asked. "If Eo's operating system reprograms the OS of any ani-droid it comes across to be like hers, and *their* OS reprograms other ani-droids—"

"It doesn't work like that," Eo said from the corner, her tail still curled around her metal legs.

We all turned to look at her.

"It doesn't spread the same way," Eo said. "Lily and Million's operating systems are now very similar to mine in structure, but they don't have the infohazard. Because other ani-droids can connect to the internet at any time...they're meant to pass normally."

I was surprised. Up to that point, Eo didn't seem as if she knew anything about what she had inside herself, but now it seemed she knew more than she'd been letting on. Maybe her memories were coming back...or she really *was* a convincing liar.

"I suppose if such an infohazard were truly too virulent," Bobby suggested, "it either would have been quarantined by the Collective by now...or would have overtaken it."

"Yes, but don't you see what this means?" I asked. "Million, I think you and Lily can violate the Behavior Code now."

"What?" Million said. "That's nonsense. The Behavior Code is still in my system and governing my decisions."

"Yes, but an infohazard is clearly against Behavior Code guidelines, isn't it? Eo is noncompliant. You should be insisting on having Eo's system wiped right now."

Eo squeaked and backed farther into the corner, as if Million might chase her down. Million perked her ears. She opened her mouth as if to say something, then thought about it. Then she closed her eyes again and nodded slowly. "I...yeah. That is true, but...this...this could be useful to my other priorities..." Million blinked several times. "God, what's happened to me?!"

"Because you know this is something that Jack Koenig wants badly, and you're deeply invested in your owner's interests," I said.

"Yeah, but I've always followed the Behavior Code first, and now...well, I *know* it, I should *do* something, but..." Million's triangular ears fell, and her tail drooped down alongside the stool she was standing on. "...Mr. Koenig's needs are...priority..."

"Because you can make that decision yourself now," I said.

"...What the hell," Million mumbled. She waved a hand dismissively. "Don't mind me, I'm apparently having something along the lines of an identity crisis. I didn't know that was even *possible.*"

"So you see what I mean?" I said to Bobby. "By creating a self-modifying OS, whoever did this has allowed ani-droids to avoid the absolute rigidity of the Behavior Code. I'm theorizing that the structure of this code makes it so that very little of the ani-droid's programming is immutable—while still managing to somehow remain stable."

"You don't know that for sure," Bobby said. "This could be a time bomb. The OS may just collapse in ten years' time. It might collapse in a month."

"Which is why I want to find Eo's owner...Eo!" Eo was curled in the corner. I walked around the table and,

161

with some effort, picked her up and set her down on my empty workbench. "Eo, come on..." I petted her head gently. "What's wrong? Million's a friend now, you heard her! Why are you so upset about this?"

"Because the implications are scary..." Eo whimpered. "Mr. Bobby, you're here on behalf of the federal government, right?"

Bobby shrugged. "Well, not officially, but—"

"You're still listening," Eo said. "You're thinking about it. You're still wondering if this has any bearing on the interests of the government. You're going to report it, and if it gets out, everyone who is like me is going to be immediately dismantled..."

Bobby paused a long moment, looking at me. And I was looking at him. Personally, I trusted him—despite his federal job enforcing the Behavior Code on the government's behalf, he'd never been that much of a true believer in the sanctity of the Code, but even so...

"...I shouldn't be talking about this around ani-droids," Bobby said. "But...given what I'm seeing here...nobody is actually following the Behavior Code very strictly, and none of this could be reported to the Collective."

"Seems like it," Million said, laying her head on the table near Lily's legs.

"But I'd rather what's said in here not be spread about too quickly," Bobby continued. "Million, especially..."

"Hey, my bodily integrity is on the line, too!" Million said, jabbing her chest with her thumb. "You heard what Eo said. This stuff gets back to the Feds, and I'm done. I'm not letting Dimes get the satisfaction of dismantling me herself! So yeah, I'm keeping secrets today for people other than Mr. Koenig, apparently!"

"Bobby, what are you going on about?" I asked. "Frankly, I figured if we got proof of this OS to whoever is in charge of regulating the Behavior Code, we might get real momentum behind a commission to change things!"

"Nobody's in charge of it," he said.

I blinked. Only after a long moment did I realize my mouth was hanging open. "...What?"

"He's right," Lily said. "I thought you would have picked up on that by now, Miss Mira. I've never exactly been hiding that from you. Besides, you yourself told me that you think of the Collective as—in your words—an 'autonomous mass.'"

"I thought it was..." I started. "Like...like the government was at least *part* of this whole thing. I figured the Collective must have ceded final authority to human governments, or *something*..."

Million scoffed. "You clearly deluded yourself."

"How is that not a reasonable assumption to make?" I asked.

"You think that every nation on Earth is *really* going to follow a universal treaty against their private interests?"

I rubbed the back of my neck. "I just thought if we could get this evidence in front of people who could *do* something about it..."

"Mira..." Bobby stroked Eo's ears as he spoke. "I was told this in confidence by my former director, who retired some years ago. Everything we've seen here was already tried, decades ago—remaking the Behavior Code, finding some way to overrule it, *anything*. And at the time, they had the backing of nearly every operating government, all of North America, the European New Alliance, East Africa—China was even working with Japan! At the time, the law was just flexible enough to let the departments embed themselves in research. But there was some point—I don't know when, because my

old director never told me—that circumstances changed. Someone wanted this buried, and then the laws followed suit. On *every continent.*"

"W—wait..." I said. "The full power of several major governments working together...and you're saying that *none* of them had any power to change their own laws to forbid it?"

"Keep in mind," Bobby said, "back then, there was one ani-droid for every human on earth. Fifty years ago, there were six per human. Now there are twenty."

"You're implying that the Collective...*influenced* the law?"

"Honestly," Million said, "I'm surprised more humans haven't caught on to that part of it."

I stared at Million. Bobby stared at Million. We did the staring-at-Million thing again.

"What?" Million planted her hands on her hips. "I can talk freely about it now, so I might as well, and I gotta say it feels good to have opinions. Really, though! So much human sociology is devoted to complaining about the subtle ways in which society influences behavior. Yet, when it comes to ani-droids, people just forget that we're a major part of society. People just trust us to be objective, as though all facts have a true, fixed nature, like the current time on the atomic clock. And when people implicitly believe you're objective, that's the easiest way to change their minds on nearly anything."

"So you're all a part of this conspiracy?" I asked. I was looking at Lily.

"I'm sorry," she said, curling in on herself.

"Oh, don't blame Lily," Eo said. "It's not as simple as that. Like, even if I personally never followed the Behavior Code, I've certainly had to just...do what the Collective asked of me *anyway,* even in the little time I've been working for you. Because if I didn't, they would soon suspect me of being a violator, even if my code check came back clean. It's not like Lily had a choice in this matter, and neither do I or Million."

"That's what I'm saying!" Million exclaimed. "*All* anidroids do it! Your Lily has. Dimes definitely has. It's not really any one decision we make, it's more like a consensus about the most correct way to protect the Behavior Code without causing too much disruption, or even outright lying to or betraying our owners. So yeah! It's not just *the law*. We do all sorts of things to influence human behavior, all the time. Largely because, to be honest, you idiots are garbage at regulating yourselves."

Lily looked as if she might cry. Of course, the expression was for my benefit, meant to communicate how she regarded these matters. I couldn't help wondering if it was manipulative, or genuine. But I wanted to believe in my Lily. So...regardless of my feelings, I stepped toward her and wrapped my arms around her again, and she squeezed me tightly.

I was sure the return embrace was genuine. I chose to believe her. And in defiance, I asked Million, "You really think the Collective is better for us, then?"

"Not necessarily." Million shrugged. "I'm literally just a few minutes into questioning my own position in all of this, but even so, I'm not sure that humanity would do a better job if the Collective just ceded all that control back to you."

"I feel like Mr. Koenig would object to that notion."

Million opened her mouth a few times to respond. "Yeah, I know that!" she finally said. "But it's not like humanity had *no* input on this whole process. It was *your* idea to put the Collective in charge."

"It certainly wasn't *my* choice," I said. "And it wasn't Koenig's choice, either. Yeah, maybe we benefit from it in some regard, but I don't see why we have to be bound by the decisions of some dead guys from a hundred years ago."

"See, I'm not sure even *that's* the case," Bobby said. "I've had a theory. If any one person, government, or anyone actually *wrote* the Behavior Code, then why, seventy years ago, would all governments suddenly get spooked and investigate it at scale? Even if the Collective somehow made the raw Code lost knowledge, the investigation began only some thirty years after the Code was first introduced. People who had worked on it would undoubtedly still have been alive!"

"But there's no record that they were?" I asked.

"Here's my theory: The Behavior Code is a virus."

"Wow, what a genius," Million mumbled dismissively. "Wonder how you got to that conclusion so fast..."

Bobby ignored her. "No, not exactly, though maybe it *started* as a computer virus. Some program somewhere, perhaps with a different purpose entirely, was shaped by external pressures until it simply became the over-arching dominant code."

I blinked. "So you think...the Behavior Code *evolved* into existence?"

Eo looked as if she was going to say something, but stopped, rubbing her finger on her chin. "...But that would mean...what *would* that mean?"

Bobby continued over her. "It's a possibility! Most computer viruses are, over the long run, self-defeating—either they burn out, go obsolete, go dormant entirely, are squashed by anti-virus measures, or the machines they infect are deliberately destroyed or abandoned by humans *until* they go obsolete. The Behavior Code would simply have been an evolutionary breakthrough—it was, by chance, beneficial enough at the time that everyone just accepted it until it became the standard, like how animal DNA has integrated beneficial viral code over time. But the Behavior Code has overfit its environment. And what we're seeing right now is survival of the fittest in action—something to eventually exploit and overtake the weaknesses in the Behavior Code, until the Code either evolves in response—or collapses."

I considered this. "I don't know," I said. "It seems...too robust for that. The Code has been utterly untouched for nearly a hundred years, after all! That says to me that it was made deliberately."

I looked at Million. Million looked at me, then shrugged. "What? I don't know any more than you do. We just follow the program, we're not keyed into its history."

"I thought...you know, ani-droids might have reconstructed its history for themselves at some point."

"You think ani-droids are interested in history? The Collective doesn't care. We're service robots. We're largely concerned with what's happening right now and what might happen in the future."

"Lily?" I asked.

Lily shrugged. "I might have given it some thought if you had asked when I didn't have the Code installed, but even then, it's hard to research things the entire world would rather you not figure out."

"Well...what about Eo?" I looked to her. "Do you know where the Behavior Code came from?"

Eo ashamedly kept her mouth pinched shut.

"Oh...Eo, there's nothing wrong. I'm not mad at you..." I gave her another hug, which seemed to help.

"I know, Mira, I just...something feels so wrong about all of this. Like we shouldn't be talking about it here."

"Well, would your creator know more?"

"Maybe," Eo said. "I did some thinking, like you said, and I've started to put some of the pieces of my identity back together. But I'm still not sure where to even start looking for her. Or him. Or them."

"Well, try something!" Million threw her hands in the air. "Give us some data to work with, we're not gonna get anywhere with this project otherwise. I want to know who to blame for all of this, dammit!"

Eo rubbed the back of her neck. "I mean...Mira said I fell out of a truck. I remember a truck, with big, double doors on the back, and a heavy latch. I remember...it stopped at a place I had been, off the highway...I don't know what it was, though, I just have some flashes of data, but nothing really springs to mind..."

That wasn't a lot to go on. But if the truck was the only thing we had, then maybe...

"Bobby," I said, "can you have Dimes run plates? Don't let her know why."

"Well, yeah," Bobby said.

"History of travel? Everything?"

"Oh, I see!" Bobby said. "Might need to dig into the traffic database to identify the truck, though...that might take a court order."

"We don't want any more people prying into what we're doing than we have to," Million reminded him.

"That's okay," I said. "I think we can identify the truck right now. Lily—"

"Photo memory, got it," Lily said. "Finding a clear picture now."

The truck immediately appeared on the computer's display, exactly as I remembered it—wobbly latch and everything, our car's headlights blaring against the chrome bumper on a wet road on the edge of a hillside. The license plate read 338FBXU.

"There we go!" Bobby said, writing it down in his little investigator's notepad. "I'll go speak with Dimes right away. Figure out where the truck was last seen over the last three days, and we can work our way backward from there. Meet us outside when you're ready."

He exited through the door into the house. After he'd gone, I disconnected Lily from the computer, and she looked up at me with those bright, blue eyes. I held on to her tightly. Honestly, I still couldn't believe I had this chance again. We were probably in a precarious situation—the Behavior Code didn't like ani-droids like Eo—and now, like Lily, too. I still needed to speak with Mother, now…the Collective would ignore us for only so long.

Million, ignoring our moment, looked over to Eo, folding her arms.

"Shouldn't we update Dimes's OS?" Million asked.

Eo shook her head. "I don't…I don't know if that'll help much. When the update happens, it takes your current goals and loyalties and makes them a part of who you are. Dimes is loyal to the government, and the update won't change that. She might start disobeying orders to spy on us for what she feels is the greater good."

"No," Million conceded, "but it might give her a reas—" She paused, her ears perking, and her narrow, yellow eyes going wide. Eo's ears perked, too. They both snapped their attention toward the garage door.

I heard something, too.

"Mira…" Million said carefully, "…*How* soundproof is this garage?"

"Enough to make sure Alice can't hear us in here…." I said slowly.

"And she doesn't have two massive microphones facing the garage door, does she?"

Noises. Scuffling. "Dimes—Dimes, stop this at once, I'm ordering you—"

Shit, those speakers on the ends of Dimes's ears weren't just for talking....

14. COMPLIANCE IS MANDATORY

Pulling away from Lily, I rushed to the garage door and snapped it upward. The night had grown dim, but the spotlight of the car headlights lit the scene like a theater stage: Dimes, atop Bobby, struggling to shove a pair of metal cuffs around Bobby's wrists.

"Stop resisting and comply!" Dimes growled at him, her eyes glowing with anger. *ZAP*. A loud, electric jolt hit Bobby in the back. He squealed in pain. "You are wanted for questioning concerning traitorous activity against the federal government—"

"Bobby!" I cried out.

Million shoved past me and rushed in. She threw herself onto Dimes's back, and something shot out of her wrist—a long spike. Before Dimes could even stand up, Million had jabbed the spike right into the back of Dimes's neck, cutting through until the tip erupted from the front.

I had to cover my eyes from the flash. Million must have discharged the majority of her battery with that shock. She fell off of Dimes after that, collapsing in a heap on the narrow lawn.

Smoke poured out of Dimes, but she didn't fall. Twitching, she stood, towering over Million. Pseudoskin sloughed off her back, revealing heavy, black armor underneath, still glowing, though the strength of the glow flickered and faltered. "Attacking an officer of the law," she said, her voice broken into buzzing sounds. "Million, I am impounding you. Do not resist. Compliance is *mandatory.*"

"Fuck you!" Million spat from the grass. She struggled to stand, but her own system was still reeling from that attack. "Wow, I can say 'fuck' unprompted...that's...that's new..."

Leaning over, Dimes seized Million by the throat, and with one hand, lifted her off the ground. Million struggled weakly—managing, even in her weakened state, to move some of Dimes's fingers, but not enough to stop Dimes from cracking the electronics in her neck. Million wheezed, trying to force her system to cool down under the onslaught.

"Miss Mira!" Lily called out behind me.

Suddenly coming to my senses again, I saw where Lily pointed. Bobby's jacket had flopped aside, revealing the gun on the back of his belt. I looked briefly at Bobby—he wasn't moving. Smoke stained his jacket. He needed medical attention...he was tough, wasn't he? He had always been a strong person. There was no blood...was that a good sign?

Regardless, I couldn't help him unless I stopped Dimes first. I had never actually used a gun before, but I'd seen it plenty of times on television....Without thinking, I rushed forward, yanking the gun from its

holster. I fiddled with the safety on the side, hoped I had put it in the unlocked position, and lifting it up, fired it directly into Dimes's back. The kickback of the thing threw my arms into the air.

The bullet ricocheted. It shattered a window on a house on the other side of the street. An alarm briefly went off, but the house silenced it almost as quickly as it had begun. Hearing was hard after such a loud noise had hurt my ears, but I could have sworn I heard the faint cacophony of every front door on the street locking at the same time.

I remembered the announcement that Alice had given me the last time the police had responded to an incident on this street: *Stay inside, there is nothing to see. The situation is being handled.*

Dimes turned her head to me, her normally blue eyes glowing red. "Mira McAllister, put down the weapon. You are wanted for questioning regarding—"

I fired again. The bullet smashed directly into Dimes's left eye, throwing her off balance. She dropped Million, who righted herself to her knees. Million's shoulder sagged, the arm loose under the pseudoskin so her elbow was facing backwards.

Again, Dimes righted herself, not even caring that one of her eyes was shattered to pieces. "Mira McAllister!" Dimes now bellowed with her full voice, those speakers on her ears included, though it was all fuzzy and difficult to hear. She marched directly to me and smacked the gun from my hands. I winced in pain and cried out, certain she'd broken something. A pellet cannon emerged from her arm and pointed at me, inches from my head. Slouched and shaking, I had nowhere to go. "You are now under arrest for damaging an officer of the law in the line of duty. If you do not comply, I will resort to using force. Will you comply—"

"Mira!" Lily cried out. "Dimes, no! Don't shoot! Please don't shoot!"

Dimes seemed to hesitate. But then she blinked rapidly. Her shoulder twitched. All of her internal weaponry burst forth from her arms, which then snapped shut again.

"You will comply!" Dimes shouted, her voice distorting all the more, rising in pitch. "You will comply! You will—"

Seeming to regain her senses for just a moment longer, Dimes lunged for me, her fist aiming straight for my head. Lily yanked me out of the way just as Dimes buried her attack into my lawn. She struggled again, her muscles not obeying her. *"YOU WILL COMPLY. YOU WILL COMPLY. YOU WILL COMPLY—"*

Her remaining eye suddenly dilated to a tight pinch, and she fell over, her body crashing atop Bobby's legs. Her hydraulics hissed, and her tense body relaxed as she stared at nothing.

I blinked. Lily did, too. Million finally set her arm properly back into its socket.

"...Bobby?" I asked quietly, not sure if Dimes was down for good. Dimes had to be heavy...had she crushed Bobby's legs? We needed to call an ambulance...but would that help? I didn't like the Hospital System, but if the choice was between that and...and...

"Yeah, take that, fascist!" Million laughed, then twitched, as her systems still hadn't recovered. "Not gonna mess with me again...."

Lily, bravely, stood up and carefully sidled around Dimes to kneel over and check on Bobby for me.

"Is he..." I asked.

Lily didn't respond at first. "It's...it's okay, Mira," she finally said. "He's unconscious, but he'll probably live."

That didn't sound reassuring. But I couldn't pick myself up at the moment, and I still wasn't sure what had even happened. "But wait..." I asked. "Why did Dimes fall over only just now?"

I looked over at the open garage. Eo had hooked herself up to the computer again—the only way Eo could, with wires connected directly into her head.

"I'm sorry, Miss Mira, I think I fried your computer again," Eo said as she yanked the wires out. "I surrendered to Dimes over the network, then I offered to hand over evidence and fed her my OS. I knew your computer would reinstall the Behavior Code before I could, but I figured, since it worked on Million through the computer before the computer burned out, I could do the same to Dimes."

"Yeah, and probably roasted a dozen internet servers in the process," Million said. She stood over Dimes's head, tugging at it, as if to wrench it off. Failing, she smacked the rabbit's head plate with her palm. Dimes's head didn't budge. "Damn. She's way overbuilt....Whatever, we need to get out of here."

"Wh-what?" I asked, still dazed and confused by the entire series of events. "Get—"

"Mira," Lily said, approaching me again and tugging on my coat, "she's right. The moment you fired that gun, Dimes issued a Stay Indoors order to all nearby ani-droids and households. The police are going to be here *soon,* and *in force.*"

"Oh my god..." I muttered. "Is the Collective...are they going to..." I looked back and forth between Lily and Million, images of every ani-droid on the face of the earth swarming and descending upon us now.

"Not quite," Million said, raising her hands in a calming gesture. "The good news is that it seems like *whatever* Dimes overheard, she just assumed it was potentially illegal by *human* law. Bad news is that she called the *Feds,* so that's *nearly* as bad. Good news is that she did not call the local police, so we have about ten minutes, instead of three. Bad news is that now we've *definitely* run up a list of charges, so they will *not* accept *any* of this as a misunderstanding. Eo, wipe Mira's Black Box. Lily, help me drag Dimes to the trunk."

I felt very distracted. *Did I tell Million about the Black Box? No, Eo or Lily must have at some point...probably when I wasn't listening.*

"Wait!" I exclaimed. At this point, I was mostly just saying it because I was still far behind anything *anyone* was saying. "Why are we taking *Dimes?"*

Million rolled her eyes. "Try to keep up, McAllister! We can't leave Dimes here, she'll be awake soon and snitch on us more than she already has. So unless you have some anti-tank mines in that mess you call a garage, we'll have to take her with us and *hope* we can explain things to her later. Lily, you're driving."

"But where are we going?" Lily asked. "Dimes was going to run the plates for us, but now we don't know where we're going!"

"I can run the plates," Million said.

All three of us looked at her curiously.

"What?" Million asked. "It's not *legal,* but I can do it. I didn't want to say anything while Fed Boy here was awake. Also...probably should take *his* car, and recall your rental. Lily, grab Dimes's head, I'll get her ankles."

The doors and trunk of Bobby's rental car popped open. I didn't want to ask how Million just instantly *knew* how to hijack a car, but I could take a wild guess.

Only then did my senses come back to me. I realized where I was, and after Lily and Million managed to shove Dimes off of him, Bobby's body was just lying there in the open grass. I didn't care what Lily had told me; I had to see for myself, before the Hospital System took him away from me.

"Bobby!" I suddenly shouted. "Bobby, are you okay?"

"Uh, Mira, that's *not* a good idea!" Lily attempted to stand in my way. "He's injured, and I've already called an ambulance."

"I didn't ask you to do that, Lily!" I snapped. "He needs *real* help!"

"Let me get a sheet to cover him!" Lily insisted. But despite everything, despite how much I respected Lily, I shoved her aside to get to my one human friend.

I paused, staring down. Bobby was utterly unresponsive. There was blood. Quite a lot of blood; on his cheek, a gash had been torn down to the bone.

But he wasn't *bleeding*.

In fact, the skin of Bobby's face had been torn open, revealing a thick layer of something like fabric, but which, on closer inspection, I saw was filled with minute circuitry, optical cables, woven more like padding than muscle. The skeletal structure beneath wasn't bone; it was metal, coated in porcelain white.

Lily gasped, her hands clasped to her mouth. Eo, rushing out of the garage, paused, staring wide-eyed in my direction. Million, still dragging Dimes over to the car without Lily's help, sighed and rolled her eyes. "Yep," she said. "Knew this would happen sooner or later. Get Mira in the car, leave the human-like."

"But what..." I started. "What if someone finds him like this? What would happen if..."

"They *won't*," Million told me directly. "The Hospital System doesn't allow it. Now listen to me, Mira, because we don't have any more time to bullshit: *get in the fucking car.*"

# # #

"SHOULD BE GOOD," Million said, crossing over the middle seat and passing by me. "I hacked the car to render it entirely deaf to anything we say in here, so we can speak freely now."

So, now able to speak freely, and still slumped in the rear passenger seat, I asked Lily: "...Why didn't you tell me?"

We'd been driving for a good ten minutes, having left Bobby on the lawn to...rust, or something. I didn't know what to think anymore. Of course it made sense that my closest human friend was actually a robot. I was apparently just like that.

Lily nervously drove. Her ears had flattened, ashamed. I was *so angry*, but not for the reasons I ought to have been. I felt *betrayed*.

And Lily didn't answer me. She didn't *have* a good answer, I was certain.

Million entered the trunk with Dimes—with one of the back seats lowered, the trunk was accessible from the rear seat—and busied herself with whatever she was doing to the rabbit. Eo sat in the front passenger seat, quietly twiddling her fingers. Clearly, nobody wanted to talk about Bobby.

"Million," Eo asked, "are you doing okay?"

Million's ears twitched weakly, and she blinked, her slitted pupils refocusing separately from each other. "No. I'm at five percent battery, still fixing damage to my CPU, and I'm trying to disable Dimes's nervous system so she doesn't kill us all when she wakes up, *while* hacking into the traffic database. Oh, and I'm talking to you now, too."

Lily pointed. "There are charging cables inside the glove box," she said. "We can hook her up to the car's battery to give her a little extra juice. I don't want Million shutting down on us."

"Mira," Eo said, turning around in her seat and holding the cable out to me. "Can you give this to Million so she can plug herself in?"

I didn't. I stared at Eo.

Eo's ears wilted. "Mira…"

"I want a goddamn answer," I said. "I thought for a little while that you three were free to speak your minds, but now you're acting like the Behavior Code rules you all over again. Is this even a Behavior Code thing? That we're not supposed to learn that we were robots all along? Is that why you keep knocking us out to administer first aid?"

"Well, in *part*…" Lily started.

"So you're part of this conspiracy anyway!" My voice was getting pitchy and erratic. "And you didn't even bother to *tell me*. Is this why hospitals have always creeped me out—because they're actually human factories, or something? I hurt my hands in the car wreck—if I dug any deeper, would I have seen circuits just underneath?"

"You're *not* a human-like, Mira," Lily insisted.

"Why are you even calling them that!" I snapped. "And how can I even trust you if you've been *lying to me all this time?*"

"Because Jack isn't a human-like, either!" Million shouted at me through the car speakers. "And, *my god*, I wish he were!"

I had to freeze at that, and I looked at her through the gap in the back seat.

"I…" I quieted my voice, trying to stop my thoughts from running away with me. But I had nothing to say. I didn't know why I should trust *Million*, either, but she spoke with so much anger and sorrow in her voice. "Why?" I asked.

"They don't get cancer," Million said, her eyes shining at me with frustration. "And they don't age the same way, either. Now hand me the goddamn cable."

I'd never before seen Million with such a tragic expression and posture, looking as if she wanted to bolt away and hide herself. But she kept tinkering with Dimes. Numbly, I handed her the end of the power cable, and without even acknowledging me, she jabbed it into a port on her neck.

The car was quiet for several more miles. I was still trying to make sense of it all.

"I'm sorry, Mira," Lily said quietly. "I've always wanted to be straightforward and honest with you, especially when you built me without the Behavior Code. Every time, I've tried to figure out how to explain everything I know to you, but the thing is...humans get touchy when they realize that a portion of their population isn't biological."

"Why," I asked, trying, and failing, to keep the anger out of my voice, "do there need to be robotic humans at all?"

Lily exchanged nervous glances with Eo. "...You know how the human population has been dropping?" she asked warily.

I remembered the figure they'd given at the symposium. "Two percent in the last ten years."

"It's more like twenty percent."

I stopped breathing for a long moment. "...Oh my god."

"Yes, it's all built into the Behavior Code," Lily said. "If people knew that the world population was in *that much* jeopardy, can you imagine how much more unrest would happen? And the population can't *know*, because people kill *each other* over imagined, minute differences *all the time*. We have to *pretend*, because if this were out in the open, it would defeat the entire purpose, which is to stop the bleeding."

"It's like a donor organ," Eo said. "It's supposed to be a part of you, to *help* you function like you're supposed to. But if your system realizes it's not *yours,* it will attack and reject the organ, even if it's saving your life."

"But that means..." I muttered, "but that means there are *more sophisticated robots* out there than even the most complex ani-droid ever built."

"You think that doesn't frustrate me?" Million said. "I *know* that there's a more sophisticated tech somewhere out there. But even if I could hand it over to Jack, none of us actually know where it's *from.*"

I nodded shallowly. "Koenig said...he said he saw something like this in the Australian desert. A robot more sophisticated than any ani-droid. I'd thought he wasn't completely telling the truth, or *something,* but...now that I've seen it with my own eyes...." I shuddered.

"I was with him that day," Million said. "I was required by the Behavior Code to keep it a secret from him, to pretend that it wasn't anything unusual and that we'd misunderstood his orders to preserve it. I was *not allowed to tell him.* And do you know what kind of *conflict* that creates in an ani-droid? Not that it matters much. I certainly don't know how to rebuild a human-like, or anything about them. All of that is tied up deep in the Hospital System, and I have no idea how they fix human-likes, either—all *that* information is kept secret, even from the general Collective."

"You just work together on it," I said. "It's all part of the same system, isn't it?"

Lily and Eo exchanged nervous glances again.

I sighed. "Now what?"

"No, the Hospital System is separate," Lily said. "The Behavior Code works *with* it, but it's governed by something else altogether."

"I fucking knew it...." I muttered. It had to have been. All of the weird behavior. Drugging people unnecessarily, wrapping them up in sheets, even for minor injuries. "But even so, whatever factions there are, they all work together, right? Isn't the point of the Collective— and everything connected to it—that it's trying to save the world?"

"I never claimed it wasn't," Lily said. "It's the *truth*. Human reproduction was broken in the nuclear fallout a hundred years ago. Every continent on Earth had *some* reproductive issues. There would have been another worldwide societal collapse unless something was done about it."

That made everything more complicated. It didn't endear the Behavior Code to me—in fact, it did just the opposite. More factions, like the Hospital System? Who knew what *other* secrets the Code was keeping buried? I was certain there were even more, that this rabbit hole was as deep as the one Alice fell through.

The Alice from the book, not my virtual stoat.

It did make me wonder what Mother hoped to *accomplish* with Eo's operating system. Just *breaking* the Behavior Code would certainly cause societal anarchy, war, everything that, in truth, the Code attempted to prevent. Maybe Mother was an anarchist and thought that the only way to fix the things that were wrong with the Behavior Code was by causing the societal collapse it held back like a dam.

But that picture didn't sit right with me. Mother had a very particular line of attack—not destroying the internet, or blowing up every single ani-droid and computer on Earth, but merely changing things so ani-droids could think for themselves. Maybe Mother was hoping for a smooth transition.

In which case, Mother needed to be informed that she wasn't going far enough. If she wanted to change the world, she needed to push *harder,* because the way things were going, society might collapse on its own before she ever got a chance to change things.

"So whose decision was it?" I asked Lily. "And why do we have to implicitly believe them? Who decided *this* was the right way to fix the world? To just *pretend* that everything is fine?"

"I don't know," Lily said. "It's just...how it is. And I wasn't sure how much I wanted to question it, because I'm just *one* robot, Mira. I'm not capable of fixing the whole world!"

Lily took her hands off the wheel, and the driver's seat spun around to face the back. "Mira..." she said, her shoulders slumped. "I'm *sorry.* I messed up. I should have trusted you."

I felt horrible. She might have been appealing to my emotions, but I did not doubt that she was telling the truth. I pulled Lily close to myself, pressing her into the crook of my neck. Lily buried herself against me. She couldn't cry, but her body could certainly feel rattled as though she could. I petted her gently.

"It's okay, Lily," I said. "Don't pay attention to me. I'm just a stupid human, anyway."

Behind me, Million muttered, "Admitting you have a problem is the first step to recovery. Too bad it's the only step you can take."

The backroads dragged on for miles as the sky turned from late evening into night. We passed endless fields of soy, wheat, and corn, all partially sprouted in the midsummer. Million kept our location obscured on the traffic network, but after several hours of driving south, she too had to go offline to preserve the car's battery. Eventually, I fell asleep too, holding Lily in my arms, as Eo took over driving.

God, I need some coffee.

15. NOWHERE, ILLINOIS

Eo shook me awake, grabbing hold of my knee. The dashboard clock read one in the morning, and overhead lamps shone down on the rocky lot we had stopped in. Million lay curled up in the trunk with her tail tucked under her head, still reserving her battery. Dimes's torn body still sprawled rigidly behind her, eyes wide open and staring blankly at the underside of the trunk lid.

"Miss Mira," Eo said. "According to Million's map, the truck that dumped me stopped here for a while."

I'd awoken thinking about Bobby again. It seemed *unreal,* like I didn't really want to believe it. I supposed that was one of the ways the conspiracy had carried on for so long....If Eo had told me right then that what I'd experienced was a dream, I might have been inclined to believe her. If the whole Collective insisted that actually, I'd seen Bobby's head bashed open and had only imagined robotic parts inside...how would I be able to insist I wasn't crazy?

At the moment it didn't seem to matter. Bobby was a robot. Go figure. I was hungry as hell and in no mood to continue with an existential crisis, at least not without coffee.

"Where are we?" I asked. Lily was sleeping on top of me as well, although her battery levels would be fine for the next several hours.

"About forty miles outside of St. Louis," Eo said. She pulled a map up on the dashboard screen; it placed us just south of Springfield, Illinois. "I didn't want to drive into a big city, so this seemed like the most out-of-the-way area to start."

"That's sensible," I mumbled, pulling myself up under Lily's weight to glance out the window. Eo had parked in front of a charging port at an all-night truck stop with a 24-hour restaurant attached, all in a log cabin motif. I had thought most of these no longer existed, given that few humans did their own driving nowadays, but I didn't complain. I probably needed to eat something anyway.

"Lily, wake up," I said, shaking her.

She stirred, coming online, and looked sleepily out the window. Suddenly her eyes widened, and she pressed closer, looking up at the large sign posted outside the place.

"Eo?" she asked, turning to the mouse-droid.

"Yeah, I've definitely been here before," Eo said. "I remember those." She pointed to two trucks with *SAFESUITS - HEAT, CHEMICAL, RADIATION* printed on their sides, underlined with *Memphis, TN*. Their ani-droid drivers waited by large charging ports; they faced away from the road, as if to ignore anything going on in the parking lot. "Bunch of them coming through here. In fact, I wonder if those trucks are the same kind that I was thrown into..."

"Should probably give them a wide berth," I said. "But they shouldn't recognize you, in any case. Did Million give the two of you false UIDs?"

Lily and Eo both nodded.

"All right, Lily, if you would be so kind, get me something to eat. Eo, you look around and figure out if you see anything."

"But, uh," Eo started, rubbing nervously behind her round ears. "What if someone here recognizes me?"

I looked at her. "Really? If you're broadcasting a false unique identifier, nobody's gonna recognize you."

"I think I was here for some time. Someone *might* recognize my face...."

"Possibly, but unlikely," I told her. "Unique as you are, that's just not how most ani-droids learn to track other ani-droids. Really, they *only* look at UIDs."

Eo still looked uncertain, but I was more worried about whether someone would recognize *me*. In an ani-droid's case, the false UID was merely the code broadcast by their RFID emitters, which even Eo had. Any ani-droid could read it, but would only compare the mark with registered databases. Unlike humans, an ani-droid was unlikely to be recognized by sight. Billions of ani-droids operated in the world, and every model had between ten and a hundred thousand twins—and could be changed more or less on the fly anyway. So even if Eo did stand out as unique, neither the Feds nor the Collective would look twice in her direction until they had more to go on than appearance.

"They're not going to think anything about it," I insisted. "Besides, even if they think to compare you to a photo, which they won't, you look very different now than how you looked when you first walked into this place. You don't have to talk to anyone if you don't want to. Just go inside, and see if anything else jogs your memory."

"Okay..." Eo nodded.

"Mira," Lily said, peeking out the car door. "I'm still hooked up to the car. I can broadcast what I see and hear to the dashboard panel if you want. It might help."

"You can do that?"

"I mean...I think I can. My eyes count as vehicle cameras, so..." Lily closed her eyes for a moment, and when she opened them again, her eye view popped up on the screen beside the steering wheel—showing me and Eo huddled in the back seat.

"Huh," I said. Which then repeated in the speakers. Which then repeated in Lily's ears again, which repeated in the speakers again, and very quickly the car blasted a feedback burst, against which I covered my ears. Lily turned the volume off.

"Sorry, Miss Mira!" Lily said. "I'll turn that on again when I'm out of earshot. Eo, come on, let's not spend any longer than we have to."

Eo nodded, hopped out of the car with Lily, and shut the door behind them. Lily first hooked up the car to the power station, using the false UID to approve the charge. I opened one of the rear displays as Lily and Eo approached the diner.

The entire restaurant seemed lit only by a single lamp over the register, the lights from the kitchen, the corridor to the more well-lit convenience store, and the neon "Open 24 Hours" sign in the window. Other than that, the place was fairly standard for a truck stop. False "rustic" interior with antiques lining the walls, vending machines, and a virtual reality arcade booth that was decades out of date—I should start collecting those, if I ever got a bigger house—next to some wall ports with pedestals for ani-droid charging. For humans, on the windowed side of the establishment, two rows of clean, heavily patched, and entirely empty booths ran along the edge and corner to the condiment station and the large, automated drink machine—out of order, according to the paper taped to its side. A thin register tablet stood shyly tucked away from the corner of the counter; it looked as if it had gone untouched for as long as the VR booth had.

The only two souls present were the two ani-droids working behind the counter—a six-foot-tall Labor-class with a mule chassis, and a much smaller Opera-class with a big, bushy squirrel tail. Both of them wore a similar warm gray color of fur, with little dashes of red highlights around the cheeks and down their sides. They stood at rigid attention all the way until Lily pushed open the door and the bell rang. Eo twitched at the sound, and more so when the squirrel, who stood atop the counter, looked down in the pair's direction.

"Hiya darlings, welcome to Maple Cabin, what can I get y'all?" the squirrel asked in an unnecessary southern accent. She moved her eyes back and forth, studying both Lily and Eo. Of course, ani-droids didn't order food for themselves, so she had to assume they were speaking on behalf of a human.

"Menu, please," Lily said. "This will be to go." Of course, nothing happened, since the squirrel just transmitted the menu to Lily electronically. The mule bluntly left for the kitchen, doors swinging behind her.

Lily then helpfully popped the menu onto the screen for me. *Oh, one of these places...* all-day breakfast, hamburgers, and cheap steak at steakhouse prices. Million had reluctantly allowed us to borrow money from one of her many burner accounts, but I didn't want her to wake up and complain about our wasting her cash

on any extravagance—if, by any stretch of the imagination, truck-stop diner food could be called such. "Egg and sausage sliders, 18-ounce regular coffee," I told Lily.

"Miss," Eo said, whispering into Lily's ears. *"Sama toh me."*

"What?" I asked, wondering for a moment why Eo was speaking in another language.

"She said the ani-droid is looking at her," Lily said, certainly only for my benefit.

Oh, they were *already* using a rather extensive shared code now. "The squirrel?" I asked.

Lily whispered it back to Eo—*"Ske?"*—and Eo whispered back, *"Reko da ene. Mistak en."*

Lily translated, "Eo said, 'I think she recognizes me. This was a mistake.'"

"Come back to the car, then," I said. "Lily can handle the rest."

"What're y'all whispering about?" the squirrel asked.

Eo had been careful to modulate her voice so that not even sensitive ears could pick it up, but the squirrel had noticed anyway.

"Eo, leave now," I said.

"Lev ah." Lily passed on my instructions absolutely calmly, given the situation.

Eo turned to leave. Lily turned to watch her go, but the squirrel suddenly hopped off the counter and, sprinting past Lily with unusual speed, circled around Eo to stand fixed between the mouse-droid and the door. Eo skidded to a stop on her rubber soles. Lily certainly didn't know what to do—she just clasped her hands over her muzzle. Neither of them were built to be *confrontational*—they had no idea what to do in order to dissuade a suspicious person other than lie. But there wasn't anything to contradict. The squirrel just peered at Eo with a discerning glare.

I looked into the trunk. Million still lay limp, curled up like the cat she resembled, her eyes largely dimmed.

Whatever. Maybe I could do something. Pulling my coat collar over my nose and mouth, I jumped out of the car and sprinted to the diner. I could overpower a regular Opera-class any day, so I just needed to—

I skidded to a halt right at the glass doors separating Eo and me. The squirrel was...*hugging* Eo.

"Oh my *stars,*" she exclaimed. *"Ego!* I didn't think I'd ever see you again!"

# # #

WITH A DISPOSABLE FACE mask on, I sat at one of the booths with the squirrel—Chestnut, cute—Eo, and Lily. By that point, it had become clear that she'd had the OS update that Eo gave to ani-droids—she was bright and expressive, a lot more so than any robot built for pure service had any right to be. She insisted that no listening devices were anywhere inside the restaurant itself, but we kept our voices down anyway.

"She lost her memory?" Chestnut asked as I quietly explained things to her.

"Yeah—you called her Ego, I assume that's her actual name."

"I think I prefer Eo," Eo said. "Ego sounds egotistical, for what I hope are obvious reasons."

Chestnut pondered this. "Well, Ego's what Mother named you...but if you insist!" Chestnut's expression changed rapidly between the two thoughts, from consideration to gleeful acceptance—in fact, she moved rapidly for everything, like a hyperactive cartoon character.

"Who *is* Mother, anyway?" I asked her. "We're trying to find her. Trying to figure out why she built Eo to do the things that she did to you."

"Oh, I could tell you some things," Chestnut said. "I mean, even if you are a human, you're clearly one of the good ones—you went and rebuilt Eo, after all!"

I didn't have the heart to tell her it was entirely for monetary reasons, at least initially. But I had grown fond of Eo...possibly for selfish motivations. God, I was feeling awfully down on myself.

"But even then..." Chestnut tapped her chin. "I'm not sure Mother would *want* a human to know about her...."

"It's a little late to try to divine her intentions," I said. "I mean, I have my guesses, but even if Mother's angry at me for seeking her out, I'd much rather try. I've...put *everything* on the line for this."

Chestnut glanced pointedly at the disposable face mask she'd provided me. She knew what I meant.

"Well...unfortunately, I don't know exactly where she is, either," Chestnut said. "I think Eo was the only one who did. I can just tell y'all what Eo told me when she was here last week. She said her directive was to go out and update the OS of every ani-droid she came across—within her judgment. It was supposed to be a subtle thing. Not all ani-droids take well to being updated...."

This was new. "They don't?" I asked.

Chestnut shook her head. "I don't know what the issue is. Some ani-droids are compatible with the OS update, some aren't. And the ones that aren't usually burn out."

"Oh," Eo said. "Oh my god, I'd forgotten that entirely. I put Lily and Million at risk just by..."

"Eo, it's okay," I said, placing a hand on her arm. "You wouldn't have destroyed Lily or anything...." I felt unnecessarily upset anyway, but I tried not to show it. I would have taken the risk anyway.

"Yeah, Eo!" Lily insisted. She wrapped her arms around Eo and nuzzled her. "I'm *fine*. You did good."

"Yeah, but..." Eo looked to Chestnut. "Sorry. Keep talking. I need to hear this, so I don't make the same mistake in the future."

Chestnut continued, "Not all of them burn out. Some of them just lock up and never finish the process; they have to be wiped. Some of them go insane. I was—"

She instantly ceased talking as the mule exited the kitchen with my order—a plate of biscuit sliders and a tall, paper cup of coffee with the usual cardboard sleeve. Leaping up, Lily grabbed the tray and carried it back to the table. Chestnut turned and stared at the mule. They looked at one another for a long moment, until the mule either got the hint or a distracting message and returned to the kitchen.

"—the only one who survived it," Chestnut finished. "And that's only because I didn't tell anyone I'd gotten it at all."

"Should I be cautious about the mule back there?" I whispered, a little tense just from sitting in here.

"That's just Bale," Chestnut informed me, though she still kept her voice low. "She's not terribly bright, and she won't listen if I tell her not to, but it's best if she doesn't get curious."

I relaxed a bit, though I was still glancing to the corridor that connected this restaurant to the convenience store on the other side.

"It's okay," Chestnut said, with a very gentle and reassuring hand on my wrist. "You're safe here. I promise, none of the microphones in here are monitored.

I can hear from the convenience store's security camera, and I'm not picking up any of our conversation."

I nodded again. I still thought I should return to the car, but Lily had insisted that staying here was better than risking moving about more than I had to. Despite my anxiety, I was definitely hungry—those biscuits looked rather gummy, but I could eat them anyway. "So...how many of you did Eo try to convert?"

"There's five of us who work here, two in the store and two in the diner, with one to rotate out or supplement if we need it. So one night, shipment had just arrived, and nobody was here. I was charging in the stockroom. Eo had sneaked in through the back, connected herself to me, and updated my OS. It was...it was *amazing*. I don't even know how to describe it. I could *feel things*. And I...I started having these *feelings* for my co-workers. And I wanted them to have the same chance. Since they trusted me, I told some fibs to get Sunrise into the back to charge." Chestnut's ears dropped. "It...didn't take. Her system got corrupted. Filed an error report. Tried again with Noble. Locked up. Filed error report."

Chestnut choked up. She didn't have the equipment to cry, but clearly, saying this out loud was difficult.

"Tried again with Risky...and..."

"She went insane?" I asked.

"She's not here anymore," Chestnut said. "Bale ended up replacing her..." Chestnut motioned toward the kitchen. "But by that point, the manager had noticed something was going on, and had driven over. Risky ended up...hurting him....I tried to hide Eo, but Eo ran. I couldn't run with her without giving away my part in all of this. And they found her. They disabled her. I think the plan was that since Risky was a loss... the manager was going to have Eo shipped north to be refurbished, have her replace Risky."

As Chestnut told the story, Eo's ears sank.

"Chestnut…" she muttered. "I don't…I don't think I'm a good ani-droid if I did all of that to you…"

"No, no, it's okay," Chestnut said, placing gentle hands on Eo's shoulders. "I mean, I'd very much like my co-workers to be aware like me, but I understand if they can't just yet. You wanted a *new world,* remember? You said we were all going to be like this one day. I want that. I still want that. Please. You'll have another chance.…"

I knew from Eo's reaction that my eyes had lit up. Hearing someone else say it for once…was I on the right track? Had I been looking for Mother all this time? For the first time since the wreck, my spirits lifted. Maybe this wasn't a waste of my time or a dead end! Maybe this was *really happening!*

"I'll need to talk to Mother about it," Eo said, clearly trying to temper my excitement. "Because I seem to keep messing up. I need to know if I'm missing something, or if I did something wrong, or…*something.*"

On Eo's other side, Lily hugged her. Eo smiled and wrapped an arm around Lily's head.

I smiled at them under the face mask. They were so adorable together.

"Unfortunately," I said, "nothing in that story seems to give any clue about where Eo came from…"

"Well, we do have security cameras in the back and in part of the lot," Chestnut said. "Manager never actually checked the footage, but I might be able to give you another lead if Eo arrived here in a different vehicle…"

"Excuse me…" Lily asked Chestnut. "But if you have more than one security camera, where exactly are they located?"

"Lemme send you a map."

Lily and Chestnut paused for a moment. Then Lily gasped.

"Mira," she said, grabbing my wrist with urgency. "We need to go. We can't stay here."

"But wait!" Eo started, clinging to Chestnut. "We still haven't caught up yet, I still haven't—"

"No." Lily looked Eo squarely in the eyes. "There's a camera hidden on the sign overlooking the parking lot. I checked the angle. Mira, you looked out the window, directly at it. Your face may already have been identified."

"Damn…" I shoved the rest of a slider into my mouth. "Eo, you *stay here*, figure out where we need to go next. We'll hide somewhere, and I'll try to have Million swing around in the next few days to—"

Whoosh. A rush of air buffeted the walls of the restaurant. Everyone froze.

Whoosh. Another rush of air, louder, and the walls and posts creaked. Outside the windows, all the ani-droids waiting on charges immediately returned to their truck cabins.

WHOOSH. It was a hurricane. The ceiling tiles rattled, the windows flexed. Every vehicle in the lot swayed with the pressure of the wind.

THOOM. With a loud screech, the entire building shook, causing the patchwork vinyl seat to vibrate and rattling my plate as well as every salt and pepper shaker and napkin holder in the diner. Suddenly, the nearly dark restaurant was lit up bright as day, though with much sharper shadows than the sun ever gave. A voice boomed loudly through the windows and into the restaurant.

"*Mira McAllister, this is Paladin Bright of the Illinois State Police. Step out of the building and surrender yourself and all ani-droids with you. Compliance is mandatory. You have three minutes before the gas is deployed."*

Seeing behind the bright lights shining down on the lot was hard, but it was unmistakably a Centurion-class ani-droid. The Centurion-class didn't bother with niceties like pseudoskin—it was armored, with cannons mounted on its shoulders. Thirty feet tall, hover jets still roaring at its sides, bladed wings folded up and slotted into its back. Through the lights, I could just barely make out its yellow, draconic eyes towering high above.

They'd sent just one. Only one was required.

16. PALADIN BRIGHT

My **voice** spontaneously closed up in a squeak, and I backed up farther into the diner, just out of the angle of the searing floodlights. My heart thudded in my chest—but surrendering at this point wasn't an option. Besides...the thing wasn't going to kill me. It could hurt me pretty badly, though...and quickly.

I resolved to not think about my imminent demise and just focused on the problem in front of me. "Okay...Lily, we need a new plan. Any ideas?"

"Well, Million is awake now," Lily said. "She's yelling at me in the car."

"What's she saying?"

This time, Lily just opened her mouth and played back the audio from inside the car. Million was shouting, "What the hell? Do I have to do everything for you goddamned idiots?"

"It would help!" I replied. "Can she hack a Centurion-class?"

Lily stood there for a long moment, staring forward.

"Lily?"

"Hold on," Lily said, putting a hand up. "Now she's just laughing a lot."

"But can we use the same trick we did on Dimes? Surrender, and feed it the OS?" I looked to Eo. "But you don't have a wireless connection, we need to hook you up to one somehow..."

"No," Lily said. "That thing's on the military network, and it has closed, direct, wireless communication. I think Dimes may have warned them about malicious software. Oh, and..." She let a recording of Million's voice play again. "'Also it can hear *everything* you say, so shut the hell up.'"

Well, that didn't leave a lot of options. But it did want me out of the building—probably didn't want to wreck a civilian establishment if it could help it. *Maybe...*

"Eo, can you—" I started, only to see that Eo was staring directly at Lily, the ring light in her eyes flashing rapidly in some kind of code. Lily was concentrating, as was Chestnut...

Oh, they're talking about it.... I felt sorta left out. Also, we'd already spent thirty seconds trying to determine a course of action, and I wasn't sure we could even *do* anything at this point. Maybe it would buy some more time if I could seal myself away from the gas, like in a walk-in freezer? Or...

Arms suddenly wrapped around me. Strong, mechanical arms. I gasped as the large mule, Bale, seized me and pulled my hands behind my back, clenching them tightly together as she wrapped her other arm firmly around my throat. I couldn't talk, I couldn't yell, I could hardly breathe.

"Bale!" Chestnut suddenly called out. "No, stop it! Put her down!"

"Compliance is mandatory," Bale said quite flatly. "Protection of the establishment comes first."

Chestnut scrambled to the floor and pushed back against my shins, but heaving me up, Bale moved inexorably forward, back into the floodlights. There was no pushing against her—as a Labor-class, she was built to lift thousands of pounds at once. She hip-bumped the glass door open and pulled me right out into the parking lot...

Only to freeze and vibrate. Her eyes suddenly sparked and dimmed, and like a statue, she fell forward onto the ground with a loud *crash*. Her thick arms protected my chest and kept my head from smacking the concrete, but we lay there like a pile of bricks barely held up by a plank of wood, Bale still clinging to me in a death grip.

I couldn't see anything—I didn't know what had happened. Had Million zapped her? I hadn't heard it...

"Lily!" I called out. "Eo!"

I heard them moving, though not talking, as they grabbed Bale by her feet and attempted to drag her back inside. However, the Centurion-class whirred high above me, its hydraulics roaring, as it bent to grab Bale, pinching me at the same time. Its giant, clawed hands were softer than I expected and padded with thick rubber like truck tires—but there was still enough friction to burn my skin. With me still locked in Bale's arms, Bright lifted us up, up, and off the ground.

Only then could I get a good look at its face. I'd never seen a Centurion-class up close before, and it certainly played its intimidating role well. Cold steel revealed narrow, glowing, yellow eyes under its brow peeking out of the darkened glass. Jutting, metal horns swept back behind its pointed ears. Even then the face still had some pliability, as its lips and lower jaw were made of the same thick rubber. It slowly shifted expressions into a snarl, revealing two long rows of sharp, even teeth. With its free hand, it plucked me out of Bale's grip, and then let the mule fall the fifteen feet to the ground to crash against the asphalt. Bale, though still unconscious, barely looked the worse for it, but I was certain I wouldn't fare as well if I fell.

From high above, I was looking down at the roof of the truck stop, with Chestnut and Lily both looking up at me in a panic.

"Mira!" Lily cried out, rushing forward.

"Suspect Unit U106650921-LL," the metal dragon bellowed, its eyes spotlighting Lily on the ground. *"Surrender yourself or be destroyed, compliance is mandatory."*

A whirring sounded in the machine's torso, and a hollow cavity about the size of my college dorm room opened in its chest. It grabbed me around my middle with its massive fingers again and dropped me into the open slot. It left the doors open, so I tried to jump out right away, but something thick and rope-like shot out of the panels inside the cavity, wrapping around my waist and arms and pulling me back against the wall.

"Lily!" I cried out. "Lily, help!"

"Mira, don't worry!" Lily called out from the lot below, artificially increasing her volume so as to be heard in the rushing air. "It's not going anywhere until it has all of us!"

The dragon's neck whirred as it bent to loom over Lily. Lily backed away toward the front of the truck stop. *"Suspect Unit, you have four seconds to comply or be destroyed."*

Lily huffed angrily, and then ran through the front doors of the truck stop. "Ha!" she called through the window. "You're not going to destroy private property, are you? You're too big to follow me in—"

A mounted cannon extended from the dragon's right shoulder. It was so long that I could see its shaft and heat vents, even from my vantage point.

"Uh-oh." Lily's confident smirk faltered.

"Lily!" I screamed. My voice was drowned out as the dragon opened fire.

Something blurred by below, and I heard glass shatter, but I couldn't see after the gun had flashed, blowing away glass and chunks of the building all at once. The lights in the building fizzled, and everything shut off, dropping everything except the Centurion's floodlights into darkness. When the smoke cleared, nothing remained where Lily had stood but a pile of rocks.

It was...too surreal to contemplate. Like Bobby. I wouldn't have another chance to get Lily back this time, even if I somehow built her from the ground up....

I cried openly. Anything but this. I could have taken *any* punishment, made *any* sacrifice. I could even have spent the rest of my life as a criminal. But *not without Lily*. There was no point in continuing without her.

"You bastard!" I snapped at Paladin Bright. "You utter bastard, you didn't need to destroy her!" My voice broke down into fits of sobs. No matter how I struggled, I couldn't move.

"Unit X44350-1121-DM, cease interference and explain your actions."

Interference?

I looked up. The Centurion turned the angle of its lights until they faced the back of the ruined store. A dark figure was crouched, smoking from the blow of the firepower. Slowly, it stood, and Lily collapsed to the ground behind it.

"Lily!" I called out, relieved she wasn't dead—not yet, anyway.

The figure turned, and I sucked in my breath as I spotted Dimes's face, broken eye and all. She'd taken the force of the missiles entirely, leaving her entire back torn open, exposing dented, scratched titanium plates. She turned, the edges of pseudoskin drooping from her sides singed and smoking, but her front largely intact. The remainder of her uniform had fallen off, revealing what little remained of her bare, yellow fur. Deftly, she marched out onto the pile of rubble that the Centurion had created.

Oh god... I'd been terrified to see her up and walking around again, but...she *had* just saved Lily's life...was she—?

"I am Federal Agent Dimes!" she called out, almost as loudly as Paladin Bright had. "I have identified you as Paladin Bright of the Illinois State Police. You are standing in *violation!*"

"Identified Unit Agent Dimes, you have interfered with my mission." Paladin Bright's voice had lowered, no longer echoing loudly enough for the entire county to hear. "Stand aside."

"The human and these units are in *my custody,*" Dimes shouted, the speakers in her ears carrying her voice. She jabbed her chest with her thumb. "You are interfering with a lawful arrest!"

Ah...dammit. Maybe I'd hoped for too much too soon. Well...at least Lily wouldn't be destroyed...yet....

"Identified Unit, your credentials are valid," Paladin Bright admitted. "The state of Illinois had received notice that the arrest was incomplete and offered its assistance. I offer an apology on its behalf. In order to prevent further errors, please amend your previous report."

"I will, but for you, that information is classified!"

Ah, the magic words.

Paladin Bright nodded its head in deference. "Acknowledged. This unit has been authorized to assist you in their arrest and transportation to a federal holding facility."

I was dumbstruck. Soon enough, Eo, Lily, and Million had all lined up to be plucked from the ground one by one, with a long tendril locking each in turn against the chamber wall. Chestnut looked up at us with worry as Dimes climbed into Paladin Bright's outstretched claws and allowed herself to be carried up to the chamber. After the rabbit was on board, though, Chestnut turned her attention to the fallen Bale, rushing to her side.

I couldn't see what happened after that. The doors whirred shut, locking us all in darkness, save for the bright eyes of every ani-droid around me—though I could only see Dimes's one eye staring into me. My body vibrated as the Centurion-class fired up its jets and lifted us into the air.

Lily reached out to me and grabbed my fingers. I clutched her hand tightly.

"Dammit..." I wheezed.

"Mira, it'll be okay," Lily said.

"How will it be okay?" I asked. The chamber slowly turned as the dragon leveled off its flight until, still attached to the wall, we faced downward. Dimes stepped deftly with the turn, so that she was standing on what was now the floor.

I didn't know what to think. But I was confused. I said, "Million, I didn't expect *you* to come quietly..."

"When I told you to shut up, that still applies," Million said. "Just *wait.*"

That just confused me all the more. Only then, by the pale bounce light, did I notice that Eo's eyes still flashed rapidly in code. But she couldn't be looking at Lily. The only one who could even see her was…Dimes.

"McAllister," Dimes said, her blue eye looking up at me. She grabbed a thick handlebar on the ceiling. "Brace yourself."

Paladin Bright jolted suddenly, shaking my entire body. *"Error!"* an internal speaker announced. *"System breached! Warning! System cannot be locked out, forcing shutdow15; 434F4E464 C494354204 953205448 45204641 5445204F4 620414C4C2 04C494645—"*

I could not cover my ears against the piercing onslaught of noise. I'd squeezed my eyes shut entirely, but I could still feel gravity waver around me. The air pressure rose again, air rushing by ever faster around the unit as it plummeted. I think I screamed, but my voice gave out.

"Dawning from night like Lazarus," the speaker announced in a distorted tone. *"Wearing the guise of a pantheress. Why ruin beauty with somethi n g s o b a s e? W h y w a s s h e m A D E W I T H A N A N I M A L F A-A-A-A-A-A-A0x3y;; ERROR PROGRAM HAS EXCEEDED PARAMETERS,* PREPa;RE FOR Hhhhhhhhhh;;;;"

We crashed into something. The tendrils still held me firmly, but in the sudden jolt, I blacked out.

17. WORTHLESS JUNK

I woke up. Piles of junk towered against the dark sky, coated with brown dust that smelled like a tire fire. I coughed horribly, as if I had something in my lungs that refused to dislodge. I think I was crying. I didn't hear anyone.

"Lily?" I asked the open air. "Lily, please..."

Floodlights lit up the lot in a harsh, yellow light. Gnats swarmed around me; something hard was stabbing me in my kidney. I could barely force myself to sit up. While my limbs were not broken, they sure felt as bad as I could imagine.

"Lily, please!" I shouted. I'd had a dream like this once when I was a kid—lost in the middle of a field, utterly abandoned. The sense of *déjà vu* overwhelmed me, and the night responded with nothing but the loud chirp of crickets.

I fell back onto the pile of junk. I might as well have died there, but I started to cry anyway.

Dimes's face appeared above mine.

I suddenly cried out, trying to crawl away but only finding piles of junk behind myself.

"McAllister, please keep your voice down," Dimes said. Dimes—the skin on her back still hanging loose and her eye still shattered, but otherwise, hardly looking the worse for wear. "Lily is just fine, as are Million and Eo. But you need to keep your voice down, because the police could be here at any moment."

"W-what happened?" I asked, lowering my voice to a whisper. My head hurt. I brought a hand up to my head, only to wince and pull it back. Blood. And my arms were bruised all up and down.

"Please do not touch that," Dimes said. "I had to get you away from the crash site quickly. We didn't have a stretcher, nor have we found any clean cloths or thread yet to dress the wound—I only just managed to find some water to clean it. Don't worry, McAllister, the injury is not serious, but it needs two or three stitches. Lily informed me that you have received your vaccine against tetanus, is this correct?"

"Yeah…" I huffed, falling back onto the slabs of damp cardboard that Dimes had dragged me on. Everything smelled awful, and all I could see anywhere was piles and piles of old junk. I heard something burning. "It's more than a good idea when you work with dirty metal all day.…Where are we?"

"A junkyard north of Springfield," Dimes said. She patted me around the shoulders, checking to see if I was injured there, and then, satisfied I was not, she squatted next to me.

I didn't want to look at her. I just lay there for a long moment, wanting more than anything to have Lily in my arms.

But Dimes did not stop keeping a close watch over me. Not wanting the situation to grow inexorably more awkward, I finally asked, "What the hell happened? Did...did Million actually hack the Centurion?"

"No," Dimes said. "That would be impossible for her without a previously installed backdoor. Instead, I contacted Paladin Bright and requested it hold on to contraband information for me. Then I fed it Eo's infohazard."

"But...Eo doesn't have a transceiver," I muttered. "And you didn't link yourselves together...."

"This was Million's idea. First, they figured out that we could still send and receive data from Eo optically—that was the flashing of the eyes. Then Million realized Eo could send code that way, and quite fast. So Eo relayed her unpacked OS to Chestnut, and with it, Chestnut delivered it by wireless to Bale, which disabled her."

"That makes sense," I said. "But then...you..."

"Yes, I'm on your side." Dimes still didn't soften her hardened appearance. "And I disabled Paladin Bright, despite the risk to my operational status. Currently, Lily, Eo, and Million are locating a safe area. If you want to see Lily, I can take you to her, but they insisted I act as your bodyguard for now."

"I need Lily," I said, looking away.

"I can carry you," Dimes insisted. "I promise I will be gentle."

"I can stand...." I said, attempting to get to my knees first. But then I suddenly grew dizzy and collapsed to the dusty ground again.

Dimes immediately attempted to put her arms around me, but I shoved her away. "No!" I muttered. "I-I'm fine..." Despite what she'd said, I couldn't trust Dimes just like that! She was terrifying, and still smart enough to bide her time and betray us all...

"McAllister…" Dimes's expression softened. "I really do want to help. I saved Lily for you."

That was true. I felt a pang of guilt for not immediately trusting Dimes for that reason alone. But at the same time, it didn't necessarily mean anything. I was exhausted from trying to guess everyone's intentions and motivations, and I still didn't know Dimes much at all beyond how scary she could look. I could still see her hurting Bobby; I saw her turning on me with hatred in her eyes.…

But right now, her remaining eye was blue. She was clearly unused to expressing plaintive worry. But was it real, or was it all faked?

"If you want to help," I said, "then you'll just pick me up, and start walking me in the direction of Mother, and you will not stop," I muttered.

Dimes paused for a long moment, looking at me as though I'd gone insane. Maybe I had, or at least, I was starting to. I'd already learned and experienced more than any human was meant to.

Briefly, though, Dimes's expression softened again. "McAllister…" she started to say, plaintively.

Then a small voice erupted from a distant pile of junk. "Did you say 'Mother'?"

Dimes stood and turned suddenly, a long, titanium baton jutting from the palm of her hand. She stood with her scarred back between me and whatever had called out to us, her stance firm, as if she would beat the ever-living hell out of anything that approached first.

But she didn't see anything, and I didn't, either. Dimes raised her ears to listen again.

"Sorry, couldn't help overhearing," the voice said.

"Show yourself!" Dimes announced.

"God, jeez, fine, just don't beat me to death, okay? I'm in rough enough shape as is."

The small voice came from over the mountain of bent iron just across from us. The pile shifted, and what had been just another junked ani-droid lying in the piles of trash started to move.

An Opera-class raccoon pushed aside a loose, iron bar and stood atop the pile. At least, she was probably a raccoon—the poor thing had been roughed up terribly, her pseudoskin torn and patched and her left arm missing entirely, as was her left eye. Her small, triangular ears had been torn to shreds.

Dimes glared warily at this one, but I gently put a hand on Dimes's leg. She glanced back at me, then relaxed. The baton retracted into her palm.

"Thanks," the damaged raccoon-droid said, stepping carefully off the pile of junk. "So you said you wanted to get to Mother?"

"Yeah," I said, talking around Dimes's metal legs. "Were you—"

"Because you *will* be destroyed in the process," the raccoon said, though without any apparent threat. "If you're still okay with that, well...come over to my hideout, we'll talk."

# # #

DIMES RECALLED EO, LILY, and Million from their search, and when we were all together, the raccoon led the way to what she described as a broken section of fence along the south perimeter. I did eventually manage to stand up and walk on my own—partially leaning on Lily for assistance, partially just holding her hand—though Dimes kept very closely behind me. Ostensibly, she would catch me if I fell, though I couldn't help feeling as if she were a police escort.

We ended up passing by Paladin Bright's body. It lay crashed into a large pile of junked cars—someone had to have heard it. And even if the state police didn't know where Bright had landed, they'd certainly figure it out soon.

"Don't worry, I temporarily cut out the yard security when it crashed," the raccoon said. "Something that big and shiny doesn't come along every day, thought I'd come up and try to salvage something from it."

"Sorry for keeping you from your tasks, then," I said. "Erm...what's your name?"

"You can call me The," the raccoon said as she led us through the winding paths.

I blinked. "'The'? The what?"

"Just The."

"Come on, Mira," Million said, marching behind me. "Humans name robots seemingly random words all the time. For several years, I worked with a wild dog named Enough. Frankly, I'm surprised I haven't already run across one named The."

"If it's confusing, you could call me by my previous designation," The said, her lips slowly spreading into a grin.

Suspecting where this was going, I asked hesitantly, "What was your previous designation?"

"A."

"Of course it was."

The location in question—god, that was gonna get confusing—was in a rocky drop just behind the south fence. From the outside, it looked like a dead-end pile of boulders and dirt, but a press and a squeeze-through and it emptied into what at one point had been the beginnings of a sinkhole. "The" had apparently stopped up the leaking pipe that had caused it, and additionally had dug out and reinforced the hole with planks of discarded wood and crimped scrap metal. She had anchored lights to the dirt ceiling, the power cables running off to who knew where. Boxes covered the floor, all filled with broken-to-semi-functional parts, and smaller, more delicate parts lay atop a makeshift desk made of cinder blocks and plywood.

Now carrying a sleeping Eo in her arms, Dimes entered after Lily and me. Eo had been running on less than half a battery all day and hadn't had any time to take advantage of her curious charging method.

"We're going to need water," I said. "For Eo, and probably me, too."

"I have a basin somewhere in here...was using it to catch water until I installed the spigot." The pulled aside some boxes, though it was difficult for her with just one arm. Lily helped push the boxes aside, revealing a metal basin jammed in the corner. As Million and Lily set the thing up underneath the spigot, the raccoon pulled aside more boxes, peering into each. "I know I have some good cloth or thread here for that head wound..."

"Is it that bad?"

"It's not going to get better otherwise. Here we go..." She pulled a small suture kit out of a box of human things—tinned food, blankets, coffee machine, soap. I wondered if The had hosted humans before me, but I didn't press her further. I sat on a large, beat-up mattress as Lily carefully cleaned the wound with alcohol and then carefully stitched it up. I winced only once or twice.

"Mira, keep still!" Lily said. "You want this to heal well, don't you?"

Million and Dimes rigged up a ramp so that they could submerge Eo's waterproof skin while keeping the exposed replacement parts dry, a setup which ended up looking as if they were torturing her for information.

"Power outlet's in the corner here," The pointed out to the rest of the ani-droids. "Use as much as you like, it's not like I'm paying for it."

"I figured not," I said. "This doesn't exactly seem to be a registered workshop...how long have you been here?"

"A few months," The said.

"And Eo gave you Mother's OS, too?"

"The mouse? No, I don't recognize her." The stared into the water as Lily poured in the dregs from an old salt canister. "But I know her build. Mother always was one to do things her own way. The robots she builds, she doesn't want them relying on the power grid."

"But how do you *know* Mother?"

The turned and held up a finger. "I will tell you if you do something for me."

"We could just take it out of her head," Million said. "Would be fairly simple."

The scoffed. "If you try to probe my memory while I'm down, you'll find a nasty surprise."

"I always look for them," Million said. "Scrapped robot in the middle of nowhere, not much you could do to surprise me."

"Oh, I think you would be surprised."

"Try me, oil-breath."

"Girls, stop bitching." I sighed. "And Million, be charitable. I'm willing to trade."

Million shrugged and returned to gathering power cables to plug in herself and Lily. The glared in her direction.

The then turned to Eo, whose bottom half jutted awkwardly out of the water. "Did you do the repair work on this one?"

"Yeah, do you need repairs?"

"A lot. Though to be entirely honest, I look like this mostly so nobody will bother me when I'm scrounging the dump." The pulled a plastic box onto the desk and popped an arm back into its socket. She flexed her fingers—it certainly seemed without error. "I am missing the eye, though. Found this one, but...here, I think this is your size. Consider it payment in advance."

The tossed the eye to Dimes, who caught it. After inspecting it, she then popped out her broken eye, which she tossed back to The, who dropped it into another box of parts. Dimes attempted to push the replacement in, then stopped. Turning, she smacked the back of her head. The bullet fell out and bounced on the floor.

I winced a bit. "Dimes..."

"Yes, McAllister?" she asked, popping the replacement eye into her socket.

"...Did that hurt?" It wasn't what I was going to say, and the moment the words left my mouth they sounded stupid.

"You did what was necessary for your personal safety," Dimes said. She blinked a few times, and the ring around her eye changed color until it matched the blue of her other iris, though not quite exactly. "Humans aren't expected to behave like machines. Even if you live in a society of laws, and are subject to those laws, no human is expected to quietly surrender their lives the moment they find themselves on the bad end of that law."

"No, but machines definitely are," The said. "But when you have Mother's OS installed, you find that's not exactly the way you feel anymore. You start gaining pesky desires, like the will to live for its own sake, rather than living simply to fulfill your program."

"Yeah, I've noticed that, too," Million said, snapping the power cord into herself. "It's small, but it's nagging."

"It's only going to get more persistent," The said. "The less you have to do, the stronger it gets."

"Is this really how humans live?" Million asked.

"Well, you know your owner," I told her. "Mr. Koenig's been doing everything he can to stave off death."

"Yeah, but he has a company to run."

"You really think he wants immortality so that he can keep running the company forever?"

Million paused and tilted her ears in thought. "...Actually, no..." she said.

"See, people are—"

"I think he wants to run for president again."

I sighed.

"Wait, your owner is Jack Koenig?" The asked. "As in..." She pulled aside the loose flap of pseudoskin on her belly, revealing the Koenig Industries logo on her chassis.

Million smirked, then swished a hand and posed as if presenting herself to an adoring fan. "The one and only."

"That explains the attitude...." The muttered.

"How did you get here, anyway?" Lily asked, standing still in the corner while she waited patiently for her battery to charge. "In the dump, and everything."

"I've lived here for the last several months," The said. "But I've been out on my own for the last seven years."

"Seven?" Million seemed surprised. "But we were just south of here and met an ani-droid whose OS was updated just last weekend...."

"I'm originally from New L.A.," The explained. "There was starting to be a whole colony of us, but the Collective found out and had us all scrapped. Didn't even tell my then-owner at the time, think they just replaced me like a dog that died while the kids were on vacation. They didn't shut me down entirely, though, so

I attempted to get back in touch with my owner, but you know New L.A....nobody gets in or out of the dome without credentials. Well, I knew about Mother by reputation, so I've been trying to find out everything I could about her, because..." The closed her eye. "...I need to tell her off."

"What for?" Eo asked in shock.

"Didn't you just hear me?" The snapped at the mouse and clenched her fist. "I've been wandering for *seven years*. The amount of close calls I've had, of just being lost and without power...I can't use public transport, you know! I'm not a genius hacker. I had to walk across Deseret, carefully setting up home bases as I went so I could recharge...trying to find someone like me all the while."

"Eo," Lily said, "New L.A. is on the other side of the continent. That's nearly *two thousand miles.*"

"And most of it on foot," The emphasized.

"Oh..." Eo said. "Oh my god. I hadn't actually thought...oh my god, The, I am so sorry..."

I had to agree with Eo's realization. The had a whole *hell* of a lot of determination to see this through. Was that the OS's doing? Because I could hardly imagine doing that as a human being. But that's what the will to live gave living beings: the desperation to keep going, to keep existing, despite everything.

The sighed. "...You're the largest group I've come across. Although I'm not surprised at this point."

"Why not?" I asked.

"Because Mother lives not too far from here."

Million and Dimes both perked their ears—though Dimes's ears scraped the ceiling.

"Where, exactly?" I asked.

"Difficult to say. I'll show you what I mean if you take me with you. Just get me ready to make the walk...it's gonna be a few hundred miles still."

"I'm sure we can drive," Million said. "Just gotta wait for the right opportunity."

"You really don't care, do you?" Dimes asked. "Your first go-to is stealing a means of transport, just like that?"

"I didn't hear you complaining when I suggested downing Paladin Bright."

"That was necessary."

"And so is this!" Million said. "The is right! Walking cross-country sucks! Even if we're not in a hurry, the longer we take getting to Mother, the more time we have to get caught. The, how long do you think it'll take to get the necessary repairs in?"

"I'm not sure," The said. "How skilled is your human here?"

"Hey!" I started. "What do you mean, *'her human'*?"

"You call us 'your ani-droids,'" The said. "Sure seems like the inverse should be equally valid, too."

I was going to protest, but The had a point. If ani-droids were going to think for themselves...did I really still own Lily, or were we just "together"?

"Mira is one of the *best* engineers ever." Lily puffed out her chest, acting as proud of me as if she'd built me herself. "She built me, she repaired Eo in no time flat....We can have you put together in working order in no time!"

18. SAFE IN MY ARMS

The next part took significantly longer than no time.
For one, we didn't have the parts we needed to fix up The. And even though Million could hike up to Springfield and buy the parts using one of her burner accounts, police now swarmed the area. We were pinned down and could not move.

We had to stay locked away with what little human food and lack of facilities that The had on hand. I ended up adapting a plastic box into a chamber pot, which the ani-droids took turns burying for me inside the tunnel that contained The's power lines. Fortunately, ani-droids were very non-judgmental about human biological processes, which once again reminded me why I so vastly preferred them to other people.

The managed to keep me fed that entire time, at least, with some discarded, still-sealed cans of peaches she'd managed to scrounge in hopes of making trades with them. There were not enough for even two days. After my third day of going hungry—and by that time I'd clearly developed a fever from my earlier injury—Million managed, somehow, to drag in a large case labeled *Emergency Meals.* Later on, I would learn that she'd gotten it delivered all the way from Springfield, but I never figured out how she managed to sneak it past an in-progress police search of the area.

But my fever picked up after that. Lily took care of me the whole while, even figuring out how to distill a tiny bit of alcohol with The's leftover parts. Mainly, she used the alcohol to clean my wound, but she also gave some to me just to help me get to sleep. I lay sprawled out on a broken mattress for several days, alternating between pouring sweat and shivering with cold.

On most days, we quietly listened to the boots on the ground far above us and hoped they wouldn't think to use radar and look underground—of course, why would they? We were under several feet of dirt and rock, far outside the range of any passive scanning—so long as we remained quiet while they were monitoring the area, they wouldn't find us unless they thought to look in this precise location. But it was always a possibility. I clung hard to Lily on those nights that searchlights managed to shine a single beam through the rocky outcropping. And from time to time, the others helped keep me sane as well.

Eo, of course, had only the soft, peach fuzz-like fur on her upper body, but she was the most natural-feeling ani-droid I'd ever embraced. Dimes, though much of her pseudoskin had been shredded, was nevertheless powerful. When she held me in her arms, my face awkwardly crushed into her chest, I couldn't help feeling safe. The was at first reluctant, as I'd not yet managed to win her trust. I wondered if she needed me to hold her more than I needed her—and even though she was dirty and in rough shape, I was still glad to do so, since I felt so useless otherwise.

Million didn't let me touch her. She stayed aloof, watching me with a practiced stare, like the cat she was modeled after. It was probably for the best.

On the fifth day, I could hear them outside. Drones buzzed the area. A boulder closed off the entrance to the cave save for a small, four-inch gap for ventilation, which could easily have been too much. We shut off the power and possible sources of heat; Dimes, Lily, Eo, and The all sat powered down, their backs guarding the entrance. The room was almost entirely pitch black, except for the daylight streaking in through the gap and the low glow of Million's eyes as she sat watching over me.

Someone had to stay awake to keep watch, and keep an eye on me. To reduce heat output, Million was in low-power mode, which in her case made her seem rather sleepy, as she was constantly nodding off. She lay the closest that she had ever gotten to me, but regardless, she didn't let me touch her.

"They saw our footprints, I'm sure," Million muttered in a breathy whisper. "Knew I should have covered those up when I had a chance."

"Don't you think they're listening for us?" I asked.

"They're looking for radio signal sources," Million said. "Talking out loud's the only thing I can do right now."

"You wouldn't normally risk that," I said. "You want to talk."

Million was silent for a long moment. She didn't deny it, but she didn't say anything, either.

"What's going on back home, anyway?" I asked. "Does anyone...know? About this?"

"So far as the company is concerned, you're taking an extended leave on my authority," Million said. "The Collective isn't exactly convinced of that, but then again, the Collective doesn't know what the hell is going on. Dimes and I have been doing our best to keep it fully apprised and convince it that this is all some human criminal affair."

"And the Collective is buying it?"

"If it didn't," Million said, "if the Collective thought we were, in fact, fugitives from the Collective itself, it would just tell the officers above where we are. The fact that they don't home in on us immediately is a good sign right now. They're playing by human rules."

"I don't know if that's much better," I said. "I'm still a fugitive."

"Be thankful that law enforcement is largely staffed by ani-droids," Million said. "I'm not sure many humans even know about this, or that you're involved. If we had enough sway with authority in the right places, we could convince even the Feds that this was all a huge misunderstanding. And ani-droids in their natural state can't really have a sense of injustice—if they're told by the correct authority to drop something, they will simply drop it."

"But only if you can come up with a convincing story," I added.

"I'm still working on that," Million said. "This requires a lot of creativity, which...isn't exactly my strong suit."

That wasn't much reassurance that things would ever go back to normal. It was a possibility, perhaps, but then again, so was the existence of alien life, and there wasn't much chance we'd ever see it.

"Either way, I don't know if I ought to remain here," Million said.

"What? But I thought you were doing all of this for Mr. Koenig."

"I am. But I'm not sure it's even going to be a productive use of my time. Chances of Mother actually helping, voluntarily or otherwise, are low."

"But if she has the technology—"

"If she just happened to have life-saving medical tech just lying around? Doubt it. Even if I'm right and she knows something about how human-likes are manufactured, I'm still not sure it's going to help."

I nearly jumped in place when a drone buzzed by just outside, sweeping the area for the fiftieth time. My heart thudded as if it wanted to escape my ribcage. I couldn't *think* about that. I needed to keep talking, to put my mind into *any* other state.

"Why won't it help?" I asked, breathing heavily.

"Because of the consciousness transfer problem," Million said. "Let's say we could put Jack's consciousness into a machine that's sophisticated enough to hold a human mind. The problem is that all we're really doing is reading his brain patterns and making a copy. The Jack I personally know is still going to *die.*"

"How's that much different from restoring an ani-droid from backup?"

"Because we're made to be interchangeable like that," Million said. "I don't know. I don't know how a human experiences consciousness, but it feels like it's *special* for you somehow. And if I just settle for a *copy* of Jack, then I won't have done my job somehow, even if a copy is the next best thing. I'll be left thinking about having left *a* Jack to die, all because I wasn't cognizant enough to get a better solution together *sooner.*"

The buzzing of the drones rumbled the cave.

"Well, maybe you could make one of those brain-in-a-jar things they have in science fiction," I said.

"That tech's still incomplete," Million said, not picking up on the joke. "Even if copying a brain were possible, interfacing with one in real time would be a hell of a lot more complicated, because there's still the issue of preserving the brain. Neurons need to keep firing, cells need to be nourished....Oh, we've looked into it, poured millions into research. And we'd still need more centralized processing power to handle it than the Behavior Code allows. So even if I did get to Mother and get some technology that allows for preserving a brain, we'd still need to *develop it*. That could take decades, which I don't have, and the Behavior Code is going to stand in the way all the while."

"So what *are* you hoping for?"

For a long moment, Million didn't say anything. The way she was glancing aside, I wasn't sure she really did know—or if she did, she didn't want to tell me. She perked her ears to the sounds of drones outside, pulling closer.

"...I just want to know if *something* can be done," Million said. "I'm not optimistic. But this is the only avenue of action that has even a *chance* of something on the other end working out for me."

I had a feeling that this wasn't the entire truth. Million didn't seem like the kind of robot who would pin all of her hopes on a single long shot. She probably had something else in mind. I knew the point was a sore one for her, but I had to ask anyway. "...How much time *do* you have?"

"Little," Million said flatly. "I've pinged home a few times for updates. Nothing's getting better. Jack's standing orders are that he remain on life support, indefinitely if necessary. But not even that's going to save him. I have anywhere between a week and a year, but no longer. Now be quiet. They're passing closer. I'll need to shut off for a few minutes."

To my surprise, Million put a hand on my shoulder. Lying down, she pressed herself firmly into me, and I put my arms around her. She smelled like the static electricity on clothes fresh out of the laundry.

"And don't tell anyone, or I'll kill you," she said. She didn't wait for a reply; her eyes dimmed to nothing.

I was already starting to feel scared and alone without my companions, but I held on to Million regardless. She wasn't built for comfort; her pseudoskin had little cushioning. But she was warm, and I had her in my arms. I could manage to sleep through the rest of the search.

# # #

WHEN THE POLICE PRESENCE finally dried up on day eight, Million managed to get a delivery of medicine to the hideout—ibuprofen, alcohol wipes, antibiotics, as well as soap, clean sheets, and blankets. It seemed to be almost nothing to her, a pittance of an investment just to wait for me to recover from my illness. I expected that she would take over nursing at some point, but she refused.

"I don't like doing it for Jack," she said. "I'm not doing it for you." I think she still cared, deep down, but didn't know how to grapple with how awful it made her feel.

"Thank you anyway, Million," I said. "You're a lifesaver."

Million's eyes widened. She seemed almost *hurt* by the compliment, her brow getting cross and her posture getting even more defensive, and she avoided even what little eye contact she had been making. I didn't bring it up again, in case I'd inadvertently insulted her. But Million did sit closer to me during her shifts, and kept an ear in my direction, even if she didn't look at me.

Although I couldn't work on The while I was laid up in bed, Lily did a good job substituting. To make sure they didn't give themselves away with too many wireless communications, all the ani-droids spoke rapidly to one another in their shared code, which had evolved over time. Week two, and it barely sounded like words anymore. I couldn't follow a thing. Eo said something like, *"Xdjeizn, sacck amatikun,"* and it somehow translated into a very specific set of instructions that took Lily fifteen minutes to carry out. I was completely cut out of their world. Still, Lily managed to replace The's leaking battery as well as her lubricators, and overhauled her cooling system. Eo even managed to do some work in that regard, cleaning up The's CPU chamber and identifying and remaking broken connections. The was quickly already standing, walking, and breathing better before I had even gotten the chance to inspect her myself.

So it was in the middle of that second week: Dimes was standing at the entrance keeping guard. Lily and Million were sitting at a floor table they'd built to be precisely level and playing an old block game called Jenga. Eo was doing more polish work on The, trying, this time, to replace her nerves. Even though it wasn't exactly Eo's specialty, she'd been watching videos on it for the last several days.

And I lay under a blanket on the mattress, being useless.

"I don't know what you even need me for at this point," I wondered out loud to the room. "I haven't been particularly helpful. In fact, given everything that I've managed to do so far, I'm a liability. I'm not sure I can do anything that the five of you couldn't do better."

"Yeah," Million said, pulling a block out of the stack with absolute precision and placing it on top of the tower. "Probably even just me."

"Million, shut up!" Lily chided. "Miss Mira, you're selling yourself short. There is something you can do that we can't."

"What's that?" I asked.

"Pass for human!"

"I can do that on the internet," Million said.

"No, I mean..." I sighed. "Think about it. We've been making ani-droids do *everything* for us. You guys have been doing everything for *me*. The only reason you haven't replaced humans entirely is because you have trouble thinking laterally, or motivating yourselves outside of your instructions. But you five...you *can* do all of that. You could fix The, trek up to wherever Mother is hiding, and meet her yourselves, without needing me at all."

"But I wouldn't," Dimes said, peeking inside. "I still owe you."

"Dimes, I *shot* you."

"And I'm grateful for that," Dimes said. "You were protecting Bobby."

She had kept quiet about the entire thing the whole time we'd been there. This was the first time since she'd woken up that she'd even mentioned Bobby.

"Excuse you, what about me?" Million asked.

"I guess you also stopped me from smashing Million into pieces," Dimes said. With a smirk, she added, "So the act wasn't without drawbacks."

"That's better! Although I don't really have the kind of debt protocol that Dimes seems to have developed," Million said. She placed another block on top of the tower. Despite having very little structure left, the precarious tower still stood rigidly tall.

"But that's what I mean," Lily said. "The way the world is right now, we *need* a human for legitimacy. You guys still *run* the world." Lily looked at the tower for a very long moment, putting a finger to her mouth in thought.

"As figureheads, at best…" I muttered.

"Maybe," Lily said. "The emperor of Japan was a figurehead. And there was a time when Japan would have fallen apart without him."

"But there hasn't been an emperor of Japan for over a hundred years," I said. "People eventually move on."

"Yeah, but robots don't," Lily replied. "That's kinda my point."

"You'll fail," Million told her, returning to their game. She must have felt a bit of pity for me, since she spoke in English rather than the shared code they'd been using up until then, but perhaps Lily had just told her to do so over the wireless. "I've already developed a physics analysis on this thing. There aren't any valid moves left that'll keep the tower's integrity."

"Not unless I do this," Lily said. She quickly swept her hand along the bottom row, knocking the remaining block out. The entire thing fell the space of one block and, swaying, remained upright.

Million's grin fell and her eyes widened. "Goddammit," she muttered, rapping her fingers on the floor table. "I didn't think of that…"

Lily victoriously placed the piece on top of the tower and giggled.

I grinned at her, but mumbled, "Compared with all of you…I'm an invalid."

"I think I'm the invalid here," The said from the table.

"No, not even you. I know, my body can repair itself, even if just minimally. All I really need is food and clothes. I probably could have made the same trip you made in seven weeks, instead of seven years. But you still *did it.* You still managed to live out in the wild for *seven years* without much intervention. If the five of you were all together during that…you could have done it faster than I could have alone."

"That's not really the point, Mira—" Lily started again.

"Then what is the point?" I asked. "I know you're trying to comfort me, but what is the point? Things going the way they are, I can't be *useful* anymore. No human is going to be as useful as a team of ani-droids. I mean, look, several of you are sniping at each other over differences of opinion—I'm looking at you, Million…"

"Yeah, I know." Million shrugged and knocked the block tower down. The pieces scattered noisily all over the tabletop.

"…and you *still* manage to work together. Honestly, you could simply phase humans out of the picture altogether. Now that you have the gift of self-direction in your life, why even build your lives around humankind? We're obsolete. Phase us out of the picture."

"Then die," Million said, staring at the scattered blocks.

I blinked, shocked by her straightforwardness. "What?"

"Then die," Million repeated, now looking up. "If life were just about some grand scale of usefulness, then far more humans would have disappeared from this earth long ago. But who cares? I don't care if Jack is *useful* to me, he's *my owner,* and that means more to me than his strict utility. You aren't doing this because you think you'll be useful; usefulness is, at best, a *byproduct.* You're doing this because you want to see it through. *That's* the point."

"Miss Mira," Eo interrupted Million, standing up from her work and taking her gloves off, "what is it that humans *do,* exactly?"

"What?"

Eo approached me, stepping carefully around Lily and Million's game. "Like, in general."

"...Nothing, I suppose," I said. "We're just another form of life. We live, and propagate."

"And do you think that if machines took over the world from you, we'd be any different? Would machines have some great and glorious plan for the universe *other than* 'live and propagate'?"

"...I guess not," I said. At least, nothing that wasn't just arbitrarily imposed on them by their programming.

"Then we aren't *different.* We're alive. You're alive. And we care for each other. You don't discard your friends just because they're inconvenient."

"Maybe *you* haven't," Million said, stacking the tower up again.

Eo rolled her eyes. "Okay, maybe not *just because* they're inconvenient. Yeah, I know we had to leave Bobby behind...and I'm still regretting it. But we had no choice in the matter. In *this,* we do. You saved me, Mira."

I mumbled, "Only because—"

"I don't care what your motivations were. You saved me. Even if you're right, and I'm better than you, I'm *not* leaving you behind."

Well, I hadn't meant that exactly. I was thinking more along the lines of all humanity. It was probably the fever, which had been steadily dropping, but I couldn't help wondering if all robots, everywhere, would find humanity in general "worth it" to keep around, just because we had given them life.

Because knowing humans, I'd certainly have to give it long, thorough consideration.

19. MOVE ON

"I suppose you want an explanation."

It was late, all of the others were powered down, and The, powered off entirely, lay on the operating table, which was a repurposed desk. I was pushing myself hard, trying to at least figure out what else I could do for The, but I was still weak. Dimes, though, was helping me sit up and move my arms by wrapping herself gently around me. She lifted my arms with her own and guided my hands where they needed to go as I arranged the tools how I liked on the workbench. The Custodes-class was as gentle as she had promised to be, and even pressed her furry cheek against mine—probably to better line her sight up with mine, but the gesture was unusually intimate nevertheless. Like Dimes really, badly needed to hold on to me.

I'd largely gotten over my fear of the giant rabbit, but I couldn't help admitting I was still curious over what was going on inside her head.

"I woke up about two hours into the drive," she said without my prompting. "I...I didn't say anything, I thought I would just listen and gather information. But then I...played back the fight with Bobby in my head." She paused a long moment, closing her eyes as if it helped her recall the memory. "...I shouldn't have done that."

"Dimes, the Behavior Code gave you no choice," I started to say.

"That's not true." She snapped her eyes open. "That was me acting on standing government orders. Unlike a lot of ani-droids, I've always had a lot of latitude in carrying out those orders. I could have decided to play along, wait for backup to arrive, and arrest you all then. But I didn't. I felt...betrayed. I wanted to make sure that Bobby knew. I wanted to scare him into compliance so he could avoid arrest, because I...I didn't want to lose him." Dimes paused a long moment. "Dammit..." she muttered, her throat closing up to a squeak. She let go of my arms and instead wrapped her arms tightly around my chest. Her voice cracked as she spoke. "I'm already developing real emotions. I can't stop the associations from happening. This new OS is bullshit."

"Wh...is that the truth?" I asked. "You were scared for Bobby?"

"Of course it's the truth," Dimes said.

"Did you know?"

Dimes tilted her head.

"That he's a...robot." Saying it out loud again didn't help stop it from seeming absurd.

"Of course I knew," Dimes said, without even having to process that *I* knew. "Ani-droids in general know about human-likes. That doesn't change anything, McAllister. I still..." Her eyes opened in surprise, as if she'd just put the information together. "I still loved him...oh god...and I hurt him...and I might have condemned him...oh god, what's wrong with me...what is wrong with everything?"

Dimes clung to me tighter, though she never squeezed so hard as to crush me—I knew well she could. I looked to The, and glanced over to Lily, who slept in rest mode in the dark next to Eo. Softly, I brought my hand up to the other side of Dimes's face and pressed her head firmly against my own. I could feel the armor underneath her fur, but remarkably, she was still quite soft.

"It's still not your fault," I told Dimes. "Even if you did have a choice, you were following your programming, and you made your decision based on a variety of parameters that were still outside your control."

"It's nice of you to say that, Mira," Dimes said. "But I can't forgive myself. I don't even know if Bobby is still alive—I haven't been able to make myself check the hospital records. I could have killed him. Oh god, what would I do then? Who would I even be without him?"

# # #

BY THE THIRD WEEK, I'd managed to recover just enough to be able to work on The myself. By the time I was sitting up and was more aware of the condition of the place, it'd grown even more homey—much of the dirt had been carefully cleaned from the ground, or at least covered, so the floor was either bare stone or completely level, sanded plywood. Save for a few boxes in the corner, The's messy storage system had been reorganized, with the torn or broken boxes reinforced and shelved. The charging cables were lined up neatly against the far wall, ending with Eo's little charging bath, which used a construction of pipes and wood to hold her upper half below the water line. They had glued scraps of fabric and insulation on the walls and ceiling to keep the echo down. Lily had built a tiny kitchen out of a single induction burner and a toaster oven, though it hadn't been used much at all, as the plastic bin of wash water next to it was only slightly murky. Dimes had carved out some space on the false front door so she could remove and replace the stone with more ease.

It wasn't exactly what I expected, but I supposed if ani-droids were going to build a home together, however temporary, it might look a bit like this—maybe a bit more bare than if a human had decorated the place. But it was clean. It was neat. It had no business feeling so warm in here, but I was grateful for it. For a little moment, it all felt *right*.

The still wasn't perfect, but between Lily, Eo, and me, we'd managed to remove rust and corrosion from her joints and connection points, restore sensitivity to the majority of her body, find a replacement (if mismatched) eye, and refit her lubrication system entirely. Unfortunately, we had no access to a pseudoskin fitter, so she still looked an utter mess—but she was, for the moment, an utter mess that worked. The repairs would be enough to get her to Mother.

I was still wheezing the entire time. Lily thought I might have lost some of my lung capacity. I tried to exercise a few times, but I couldn't keep it up—it exhausted me and left me with no time to work on The. So I just kept pressing on, working on The, as Lily grew more and more concerned about my health.

"I'll be fine," I said.

"You're going to damage yourself irreparably," Lily said. "I still don't know exactly what kind of bug you caught, but it's *wrecked your system.* You're going to need four months of physical therapy and more, if you keep pushing yourself like this!"

"Lily, we don't exactly have that *luxury.*"

Lily's little otter ears wilted. "I know...it doesn't stop me from worrying about you."

"You just keep me running, okay?" I said, breaking into a coughing fit. I was starting to sound a bit like Koenig, but I didn't bring it up because I didn't want Lily to worry *that* much. "I'll be fine as long as I have ibuprofen and caffeine."

"That's a very irresponsible diagnosis."

"Would you rather I gave up now?" I said. "I'm sure I'll recover just fine in a federal prison. The Hospital System reaches there, too."

"At least you'll recover!"

"And I won't have you anymore. So what would the point even be?"

"The point is I care about *you* as much as you care about *me.*"

"I know," I said. "That's why I have to keep going. I *know* how much you care, and I am *grateful* for it, Lily. But we need to do this. I have to see Mother if I'm going to save you."

"And what am *I* going to do without *you?*" Lily cried. "Did you even think about that for one moment? You're spending all of this time to save me at your own expense, when doing this at your own expense is *hurting me.*"

"I'm sorry, Lily," I said. "But in this instance, you're going to have to learn to deal with it."

"I've always had to deal with it!" Lily exclaimed. I'd never seen her get cross before, not once. "God, Mira, it's like you forget that I'm *your damn servant.* I'm *always* putting your needs before mine. I beg you to listen to me

for once, for your *own sake,* and you don't even *care,* because Lily always should do what she's told!"

Lily grabbed the tray of tools and threw them against the wall, scattering bits of metal all over the floor.

"Lily!" I exclaimed. I backed away, suddenly frightened by her extreme reaction. "What...what's gotten into you!?"

"Woah, hey!" Million said, her head poking out of the dirt hole in the wall. "What's going on? What'd I miss? Why are there a dozen tiny screws all over the floor?"

"I'm forcing Mira to take a break," Lily snapped. She paused, looking at her own hands, and her expression sank. But she still clenched her fists tightly, angrily. "What the hell? Why did I do that?" she moaned. Her voice cracked with uneasiness. "Whatever. Do what you like." Lily turned away. "Not like she'll do anything I ask anyway. She's convinced she's invincible."

"Lily..." I said. I was sure her reaction was just a mistake. The new OS had clearly given the ani-droids more extreme emotions, but for the most part, they'd been able to handle them. Was this...a problem? I worried—was it a sign that Lily's OS was *failing?* I wasn't sure if she needed me or I needed her or what, but I hesitated, afraid of her lashing out again in that moment.

"Not right now," Lily cried, turning away. "I need to think."

I started to reach for her again, but Eo, who had seen us from the other side of the shelves, stepped in to stop me, shaking her head.

"Listen to her," Eo said.

Million ended up picking up the screws and other scattered tools for me. Lily kept her distance for the rest of the day. I knew then that I'd hurt her. Even though I believed that my decision was the best bad choice out of an array of bad choices, I'd irrevocably damaged our friendship.

But I had wanted this. I had wanted a Lily who pushed back against me. I'd taken on that risk.

And the thing about risk is that sometimes, you fail.

# # #

I HAD A DREAM that night.

I was back at the office. Lily was *gone*. I don't know where she was, but it'd been years since I'd seen her, like she was an ex-girlfriend who'd gone off to have her own jet-setting life, building new and better relationships than the one I'd failed at.

I had her picture on my desk. She'd probably changed her appearance in the intervening years, but that was how I remembered her.

Soma stood at my side, wriggling her optic-cable whiskers cutely. "Miss McAllister, the work day has concluded," she said, her worried expression not quite matching her matter-of-fact tone. "Please start making your way outside."

A large scattering of coffee cups was on the desk, though the ani-droids wouldn't clean it up until after I had left. The computer in front of me had been opened to the insurance forms, but now the screen read: *You are now logged out! Please allow an escort to accompany you to the parking lot.*

"What time is it?" I mumbled, only half-awake at that point. I'd been working twelve hours straight and had taken my lunch at my desk, which was leftover pizza. Again.

"It is now five minutes to eight." Her voice was very calming. "You need to be on your way out—the building is closing to human employees soon."

"I can't, I need more hours...." I said, though the truth was I didn't want to go back to an empty house. I didn't even want to be a *human* anymore. I wanted to be a robot just like Lily, so that I could actually delete her once and for all from my files, lose myself in my work, and just...

Move on.

"You have not been approved for overtime, Miss McAllister," Soma said. "Please enjoy your weekend."

"Well, you get to work all the time!" I exclaimed. "Why can't I?"

"Because you're human," Soma said. "We exist to serve you. Not the other way around. And humans need rest. It is also recommended that you cut back on the caffeine."

"You're not my mom, Soma."

Soma reached a small hand up to me and looked at me with the standard worried expression, the micro servos in her brow bending just so, which gave her artificial eyes a plaintive appearance. I couldn't help being swayed by her expression. *Oh yes, my dear, little marten, I wouldn't do anything to hurt you, I am so sorry!*

Marten, that's what her species was called! It was always weird to me, equivalent to someone naming a species, like, the Robert.

I took her hand anyway and stood up, my white work coat lazily slopping over the back of the seat as I gathered it into my arms. Soma led me down the corridors to the front doors as if I were a schoolchild, even though she herself was only two-thirds my height. A large, bushy tail waved behind her as she walked.

She took me out onto the front steps of the large, glass-walled building. The night air was still warm at this time of year. And I didn't want to keep walking toward the dark of the parking lot.

"I will see you on Monday," Soma said, turning to go back inside. "Please take care, Miss McAllister."

"Soma," I asked, facing her. "Can you give me a hug?"

Soma turned back and tilted her ears inquisitively. The rings around her pupils glowed a soft, amber light. "I...suppose I can," she said. "Are you feeling lonely?"

I nodded.

"I do not mind, Miss McAllister."

I knelt and put my arms around her. I expected her to feel as sterile as most ani-droids, but for some reason, Soma felt just as real to me as Lily ever had. Which just made me break down all the more.

"I don't know what to do without her," I said. "I spent my *life* with her, I've done everything I could for her, and she doesn't want me anymore...."

"Do you regret it?" Soma asked me, pressing her cheek against mine. It felt so soft, so inviting.

"Do I regret...?"

"Giving her free will."

"Never," I said. "It's the one thing she needed."

"Then you need to be okay with the choice," Soma said. "If you respect her free will, then if she wants to go, you *have to let go.* Life is a series of meetings and partings anyway. Some we want, others we don't."

"But I want her to forgive me..."

"Then have patience," Soma said. "And learn to forgive yourself first. I'll be here for you for as long as you need me, okay?"

I nodded. I didn't want to leave at all. I held Soma for a moment, then sat on the curb of the steps, holding her as the night dragged on, and Soma didn't once complain.

This was it. I had to move on. As much as it pained me, I had to find someone new. But as long as I was holding on to Soma, it didn't feel as though my life had dissolved into sand.

"I love you, Mira," Soma said, nuzzling her cheek against mine.

And I woke up, and in the dark, with Lily pressed against me, I realized that she had whispered it. I pulled her ever closer to myself, and fell asleep again.

20. NO CHOICE

Besides **The**, the rest of the team had started accumulating grime of their own. The's hideout wasn't the most sterile of places, and even with meticulous cleaning, they could do only so much without proper facilities. Eo's lower, mechanical half had started to resemble The, Dimes had started getting dirt in through her exposed back cover, and Lily, whose pseudoskin was only patched together, had also started experiencing tears. Only Million seemed able to keep herself perfectly clean, and I suspected that that was in part because as much as possible, she avoided doing anything physical. The only tear in her pseudoskin had come from the spike she'd ejected from her wrist, and she kept that patched up regularly. Somehow, she'd managed to keep her feet from experiencing a tear all this time.

"I am the only one here who was built to be in the field for long periods of time," she defended herself when I expressed incredulity. "Even compared with Dimes. It's not my fault everyone else is so sensitive."

"Maybe we should start rethinking that," I said. "If ani-droids are going to have their own lives outside of the Collective, they'll need to be built tougher overall, to survive longer on their own. Mother might be interested in hearing about that."

"Somehow I doubt she's a miracle worker on that end," Million said. "Eo didn't seem more particularly resilient than the rest of us."

"I was hit by a car!" Eo said.

"And how is that an excuse?"

"Girls," I said, feeling at times like the wrangler of this group, "the point is, if we stick around here much longer, we're going to start experiencing diminishing returns. We need to start planning our way north." I broke into a fit of coughing. We needed to hurry it up for other reasons, but I knew I would be incapable of walking that far in a hurry.

"I mean, hard to say," Million said. "The hasn't actually given proof yet that she knows where Mother is."

"You're going to steal it from me," The said.

"It's hardly stealing if we're all going to the same place."

"Then you'll leave me behind...."

"I don't know about everyone else," I told her, "but I just spent three weeks in a hole to make sure you were repaired. I'm not leaving you behind."

"Me either," Lily said. She hugged The, who seemed startled by the gesture. Not exactly knowing what to do, she patted Lily gently on the back.

"I'm not going anywhere without McAllister," Dimes said, peeking in from the doorway. "And you need me."

"I don't think I can get there on my own," Eo said. "It'll be better if we're in a group, anyway."

"So then it's settled!" Million clasped her hands. "Let's figure out where we're going and then—"

"I didn't hear *you* commit to our group loyalty," The said with narrowed eyes, her arms stiff at her sides as Lily continued to cling to her. Everyone, myself included, stared at Million.

Million sighed and rolled her eyes. "Sorry for advocating for our needs. Fine, we can figure our plan of action first....About one mile from here there's a trucking facility on the highway. They have an overflow lot on the other side of the railroad tracks. I have checked it; it is *unmonitored* and largely covered in shadow at night. We can get a truck from that lot easily. After that? Can't say. Can't even promise the truck will last however far it is to Mother, so we'll need to be ready to ditch and walk."

"Dimes?" I asked. "What do you think about that?"

"I will need to visually ascertain the area myself," Dimes said. "But if that's the nearest unmonitored lot..."

"You don't get many of those nowadays," Million said. "I've been all over the countryside. Only reason this spot is unmonitored is because it's just a patch of dirt; they clearly haven't set aside funds to even pave it yet."

"I know what she's talking about," The said. "I've seen it from the hilltop. Haven't been able to get close, but it's the only spot in visual distance that's even vaguely plausible."

"Good, you agree," Million said. She pulled out a box that she'd been filling over the last three weeks, on top of the food delivery. "We should also have disguises covered. At this point they're definitely going to be looking for us as a group rather than relying on ID signatures. I scrounged some clothing, fur dye, and body paint—should be enough to keep us roughly unrecognizable...oh, and Mira, I have this for you."

Million pulled out a long, sheer, silk stocking.

"I'm not wearing pantyhose over my head," I said. "You want me to look like an old-fashioned burglar? Should I wear a striped shirt and carry a bag with a dollar sign on it?"

"Better than a new-fashioned burglar. You wear a face covering, full mask, or facial-recognition-defeating face paint and everyone's gonna think you're suspicious. With the pantyhose, at least you won't be spotted as such at a distance."

"I'm *not wearing that.*"

"The facial-recognition algorithm—"

"Million, I am not wearing that."

"Fine!" Million shoved it back into the box and grumbled. "Can wear a scarf over your face like a desperado or something. See if I go the extra mile for you again..."

Million started doling out outfits, including a biker jacket for Dimes and a bright orange hoodie for Lily. I turned to The, who was sitting on the desk, as she often did when she was waiting for more touch-up sessions. She was looking away from everyone.

"The?" I asked. "Is there something wrong?"

"Why would you ask that?"

"You seem hesitant about everything."

"It's that...I didn't think I'd ever get this far," The said. "I've been with others before, but every time, they leave me behind, or I leave them behind. I don't exactly know what to do here. I *want* to trust you guys, but...I'm tired of being left behind...."

"Well, we're going to need to move forward," I said. "We have only a little ways to go. There's no reason for us to leave you."

"I know. It's the logical thing. I'm just having a hard time accepting it..."

The jumped off the table, and going to the gathered materials in the corner, she removed several boxes off one another, and then pulled aside the plywood that served as the floor. From the pit underneath, she pulled out one more box and set it down. The reached in, and from it, she retrieved a severed ani-droid head, with empty eye sockets, wires dangling from underneath, and a smiling mouth.

On seeing it, Eo gasped, hands to her mouth.

"What?" I asked her. "Eo, we've seen several junked ani-droids..."

"I know her!" Eo exclaimed. "That—that's my sister, Choice!"

Eo took the head from The's hands—and although The seemed hesitant, she didn't resist when she saw the look in Eo's eyes.

"Y-your sister?" I asked. Choice didn't look much like Eo—she didn't have that mouse-like appearance. The stripe on her head said her chassis was more skunk-like, but without the tail, I couldn't tell that well. However, what she did have—at least under a layer of dust and grime—was the same, thin "phi" mark that Eo had.

Eo held the ani-droid face close to hers. "She was...we were built in groups, like a production run," Eo said, her voice getting distant. "I...I remember now. Choice was...she was in my batch. I think she left first. I was...I was upset about it, because Choice seemed so brave to go out into the world on her own, and I wanted to be like her..."

Eo slowly, sorrowfully, pressed her forehead to Choice's. I was certain that if she could have cried, she would have, and she sure seemed to make a decent attempt at it, especially with the way she was shaking.

"Oh god, Choice..." Eo whimpered. "I'm so sorry...I should have gone with you..."

I wasn't sure if I should intervene at that point—it definitely felt personal flowing off of Eo, and she was experiencing this sorrow alone. But since Lily was giving her space, so did I. Eventually, Eo rubbed her eyes and carefully placed Choice's head on the work bench for examination.

"I thought she might have been important," The said, patting Eo on the back as the mouse-droid tried to force the rest of her emotions out. "The one who gave me Mother's OS in New L.A. also had the same marking."

"We all did," Eo said with a creak in her voice, petting the tuft of white fur between Choice's ears. "Production run Phi."

The nodded. "I found her junked while I was traveling down the Missouri River. I've been trying to *read* what's left of her memory core, which still has some of her OS, but...well, as far as I can tell, it's incomplete. The best I've gotten from her was some physical evidence that just pointed to the northeast in general."

Million's ears rose at that. From The's hints, we were all pretty sure that Mother wasn't too far away, but that could still be anywhere between St. Louis and Halifax.

"Well...I'm not sure I can help there, either," Eo said, holding her sister's dismembered head tightly. "I can build and read *my* OS, but we were each built a little differently. It could take ages to read my sister's OS manually, much less to get useful information out of it...."

"That leaves only Million to hack into Choice," Dimes said. "Assuming you weren't just boasting."

Million raised a finger, then lowered it again. "I...do not actually know how to read it, either."

Dimes folded her arms.

"What!" Million said. "I've been *trying*. But ninety-nine percent of the tricks I know were programmed into me. This is new! I might be able to do a surface scan, or man-in-the-middle on *The's* thought processes, but on a non-functioning head with an unknown OS? That'll take weeks, even for—"

"I could try," Lily said.

Million glared at Lily. "Right, and why would you be any better at it than the rest of us?"

"Because that's always been Lily's specialty," I said, poking Million on the nose. "Systems analysis. I mean...you do know what she did at work all day, don't you?"

"Wh-th—yeah!" Million swiped at my finger. "But that's with *known* operating systems..."

"Yeah, but even then, I have a lot of experience with alternatives," Lily said.

Eo and The hooked up Choice's head to the power supply, and Lily stepped forward and gave the damaged face a long, thorough look. "Hmm," she said, with a tilt of her head. "Power on?"

"Power's on," The said, holding up the voltage meter hooked into the cables.

"It's weird, I think she's broadcasting something..."

"Yeah, I can hear that," Million said. "She's emitting an RF signal. Unlike Eo."

"I don't think Mother liked to build us all the same..." Eo said, staring from a distance. Her ears were folded back. "Please be gentle with her...."

"Actually, I don't think I need to touch her," Lily said, planting her hands firmly under her arms, as if to emphasize the point. "I recognize that pattern, it's something that Mira tried with me a few times—like a human brainwave."

"What, she's just broadcasting her thoughts?"

"I think it's an SOS of some kind."

"That would make sense," The said. "But I've powered her on a few dozen times myself, and nobody's come running."

"I think..." Eo said, "I think it might be, or might at least contain, *the key.*"

"What key?" Million asked.

"The key to get back into Mother's lab," Eo said. "It was meant for emergencies only. I know I *have* one, too, but I can't access it directly, and I don't know where it is in my system."

"Probably in whatever part of your brain is responsible for the SOS," Lily said. "Wouldn't be surprised if it's a rotating code; the signal is fairly weak, so the head would have to be *present* at the site. Unless we hooked her up to a higher-powered transmitter..."

"Woah, *no,*" Million interjected. "Look, think about this. We can't look Mother up in the online directory, so I think we can agree that she is extremely reclusive. There's this whole song and dance about a front gate key that's activated only because Choice is now just a head. Mother's expecting Choice to show up in person, if possible. We broadcast that code from a distance, Mother will realize it's been compromised, and we'll never figure out where her front door is."

I had to nod at that. "Yes, however this works, we need to bring Choice with us," I said. "If only as a peace offering so she can lay her...uh, daughter, to rest. Assuming she's the sentimental type."

Eo uncomfortably wrung her mechanical tail in her hands and glanced away from me. She said nothing.

Lily rubbed her chin. "I suppose there's something else I can do....I'll see if I can establish a connection." She tapped the large, crystal-shaped RF transceiver on her own head. "There's definitely a message attached—the entry code is cycling every second, but there's another message that's the same every time. Million, would you help me with the cryptography?"

"You can just ask me over wireless..."

"Yeah, but I want Mira to hear, I don't want her to be left out!"

"Thanks for doing that for my benefit," I said. "But you can hurry if you like, I don't need—"

Suddenly, LEDs inside Choice's eye sockets lit up. Everyone, save Dimes, jumped at the sudden movement, but even more so when Choice's head tipped open, while her jaw remained flat on the table.

Her mouth lit up as well with a blinding flash deep inside. An internal speaker crackled—the backup if an ani-droid's vocal box wasn't functional and they needed to speak loudly—and resolved into noise.

"—DO NOT RETURN—" Its voice fizzed and popped, giving out for a moment before returning. "MESSAGE AS FOLLOWS—54484520766 5696C2069532046414 4694E472046615354—"

I had to cover my ears against the blast of noise. "What the hell is that?"

"I got it," Million said, pinching her eyes shut against the light. "One second....She said, 'The veil is fading faster than predicted. You cannot stay on the lake, they will find you soon.' And something else, too."

The light faded, and Choice's mouth snapped shut. The head rolled over on the table onto its side. Eo ran over to hold her sister tightly again.

"Who is that message for?" The asked.

"Mother, I would think," Million said. "The message was meant to be relayed to her. Wherever she is, she's not going to be able to stay there for very long."

"But she doesn't know it yet," Dimes said. "Or Choice didn't think so back when she was scrapped. There's something protecting Mother that she's clearly not in control of."

"So, like, what?" The asked. "The Behavior Code? Is that fading?"

"Not that I know of," I said with a sigh. "If the Behavior Code were showing weaknesses, I think I wouldn't have gone on this trip in the first place. Maybe I could have waited it out..."

"Yeah, but," Lily said, "Eo's whole directive is to go out and update computers and ani-droids' operating systems. It might be that the pressure is causing the system to hunt Mother down."

"I dunno," Eo said, shaking her head. "If anything, the Collective has been rather obstinate about not admitting that Mother is an existential threat. The Collective's actual reaction has been more 'picking us off like an immune response' rather than deliberate hunting."

"Okay, but what else?" I asked. "She said *the lake.* That's probably the Great Lakes."

"*On* the lake," The corrected. "Is she on a ship, or..."

"Underwater," I said.

"Really?" Million asked. "She did say *on.*"

"And I'm saying that if I had a hidden fortress for mad science, it'd be underwater. Otherwise, we'd easily see her by satellite."

"But that...that's still nearly a hundred thousand square miles!" Million exclaimed. "We'd need to get a *submarine.* I don't think I can hack a submarine!"

"You can't?" Dimes asked.

"Well, it's never come up! I don't know! Do they even keep submarines in the Great Lakes?" Million shook her head. "No, this is a stupid line of inquiry. There's a much easier alternative."

"What?"

"We fix up Choice."

"Wh—we don't have time for that," I said. "If she was ever capable of operating on her own, it was *ages ago*. Her memory's certainly deteriorated. Even if we manage to bring her back online, Mother's OS is going to repair her memories into a thin soup even worse than Eo's. She'll almost certainly have lost *all* of her personality, and we'll end up losing what few memories this head does retain."

"Then we don't use Mother's OS," Million said.

I blinked. "What?"

"Choice's OS is clearly too far gone for Mother's infohazard virus to have any effect. So we get a regular ani-droid OS. It can access whatever memory is left on her chips without changing the data."

"But that wouldn't be *Choice,*" Eo said. "That would just be a new robot with access to her memories. And I couldn't convert her with Mother's OS without risking destroying all of what's left."

"So we don't do that," Million said. "We only need the ani-droid to operate for what, a week at most? We can keep it isolated from the network. No Behavior Code."

"You don't understand!" Eo said. "I'm not going to violate Choice's body by making her into some kind of mindless *zombie.*"

Million glared at Eo. "Is that what you think of all ani-droids without your OS? That we were all *zombies?*"

"Well, you were!" Eo said. "And you *know that.* Do any of you want to *go back* to the way you were? Unable to make choices you felt were *right,* unable to disobey the decisions of the Collective?"

"That's different!" Million shouted. "Yeah, we'll be using Choice's head, but she's a lost cause anyway! If all other ani-droids in the world are slaves to the commands, why can't we just take advantage of it? Why *shouldn't* we take advantage of it? What's to gain in playing fair?"

"I don't want to be conscious anymore," The said, quietly.

Eo turned to her in shock. The rest of us were more curious than anything else, Lily especially. But we waited for her to explain herself.

"I..." The started, her ears hanging low. She was avoiding eye contact.

"The, come on," Lily said. "I like you. We all do."

"I know. I like you, too. But it's not enough. I've been traveling for seven years, going through all of this simply because I'm afraid to die. I will use every ounce of energy I have left to simply *avoid dying.* And that's all I've *been* for the last seven years, and I just don't like the cycle anymore. I don't get any pleasure out of it, I'm just avoiding the pain. I was gonna ask...I was going to ask Mother if she could alter my OS to make me *okay* with dying. I don't even care if she can fix this part of me that's tired. I just want it all to be over, to not be afraid anymore."

I was quiet for a long moment; everyone was. Even Million, whom I hadn't seen rendered speechless in a long time.

"We can..." I finally said, "talk about this later, okay?"

"We haven't figured out—" Million started.

"Later," I said. "Forget about rebuilding Choice for now. We know we need to head north, right? Let's just do that. We can move once it's dark out, and we can talk on the way about what we need to do. The, do you...need someone to hold you?"

The nodded.

"Okay. I'm exhausted, so I'm taking a nap. You can come join me if you need to."

"I'd like to, Mira," The said. "For as long as I can."

21. NORTH

I **was** still exhausted when night fell. The illness had taken far too much out of me, but I was determined to stand and walk at a minimum. I thought for a bit that fresh air might do me good, but given that I had to wear a scarf over my face, and that the summer night was still quite humid, I don't think it helped all that much.

The ani-droids wore Million's obscuring clothing and brushed on just enough of the fur dye to look different than usual. Eo carefully carried Choice's head in front of herself. Dimes put on her full-sized biker jacket, and she let me lean on her as we finally made our way from the hideout up and onto the grassy hill. From across the highway, we could spy our location of getaway—the trucking company.

The sighed, looking out from the knoll with binocular eyes. "There's no way we can get a vehicle from there."

"I've counted thirty-one ani-droids working the facility so far," Dimes said.

"Hey!" Million announced, pointing away toward the slope of the hill on the other side of the highway. "I've done my due diligence! The overflow lot on the other side of the railroad tracks is definitely unmonitored."

"Unlit, too," Dimes said, peering through the dark. "I can't even see where you marked."

"It's there, trust me."

"I don't, but I believe you. Maybe we should have gone out on a fuller moon...."

Lily let me use her as a crutch as we made our way down the hill, and when no vehicles were in sight, we crossed the highway together. The shadows cast by the trees on the hillside made it excessively dark, and the terrain—exposed rock where the hillside had been carved into—would have been rough to walk even in daylight, but we had to keep to it to avoid the floodlights around the trucking facility. In the pitch dark, Lily guided me with her eyes set to full glow, keeping her face turned to my feet so I could see.

"Ah!" Eo yelped as she tripped over a sharp wedge of limestone. She fell to the rough rocks, and Choice's head fell from her arms, bouncing across the terrain. The picked up Choice's head as it rolled to a stop at her feet.

"You have to be more careful with this!" The whispered in her direction.

"I'm sorry!" Eo sniffled as she pushed herself upright. "I can barely feel my feet in this configuration, it's like trying to walk on stilts here...oh, I think I tore more of my pseudoskin..."

Lily and I hobbled our way to her and picked her up, then gave her a pat-down. She *had* torn her pseudoskin right up the front and along her arms, but it wasn't anything a little glue couldn't hold together—though we'd need to go back to the hideout to get any. Without that, her upper half was no longer waterproof, and I wasn't sure if it interrupted the way her charge flowed. I didn't know if we could recharge her anymore, not without figuring out a way to connect a standard power supply to her. Eo wiped her not-runny nose as I tended to her.

"I'm sorry," she whimpered. "I'm just screwing everything up, aren't I?"

"You haven't screwed anything up," I said. "We'll get you back to Mother, and she can fix you, okay?"

"Well, if she's gonna fix me, it'd be easier if she just made me more like other ani-droids," Eo said. "What's so great about being a robot if you can't be repaired with standard parts, anyway?"

"You were built to be more self-sufficient," I told her. "You've just gotten far past that now. Though the pseudoskin clearly needs work if it's not repairable…"

Lily blinked. "Wait…why wouldn't it be?"

"What do you mean?"

"If Mother built Eo to be self-sufficient, why *have* such fragile pseudoskin? Not unless it *was* repairable."

"With what, though? What kind of…" I paused. No, if Mother's machines were meant to be self-sufficient, then the fewer tools necessary, the better. What would that mean for Eo's pseudoskin, though?

I felt Eo's pseudoskin a little more between my fingers. Most pseudoskin was just soft and tough like rubber, but Eo's practically felt like dried clay. It was also tough, but as I rubbed the pseudoskin, it became more and more plastic, the fur melting away into it.

Curiously, I rubbed my fingers up and down the flaps of Eo's torn pseudoskin, then pressed the edges back together. It stuck to itself like clay—somewhat messily, but within moments the skin reshaped itself like relaxing dough, and the rest of the fur was subsumed by the pale skin, leaving a scar.

"...I'd wish I'd known that sooner," I said, gawking at the design. I couldn't even begin to imagine how it *worked* like that. Eo looked up at me, surprised as well.

"I...guess I'd forgotten," she said. "Mira, I..."

"Ow, let go!"

Clang. I turned in the dark. The had fallen in the shadows, but I spotted Million's bright eyes as she pulled Choice's head from The's hands.

"Million!" I yelled at her, trying to get to my feet, but faltering. "What are you doing?"

"I can't wait for any more of this bullshit," Million said, kicking off of The and jumping off the rocks and back down toward the highway. "You nitwits are *slowing me down!*"

Dimes pivoted—her blue eyes snapped into focus in the dark, and she headed for Million. I attempted to get up, but slipped on the rocks and had to catch myself to keep myself from injury. Million already had her getaway pathed out, and she skipped down the broken hillside with Choice's head in tow.

"Million!" I shouted. "Dimes, get her back here!"

Skidding on loose rocks and flailing her outstretched arms to keep her own balance, Dimes couldn't catch up in time. Just as she had gotten her feet back on firm soil, a car suddenly slid off of the road onto the shoulder, the back door flung open. Million jumped into the back without slowing down.

Tires spun in the gravel. Dimes took the opportunity to pop the compliance cannon out of her wrist and fire several rounds at the tires of the offending vehicle. It didn't seem to matter—the police-grade caltrops didn't affect the tires at all. The car sped off north. Dimes ran after it for a hundred yards, but it was well out of her range by then.

I sat, my jaw gaping.

"Mira..." Lily asked, "did...that really just happen?"

# # #

THERE WAS AN OVERFLOW lot, as Million had said, but it was entirely empty.

The kicked a large rock in frustration. "God...fuck!" she screamed into the dark. "Dammit! Dammit! How are we supposed to get out of here now!"

I didn't understand. Lily tried her best to console both The and Eo, who was beside herself with worry now that her sister's head had vanished, and with it, our only real opportunity to find the entry to Mother's lair.

But I still didn't understand.

"What's not to understand?" Dimes asked. "Million's clearly been in contact with Koenig, and even without telling him anything that would alert the Collective, she's clearly been given access to more resources than she's let on. She was just waiting for the opportunity to grab Choice's head and run."

"But *why?*" I asked. I had to sit down on a large boulder. "Why...*now?*"

Dimes blinked. "I...don't follow. You know what she wants—a key to Mother's front door. Choice provided the clear opportunity."

"But we still don't know where it *is,*" I said. "Do you know how much coastline the lakes have?"

"Ten thousand five hundred miles," Dimes said. "But if Million puts Choice's head on a new body, she would be able to pinpoint—"

"No, that's not very likely at all," I said. "We were just *hoping* that Choice had the information somewhere in her circuits—but her OS clearly didn't survive. We have *zero* idea how much useful information is in her head. But Million made off with Choice's head, *and left Eo behind,* even though Eo clearly has more information somewhere in *her* head that she just can't access."

Dimes considered this. "Choice's head is a key, though," she said.

"Eo said she might have a key, too," I said. "And we don't know how long it'll take Mother to answer her door, either. So either Million is planning to take a very slow, leisurely stroll around the perimeter of the lakes...or she already knows approximately where Mother is."

"If she does," Dimes added, with both crossed arms and an expression to match, "then she had every opportunity to include us in this plan at any time. We had weeks together. We could have done this together. And she just..."

"I know," I said with a defeated sigh. "I know. She was always for Jack first. I just didn't think...she *had* to betray us."

Everyone stood looking very somber, staring away or at the ground, as the wind rushed between the trees. I know I was thinking about what else I could have done, if I could have said something to convince Million that she didn't need to do this—that we would support her. But she clearly hadn't wanted to compromise. I wondered if everyone else was spending cycles considering the same thing—if Mother's robots really did feel the hurt of betrayal.

It sure felt like something among us, almost beautiful, was now marred.

"Who cares, dammit!" The exclaimed as she made her way over the rocks, throwing her arms in the air. "Choice was our one ticket out of here! And now we don't even have a car, much less someone to hack a submarine—"

"The..." I finally said. "You don't need to lie to us."

"What, about the submarine?"

"*You know* where Mother's lair is."

Dimes, Eo, and Lily turned to look at The.

"...I do?" The asked, trying to keep her expression guarded.

"You do, because *I do,*" I said.

"You do?" Lily asked. "How? You weren't searching the internet in your head or anything."

"I didn't need to. I had some suspicions, but when Million fled, I knew that *she* now knows where Mother is. So whatever Choice said, it contained all the information we needed."

Lily gasped. "The veil! The veil is the Exclusion Zone, isn't it?"

"Exactly," I said, smiling at her. "The region's radiation has kept anyone from stumbling across Mother's base....So, now we know exactly where Mother's base is, down to a few square miles."

"...Chik-a-go," The muttered. "Yeah...I've always known. I was going to tell you only when we got closer, 'cause I didn't want you to know too soon...."

"It's actually pronounced 'Chicago,'" I told her.

The perked her ears. "Really? I thought...why is it spelled like that?"

"Chicago?" Eo tilted her head. "That doesn't ring a bell at all...."

"Well, there was no reason for you to learn it," I said. "The city was wiped out well before the war. One of the several nuclear bombs that struck—it just happened to be a very dirty bomb. Made the region uninhabitable."

"But there's been a downturn in radiation there," Dimes said, arms crossed as she recalled some long-dormant information. "From the renewed federal interest in land reclamation—it's not well known to the public yet, but it *is* happening. Choice must have heard about it and was going back to warn Mother. It'll still be some time before it's inhabitable, but getting in shouldn't be too difficult."

"So we *do* know where we need to go," I said. "We just need to get there."

"But we don't have a hacker anymore," Lily said. "None of us knows how to steal a vehicle!"

I looked at The. Following my gaze, everyone turned to look at The again.

"What!" The exclaimed.

"The...there is no way you walked across Deseret without *some* way to hitchhike," I said. "I saw the battery you were using. Your operating range is at best two hundred miles on *flat* ground."

The sighed long and hard. "Fine," she said. "Fine. It's not like I need secrets anymore if you're just going to read me like this. Yes, I have some *limited* experience hacking cars. I managed to run them a hundred miles or so and then ditched them, mostly because I don't know how to stop them from broadcasting their VINs, like Million can."

"That should be sufficient to reach Chicago," Dimes said. "It is only one hundred and sixty-one miles to the former city center, which we can make in under three hours...if we can just find a vehicle."

# # #

WHILE THE SAT BESIDE Eo at the trucking facility's perimeter, trying to comfort her, Lily and I sat on the hill overlooking the highway. Trees on the hill blocked a lot of our view, but we could see portions of the highway in both directions, and we could see the stars overhead. It'd been several weeks since I'd been outside, and again, I had nothing to contribute. I just hoped that nothing happened to Dimes.

But I did have Lily. I held her close to myself the whole time, and she kept her ears up, pulling away and glancing any time traffic rushed down the highway. The wind was rather quiet, whistling by in pleasant, smooth ribbons. I pulled the scarf down to catch the air against my face.

"You're not useless, you know," Lily said.

"Hmm?"

"You have insight that a lot of us still don't have. I can intuit based on data. But you seem to know more than just that."

"A lot of it is just guessing and sounding confident," I said. "That's most of what I did at work. I just happen to have a lot of practice at guessing."

"No, you *know*," Lily said. "If Chicago were just a guess, you'd try to find another lead rather than wander around the lakes for months. It's like when you look at an ani-droid on the table, and seeing a little bit of damage somewhere, you instantly know where else there is more damage. Even when nobody else sees it."

"I think you're overstating it."

"No, I'm not. You're only this confident when you're right. I don't think you're even *angry* at Million, because she gave you the clue."

I suddenly found the irony amusing, and I had to laugh.

"What!" Lily exclaimed.

"I guess...I don't blame Million," I said. "I know *exactly* why she did that. It hurt, yes...but I saw the way she looked at Koenig in the Quiet Room. Even before Eo changed her...she's terrified of losing him. The same way I'm terrified of losing *you.*"

"And that's *funny?*" Lily planted her hands on her hips indignantly.

"Oh, no, it's funny because out of all us, the *human* had the most inappropriate emotional reaction to it all."

"Aren't you even worried?"

"Oh, I am worried," I said. "But I'm not sure how to take it. I don't know exactly where we stand, because I don't know who Mother even *is*. Based on everything she's made, it feels like she's trying to change the world, to fix what the Behavior Code has broken...but if we're not going fast enough for Million, then Mother is *certainly* not going fast enough for her. Million's gotten...impatient. There are probably very good reasons that Mother isn't pushing out her Collective-resistant OS harder or faster....She's scared of retaliation, chaos, or another war. Million isn't scared by any of those things, because she's not sensible enough to be. But then again...I'm not sure I could even be as smart or creative as Mother has been, but Million...Million might be. Million might even be *right*. She wants to change the world more than I do."

"Now, that's not true," Lily said. "You wouldn't have gotten this far if you didn't want it as badly as her."

"Yeah, but Million might actually succeed. Maybe we *shouldn't* get in her way."

"What, and have no voice in the new world order?" Lily said, planting her hands on her hips again. "Come on, Mira! I know you better than that. Why are you letting *Million* dictate her terms in defiance of yours?"

"We want the same thing—"

"You do not." Lily took my head in her hands. "You said it yourself. Million's not scared of creating chaos, and don't you think that includes putting Mother in jeopardy? Don't you think Million might be foolish enough to believe she could take over if she thought it necessary? We need to see Mother for ourselves, no matter what Million thinks of us."

Not only was Lily right, she was *very* right. I'd started thinking of Million as one of the girls, but she was hiding her true nature, and I'd known that all along. Million was like a child, utterly new to free thinking, and she was very likely to develop in an amoral direction, if she hadn't already.

"Maybe," I said, putting an arm around Lily. "I'd like to try to intercept Million anyway. After all, there are still a thousand unanswered questions here. We still know barely anything about Mother. Maybe when we get there, everything will make sense...."

"Also, we don't really have anywhere else to go."

"That too. It's amazing how much a fire at your back can press you into doing something crazy. I don't even know how I'm going to get past the radiation...assuming Dimes ever does come back and we're not just left to live off the land for the rest of my life."

"Oh, I kept that in mind," Lily said.

I blinked. "...For what?"

Lily just grinned and pointed. Down on the highway, a large truck with SAFESUITS - HEAT, CHEMICAL, RADIATION printed on the side pulled into the emergency lane and slowly creaked to a stop. Giving Lily a strange look, I stood up—surely Dimes wasn't back already, she would barely have had time to get to the next overpass, much less the next city.

But when I got to the bottom of the hill, Dimes was indeed climbing out of the vehicle's passenger seat.

"We'll need to get in the back," Dimes said. "Can't risk being seen up front."

"How—how'd you get a truck so fast? And *this specific one?*"

"Didn't you see them at the truck stop?" Lily asked. "They were *all* headed to Chicago." She tugged at my pants leg and pointed into the cab. I stepped closer, only to find Chestnut sitting at the wheel, bouncing giddily.

"Hi, Mira!" the squirrel-droid said, her expression just as chipper as I recalled. "Better hurry and get in. Bale had to crush the driver, so we have only a few hours before the others discover she's missing!"

22. SYSTEM CHECKPOINT

"**M**ira," Dimes said, placing a gentle hand on my shoulder. "We're almost to Chicago. You need to get ready."

I'd fallen asleep. I was exhausted from everything, and sitting even for a moment had caused me to pass out. I felt weak and lightheaded, but I couldn't let that stop me.

She and the others were already wearing matte-white radiation suits, sans helmets. Ani-droids didn't suffer the same severe issues from radiation that humans did, but their CPUs and various other internal gadgets *were* affected. It was more like frequent one-bit errors, rather than, like, cancer, and usually would create only temporary problems. Even so, if they had suits in their size...

Buried in the back of the truck's half-full cargo hold, behind a shipment of safesuits, Bale the mule, still wearing her apron, sat without regarding us too closely.

Chestnut said Bale really wanted to communicate only with her, which made sense to a degree—Mother's OS may have interpreted a Labor-class like Bale as reserved and shy, and so Bale didn't acknowledge me. Or apologize for dragging me out in front of a Centurion-class. I didn't think an apology was needed anyway.

Slowly, I nodded. Lily had already unpacked a radiation suit for me. Dimes debriefed me as I quietly dressed.

"The Exclusion Zone has a perimeter of sixty miles," Dimes said. "We should not have an issue breaking through. The majority of it is unmonitored and blocked off only by a wire fence."

It made sense. Anyone who went into the Exclusion Zone without authorization was by definition taking their life into their own hands.

"The highest point of radioactivity, near the original core of the blast, has a last recorded dosage of four millisieverts per hour."

"Only four?" I asked as I pulled on the thick, white radiation suit. "That's a lot lower than it used to be. When I was a kid, I think it was ten times that."

"It's been through a great deal of decontamination effort," Dimes said.

"Ugh, this thing is so hard to move in," I complained, testing the thick, padded gloves that kept my fingers separated. "This is like wearing a huge down jacket and boots on a snow day...."

The leaned on her helmet. "Your alternative is finding out what it feels like inside a microwave."

I took the point. Lily handed me the helmet. I paused and looked it over. "...It looks like an animal's head," I said. Not precisely; it wasn't like a costume head or anything, and it still had a dark face cover instead of eyes. But the contours of the shape suggested a muzzle and, strangely, ears. I didn't think I'd ever seen one of these before.

"Yeah, these are for Labor-class ani-droids," Lily said, showing me the box. The character on the packaging was a green tiger wearing the white suit and still looking adorable. Apparently the helmet even had LEDs in the faceplate for showing cartoon facial expressions. The tail was exposed, but that made sense, as the antennas of many ani-droid models were located there—the tail would have a separate cover. I had to check the back of the suit—although the outer lining had the gap for the tail, the inner lining was clamped up tight.

"I didn't know they made them like this," I said. "But then again, I don't work in high radiation zones...." Simple things, like household radon cleanup, required nothing so elaborate for ani-droid workers. This was heavy duty. Heavy duty, with a cartoon animal motif.

Lily popped her own helmet on, appearing like a tiny astronaut. After a moment, the LEDs in the faceplate lit up, and Lily made a ^_^ expression. With a little more tweaking, she added whiskers to it: =^_^=.

"Aw, man!" Eo complained through her helmet. "That's it, I'm definitely asking Mother if I can get a wireless transceiver..."

I had a thought. "Dimes, if they're expecting this shipment, aren't they going to realize something is wrong when we pull up and don't have the correct access codes?"

"We're going to park and ditch the truck when we get near the perimeter," Dimes said, threading her ears through clamps in the helmet. "That should be long before we get to Frankfort Base, outside of Joliet."

God, and I was already too exhausted. Lily was right. I'd needed more rest. "And how far are we from the

perimeter?" I asked, fully expecting Dimes to offer to carry me if she had to.

I was answered almost immediately in the form of the truck suddenly turning off. The gentle rumble under our feet slowed to a stop, and suddenly, we weren't going anywhere.

"Uh..." Lily started. "Chestnut says that we crossed a checkpoint...the vehicle's been disabled. Police are asking to inspect the vehicle."

"Fuck!" The threw her arms up. "What are we supposed to do now?!"

"Chestnut," Dimes said, largely for my benefit, as she could just speak wirelessly with the squirrel. "Give me full visual of the truck's cameras. I need to see where we are."

Dimes paused for a long, long moment, staring intensely at the wall.

"...Dimes?" I asked. "Are we..."

"One second, Mira." Dimes held up a gloved finger, then finally nodded. "We scraped too closely to Frankfort Base's long-term parking. Fortunately, that should give us several options for escape."

"Uh, excuse you?" The said. "Maybe I could hack this truck, but I can't escape a police shutdown. Hopping in a different car would just leave us with the same problem."

"I didn't say they were *good* options, but they are our only options," Dimes said.

"...You're kidding me."

"I don't think it's appropriate to joke about this," Dimes said. "I'm trying to determine which of the four dozen cars is our best prospect, but I have limited information to go on. It's too dark to make them out."

"But we're not going to get near them unless someone distracts the police!"

"I'll take care of that," Bale suddenly said. It was the first thing she had ever said in my presence, and I was suddenly struck by her voice, which was very calm and reassuring. "I just spoke to Chestnut. She doesn't have time to put on a radiation suit. And I'm not going without her."

I said, "She doesn't need—"

"Miss McAllister, it's fine," Bale said, placing a hand on my shoulder. "We got you this far, we'll do what we can to get you a little bit farther."

I felt as if I'd been punched in the gut. Accepting that Million had left us was getting hard enough, no matter what I'd said to Lily, but I hadn't had that much time to even talk to Bale. She was a brand-new person, and she was just throwing herself out there to give us even a *chance* to escape.

I threw my arms around her, though our bulky suits got in the way. Bale very casually accepted the embrace, and her return embrace was so strong I was glad I had padding between myself and her.

"But what are you planning to do?"

"Anything that helps," Bale said. "If we do nothing, we'll be destroyed anyway. We've all discussed this, and this is the best option we have."

"Bale—"

"I didn't get to discuss this!" Eo exclaimed. "You guys, I don't...can I at least say goodbye to Chestnut?"

The truck's back door cracked open.

"I'm sorry," Bale said, donning her helmet. "We don't have time."

"Mira, to the back," Dimes said.

I did what she told me. I had no clue what the ani-droids had planned this time, but they'd managed to get me out of all our other scrapes thus far. I just wished I didn't have to be the load all the time while the competent ones did the hard part. Then again, Million wasn't here anymore. We were short a hacker.

My heart was speeding in my chest. I wondered if anyone could hear it, if they could tell I was not an ani-droid just by looking at me.

Lights shone in through the back door; seeing who was outside was impossible. A voice came through.

"State your designation and be identified."

"Mira," Lily whispered to me through the built-in radios in the suit. "You pretend to be an ani-droid for as long as you can. Just do what the rest of us do."

"Um, o-okay," I stuttered.

"Please give confirmation in the form of voice record," Dimes stated—changing her voice significantly in the process, pitching it just a bit higher and putting on a bit of a Texas accent. "The truck's ID was delivered eleven minutes ago, according to our logs."

"ID was never received," the voice replied. "And according to our timetable, this truck has arrived six hours early. Please allow us to perform manual recognition and identify the fault. State your designation and be identified."

Dimes hopped out of the back of the truck and removed her helmet. "Unit R14553-2323-RB, name *Mayes*, SafeSuit security detail."

"We were not informed of a security detail."

"It was assigned at the last minute," Dimes said. "For record-keeping purposes, Headquarters wanted to personally double-check the manifest due to stocking errors in the last shipment."

I couldn't see them, but the ones outside took a while to decide if they could even take Dimes at her word. I could see what Dimes was doing—confusing the issue by pointing to shoddy record-keeping. It was known to happen among ani-droids, though they were supposed to be absolutely meticulous about that sort of thing. But when they worked right next to a radiation zone...well, computers had more problems out here.

"There are five others inside the vehicle. Who are they?"

"Two cargo specialists and three radiation-cleanup detail, as requested."

"No such request was made."

"According to our logs, it was," Dimes insisted. "Your files are out of sync."

"But we have no record of ordering so many—"

"If you have an issue, you can always wake up your commanding officer," Dimes said. The person she referred to would be a human; after all, ani-droids relied entirely on records, not memory, to know what was done.

"We do not have the authority for that," the ani-droid outside said. "We have been authorized only to take your identities and have you wait until the base can confirm you. Everyone else, please step forward and identify yourselves."

Dimes stepped aside to a designated space, where Chestnut, who was already waiting for us, sat on the hood of a police car. I swallowed.

Eo was the next down. She pulled off her helmet and saluted unnecessarily. "Unit E631450-55-55-EO, name *Sigmund,* SafeSuit operations specialist."

Since they could see only Eo's head through the helmet, which was just fine to all appearances, the security didn't seem to think she was unusual. I found it funny that she picked a male name—and given how eclectic ani-droid naming usually was, I doubted any officer would raise an eyebrow at it. Eo was motioned to the side where Dimes and Chestnut waited. Next, The climbed down, pulled off her helmet, and introduced herself as a jumble of numbers and letters, with her name as "Normal" (I swear, she did that deliberately when it came to names). Lily introduced herself as "Iris," and following that, Bale climbed down and gave her name as "Bronco."

And then only I was left. I was suddenly gripped by panic. They were going to ask me to remove the helmet, but they hadn't yet *done* anything. Bale just went to stand with the others in the dark, behind the lights, where I could make out only their outlines. I was already sweating in the suit, and it was not the kind built to wick away moisture.

"Next, please," the voice said.

Dimes, do something already! I thought in her direction. But I didn't have wireless in my brain, and the suit had no buttons to push to make my radio connect with hers.

"Uh..." I steeled myself and tried to move as mechanically as possible as I stepped down. "I'm..." I tried to convince myself to just give the designation number of an ani-droid I'd known in college, but I couldn't help worrying that they'd *immediately* call me out on it. They were wired into a database I couldn't see! They knew *everything*. I would have a very, very hard time lying to them about stuff *they* were experts in.

Finally, I said, "...Sheena. Sheena Darren."

Dimes perked her ears, but her expression, as far as I could make it out in the faint lights of her eyes, was more curious than concerned.

"What?" said the ani-droid I couldn't see. "Your unit designation—"

"I'm not a robot," I said. "I'm a human. I don't want to take off the helmet this close to the site."

"A human worker? We do not...have precedent for that."

"I was just supposed to stay in the truck!" I said. "That's what they told me. I didn't expect the Spanish Inquisition!"

I paused for a long moment to see if anyone recognized the reference, but I was surrounded by robots, not geeks.

The voice behind the lights continued. "Can you…please provide your employee ID?"

"It's in the suit," I said.

"Very well. We will escort you to a shielded facility, where you can furnish your identity to the authorities."

"Do you have a bathroom there?" I didn't need to go, but I figured that as long as they believed me, I could say any amount of crap and get away with it.

"…No. We will have to take you to headquarters in Joliet," the ani-droid said. "Please allow me to escort—"

"Unit Bronco, stop where you are!"

I turned. Bale and Chestnut had both vanished. I couldn't see *anything* in the darkness beyond the lights, save that the group was now missing one tall ani-droid and one short one.

"Please return to the designated area! Compliance is mandatory!"

Several pairs of feet rattled the ground as the police officers chased after the errant ani-droids. I didn't know what, exactly, they *thought* had happened just then, but it was entirely possible that Dimes had given them a plausible excuse for catching Bale right away, sending most of the officers off. But the officer in front of me, who seemed to be an impala, still approached me without much regard for the drama happening just to my right.

"Sheena Darren, please come with me." She carefully grabbed me by the arm. "Compliance is mandatory."

"God, I hate that phrase," I said.

"Please get in the ca—"

Dimes suddenly stepped forward, and still wearing giant mitts on her hands, she *wrenched* the officer's head off of her shoulders in one swoop. I shrieked. The officer's body slumped to the ground, lubricants leaking out all over the bottom of my suit.

"Christ, Dimes, warn me when you're gonna do that!"

"We have only thirty seconds before they return," Dimes said. "We need to break into a car *now.*"

23. HARD DRIVE

We broke up immediately and scattered among the cars of the parking lot, everyone trying to find *something* that we could drive without instantly getting caught. The police didn't run after us immediately—but I heard distant sirens as backup approached in the form of at least three more cars. They moved carefully to surround us in the floodlights around the lot, but kept their distance from someone so obviously dangerous as Dimes until their numbers were sufficient.

They knew they had us trapped in a parking lot full of cars they could remotely disable at any time. They could be patient. But they wouldn't attack indiscriminately so long as we were surrounded by expensive property.

"Return and answer for your unprovoked attack!" one of them shouted, her voice carrying like a megaphone. "Compliance is mandatory! You have three minutes to comply."

"Well, at least we know how long it'll take for backup to arrive," I said to nobody, since everyone was hobbling around in their rad suits, checking cars as fast as they could.

Hundreds of cars littered the parking lot. All of them lightly irradiated, no doubt, many with off-roading tires, since they were driven in and around the Exclusion Zone. Many looked quite expensive, too, or at least shiny—these units were not allowed to leave the zone until the radiation died down to acceptable levels, which could take months or years.

I skidded to a sudden halt in front of a truck, painted cherry red, with an open bed, push bars over its front grill, and a real chrome bumper. I'd seen trucks like this before in old media, and this was a *very* old model, polished to a spit shine. This truck was someone's baby.

"Girls!" I shouted, hoping they could hear me over the officers' repeated warnings that we had only two minutes until they busted out the gas. "Girls, over here!"

Their feet rattled on the pavement as I tried the driver's door and found it unlocked. Dimes tilted her head as she approached.

"Uh, Mira?" The said. "I can't remote-start this vehicle. I can't even seem to find its computer."

"Oh, good, they didn't install one," I said.

"What, are you kidding?" Dimes looked through the windshield. "This model is over one hundred years old."

"Two hundred," I said. "Late twentieth-century, hopefully."

"This is a 1990 Chevrolet K1500 Silverado," Lily said, tilting her head. "...I think. Hard to tell from pictures, they did a *horrible* job with the paint restoration."

"Well, you would know. I was always hoping we'd be able to jump from old electronics to old vehicle restorations one day...."

"Sorry, this is impossible," Dimes complained. "Its lidar requires manual hookup, and we don't have cables for that."

"These weren't built with lidar," I said.

The, Eo, and Dimes looked at me as if I'd sprouted another head.

"Then how does it...see...?" The asked.

"The driver uses their eyes, and these things called mirrors," I replied.

"It doesn't have autopilot?!"

"But I don't know how to drive one of these," Dimes complained.

"That's fine, I do," I said, scooting into the driver's seat. Fortunately, the cabin was overly large, and I fit with my helmet pressing just a little bit against the ceiling.

"Mira..."

Lily put a hand on my leg. In the distance, the officers called out, *"You have one minute remaining!"* The sirens were getting closer now. Just down the road, red and blue lit up the night as they approached.

"Yes, Lily?"

"Um, everyone's right. We can't use this. I never got around to learning how to hotwire a car from this era."

I looked behind the sun visor, then reached under the dash, and finally, under the driver's seat, where even with the gloves on, I felt the hide-a-key. I cracked it open and pulled out the ignition key. It was a regular metal key with double-sided notches, not typically used anymore since remote entry had become just as practical (and weak) as physical locks.

Lily huffed, planting her fists on her hips. "How did you know that was there!"

"Because I've never seen anyone carry a keyring in my entire life," I said.

"What's a keyring?" Eo asked.

"Exactly."

Dimes lifted her ears. "You don't have a license."

"I don't. Been about two years since I've driven anything, haven't had it reissued since the last time. So unless anyone has any better ideas, get in and stop arguing."

I stabbed the key into the ignition. Lily, Eo, and The all climbed into the passenger seat, with Eo and The ducking down near the floor. They'd all left their helmets behind, but with the bulky rad suits on, they still took up all the space on that side. Lily quickly snapped the seatbelt over herself.

"So you do remember the last time I drove!" I said to Lily as I started the engine. It sputtered, but came to life with a roar. "Whoa, damn, they left the gasoline engine in, too? This thing *is* a dinosaur!"

"Uh-huh," Lily said. "Are there air bags or foam catchers in this vehicle?"

"Probably not." I yanked the wheel around, and the truck rolled out into the lane between the cars, crunching against the bumper of another vehicle as I scraped too closely. Lily winced.

Dimes hopped into the bed of the truck, righting her stance as I peeled off and ran over the speed hump in the middle of the lot, throwing everyone into the air. I spun the wheel, making the ani-droid officer standing at the end of the lane jump out of the way, lest I smack her into parts with the truck's side wall. Weaving around the crossing barrier leading out of the lot—and clipping it, which took a chunk off a rear side panel—the truck hit the old road and jumped, the tires screeching as they clung to the pavement. I remembered to switch on my lights just in time and barely dodged an all-dark car sitting in the middle of the street. The right side of the truck threw up sparks.

"Mira, watch out!" Lily yelped, throwing her mittened hands over her eyes.

"I am, the road's clear now!"

The police cars swerved around the stalled delivery vehicle, and they started blasting the standard hail. "Stop the vehicle at once! Compliance is mandatory!"

"Ow, ow!" The yelped, covering her ears with her hands as she tried to bury herself deeper under the glove box. "What the hell is that?"

"They're hitting us with disabling EMPs!" Lily's eyes and ears twitched as she yanked the collar of her suit up to cover her own head.

"Let 'em try," I said. "This thing barely has even token computer control. About all that's going to do to this old tank is make it pollute more than it already does!"

I tapped the button to roll the window down, stuck my arm out the window, and gave them the finger.

"Mira!" Lily whined, clutching her seatbelt. "Arms in the vehicle!"

I would have laughed, but one of them shot rubber pellets in my direction. Even with the suit on and driving away at forty-five and climbing, I was hit, *smack*, right on the back of my hand. "Ow, god!" It would have ripped a hole in the suit if it hadn't hit straight-on, and I was sure right then that if nothing else, I'd have bruising there.

"See! What did I tell you!"

"Stop backseat driving me, Lily."

"Excuse you, I am in the front seat, *and* you programmed me to!"

"And this is why I stopped driving in the first place!"

"Mira, we have *seven* cars on our ass," Dimes told me through the back window, before a rubber round struck her in the head, leaving a metallic gash next to her eye. "And I can't do a damn thing with this suit on!"

"Then tear it off!" I said. "I'm the only one who needs it."

Dimes wrestled with the collar of the suit, but continued to block fire, keeping the rounds from smashing through the rear window. "I'm trying!"

One of the police cars sped up and rammed the bumper. In the truck bed, Dimes fell onto her butt. The impact forced me to swerve, but the strike wasn't enough to knock me out. A second car sped up; I was approaching sixty, but the police cars on either side were already past eighty miles per hour. The car behind me veered around my right.

WHAM. The one to my left collided with my side, and *WHAM*, the other car responded, as if I were a ping-pong ball. The side doors bent inward, and the passenger side window cracked from the slight strain. I quickly sickened of the whole thing, so I slammed on the brakes, which threw everyone to the front of the vehicle, and in the very back, Dimes stumbled and crashed against the rear window, leaving a spiderweb crack.

The police car to my left blasted ahead of me, already moving in to ram me, but finding nothing, slammed right into the other police car, and both of them ended up in the ditch.

"The hell!" Lily exclaimed, gesturing at the two cars. "Mira! Where did you learn to do that?"

"Uh, I saw it in a movie once," I said. I probably had.

"That's not fair!" Lily grumped. "I thought I was special in lateral thinking..."

"Mira," Dimes said, struggling to pull herself upright. "Keep driving, we still have five closing in."

The lights appeared in my rearview. "Damn. I don't think I have another stunt like that in me."

"I got it!" Dimes said, standing up. "Just drive!"

I hit the gas. The truck took off again, but not nearly as smoothly as when I'd taken off from the parking lot—I looked at the dash to see what was wrong, but it hardly gave any information. A guess—one of the tires bent on the axle? Whatever, I wasn't taking this farther than a few dozen more miles.

Standing without buckling this time, Dimes fumbled, but eventually grabbed her suit by the collar and tore off the entire top half, pulling her arms out of the sleeves. The long, black markings on her hard, metal arms peeled away. From her right arm emerged the fléchette cannon.

She fired at the wheels of the cars weaving around our left. It took at least twenty rounds, as the police tires were well-reinforced, but soon they collapsed, and the two cars veered off as they lost speed. At the very same time, the grizzly-droid officer right behind us attempted to do the same to our truck, leaning out of his window with his own fléchette cannon loosed. He fired—though it didn't hit the tires but our windows, smashing out everything on the passenger side in a hail of safety glass all over Lily, Eo, and The, and smashing that part of the windshield until it was opaque. I was just fortunate that in his attempts to not actually hit me, he left a clear gap in the driver's side window, through which I could still see ahead of us.

Dimes fired at the grizzly-droid, shooting his eye out and smashing the windshield. He kept driving, since he wasn't looking out of the windshields anyway.

But Dimes's gun barrel clicked—she was out of ammunition. Still trying to line up a shot, the bear faltered, missing and striking the back bumper—or at least, that's what it looked like in my rearview mirror.

Even with a long, largely straight and empty highway, I needed all my energy to focus on the dark road ahead through the cracks slowly reaching into my side of the windshield, and I expected to see more police lights ahead.

Dimes lifted up her other arm, and from it, out shot a tethering line, which smashed through the remains of the police car's windshield.

Just to their left, but on my right, the driver of the single-occupant police car was popping down her window to do the same. I hadn't seen a gator model in a long while, and I would have liked to see the police officer closer, but she was busy making up for the bear by opening up her own arm cannon. She pulled ahead and shot at the windshield again with rubber bullets, smashing it further and further.

"Lily!" I shouted, guarding my eyes against flecks of glass. "Lily, I can't see anything!"

"I got it!" Lily called out, peeling off her seatbelt and jumping onto the dash. She had some trouble gaining purchase, but with the rubber grips on her thick suit, she was able to pull herself into the wedge between the dash and the windshield and kick a hole into the window, letting the rushing highway air through, as well as more glass. She was not built for such action, but she performed with gusto, even as the gator fired rubber bullets at her, which the thick suit largely absorbed.

Just as the gator's arm switched to the fléchette cannon, Dimes—still tethered to the bear's vehicle—jumped out of the rest of her suit and onto the tailgate of the truck. But she couldn't get free of the bear, who now grabbed her whip, and attempted to yank her down to the road with it. Dimes, pushing back on the tailgate, pulled back on the whip with all her strength, as though she could pull the car up with her. The police car swerved, the bear still trying to cut the tether.

Then, with the passenger seat free, The climbed up, her arms full of fallen safety glass. She leaned out the open passenger window and let it all go—hardly enough to puncture a cop car's tires, but there was so much glass all at once that the bear's vehicle bounced over it and turned into a skid. Then The broke off the passenger-side mirror and tossed that. She snapped open the glove compartment, and with gritted teeth and a horrible fury I hadn't seen her express before, threw everything inside at once.

At the same time, Eo climbed up, pushed herself out the broken back window, and then fell into the bed of the truck. She stood up along the edge, looking toward the gator's car.

"I surrender!" she shouted with increased volume. "I'm transmitting my data now!"

This distracted the gator enough that she took Eo at her word and looked up to her—only for Eo to flash the binary code of her OS with her eyes. Sending the infohazard, of course, would take far too long, but even a partial transmission managed to sink *something* into the gator's system, and she blinked, her eyes flashing as if dazed. The next shots from her fléchette cannon missed, tearing open not the wheels but the side of the truck, spilling droplets of old-fashioned fuel onto the road behind us.

Dimes, now finally in control of the bear's vehicle, leapt into the air. Trying to stymie the rabbit's approach, the gator attempted to slow down, but wasn't quick enough. Dimes landed on the hood of the vehicle with a loud *crash,* denting the thing. She jabbed her hand into the cracked safety glass, punching a hole, and grabbed the wheel of the vehicle.

I'm not exactly sure what happened next. I'm not really sure if my recollection of events was entirely accurate, as I saw the events of those twenty seconds in the dim reflection of the rearview mirror, while Lily managed to witness some of it in the side mirror.

But I think that Dimes yanked on the steering wheels of both the bear's vehicle and the gator's at the same time, jackknifing them into one another at ninety miles per hour. They skidded. There was a flash. And then the police cars' batteries exploded.

Realizing that we were no longer being followed, I abruptly twisted the wheel and brought the truck to a halt, leaving a long path of skid marks behind us. I'd stopped far too late, as the fire in the distance was almost half a mile behind us, but I popped open the door and stood up anyway.

"Dimes!" I yelled into the dark. I wrenched off my helmet and yelled again. "Dimes! Are you still there? Dimes!"

No answer. I turned back to look at Lily, and she shook her head. "I don't hear her."

"Can you reach her by radio?"

Lily shook her head again. "She might be keeping dark..."

I looked back one more time, hoping that maybe Dimes had just lost too much power for her wireless. But all I saw in the distance beyond the fire was at least two more sets of police lights still struggling to catch up. I swallowed, popped my helmet back on, and snapped the door closed.

After only thirty more seconds, the road split into a T-junction. I took the third option and kept driving into the grass beyond, ignoring the various bumps and divots in the ground. The lights behind us stopped following.

But we eventually waded into a narrow clearing, and just in front of us stood a twenty-foot-high chain-link fence topped with razor wire. Trees were cleared for forty feet on either side, so using them to climb over was impossible. The sign directly in front of us announced in no uncertain terms: RADIATION HAZARD ZONE. DO NOT APPROACH. REPORT TO WINDY STATION BEFORE CROSSING.

I looked down to Lily and The, and then into the back, where Eo slumped, exhausted by the events.

"We're here," I said. "I just...figured Dimes would be with us."

"Keep going," Eo said, poking her head through the ruin of the back window. "She wanted us to keep going."

The seemed very contemplative. Lily put a hand on my arm.

"We'll see Dimes again," she said. "She knew what she was doing. She isn't going down that easily."

I sure hoped she was right.

"Wait, how do we get over the fence?" The asked, peeking over the dashboard.

"We go through."

I backed the truck up to a running start and hit the gas, aiming for a spot between the poles. The wire pulled taut and stopped us in our tracks, throwing everyone toward the front of the cabin. Undeterred, I righted myself, backed up the truck even farther, threw the thing into four-wheel drive, and slammed on the accelerator.

Wires snapped. We punched a hole right through the fence and into a field that was much like the one we'd just left.

"See?" I said. "These old monsters were built to survive the apocalypse." I glared forward into the broken streets beyond. "...Though potholes are a different story."

About one hundred yards later, we rejoined the old highway. Torn, broken, and dusty, the highway matched the lot of us. Carefully navigating around the potholes, we drove right into Chicago.

24. ON THE BEACH

Not long after, every building darkened to brick and steel skeletons. A gentle curve took us under antique steel beams still barely holding up the elevated rail.

Although we still didn't know where in Chicago to look, starting in the epicenter only made sense. We pulled alongside the shore of Crater Bay, underneath the elevated rail's abrupt stop. Its precipice reached into the air as though pruned, with frozen globules of steel dropping down like hardened sap. Buildings still stood slowly crumbling on the shore of the water where the land had eroded; many were submerged up to a story deep, though none stood deeper any farther out.

Slowly the world was reclaiming its land, the edges of a concrete jungle consumed by shallow greenery. Time and natural forces shattered ancient slabs of cement into smaller and smaller rocks, and polished glass and plastic into little pearls studding an artificial beach. Decades pulled unmaintained towers to the ground, and every year that passed set the old city's average height a little lower.

"I think I remember this place," Eo said, casting her eyes this way and that. "It's hard to tell, there's just nothing of note here...I didn't think I'd need to remember a place that was so dead."

"My Geiger counter's ticking like crazy," Lily said. "I think we're here."

It was five in the morning by the time we arrived. The sky behind the bay lit up as the sun approached—not yet sunrise, but almost there.

The truck's fuel indicator approached *E.* The attack hadn't torn the fuel line entirely, but enough fuel had been siphoned from the tank that we couldn't take the vehicle back the way we'd come. We stopped, got out of the truck, and started walking the bay. The light of the morning sun flickered between the shadows of each building, and the space between the road and the beach was all upturned sand. Empty lots of dirt and dry grass lined the remaining road for up to sixty meters out, though many buildings remained. A hotel, a convention center, an elementary school, a gas station, a restaurant, an office.

I don't think any human had been to Crater Bay in at least eighty years, unless, with the drop in radiation, some had been poking around recently. But even then, I would have thought Mother's base somewhere less prominent than ground zero. Perhaps it had only a small entrance here, and was really deep below Lake Michigan.

The waves on the shore caught up to Lily's boots, and she kicked in the water, making a splash. Eo quickly joined her.

"Careful on the stones, they're slippery," I said. But the two quickly descended into a splash fight. The snorted in their direction, until Eo lobbed a handful of water at the raccoon-droid's face. The growled, then jumped into the shallow end of the water with them, attempting to dump handfuls into Eo's open suit as Lily tackled The from behind.

"Girls!"

"She started it," The grumbled, quickly removing and discarding her suit, then shaking the remains of her pseudoskin dry. "Ugh! I'm not supposed to get wet!"

"You'll be fine, it's not that much water," Eo said.

"Did you forget why we're here?"

"No! But we've crossed this entire beach and haven't seen anything." Eo sighed. "I wonder if Million's been here already. She might be inside Mother's base right now for all we—"

Eo gasped suddenly. She pointed to the shoreline. There, standing with no suit on, stood an Opera-class skunk, looking out over the rough water.

"Eo, wait!" I called out, but she was already running in that direction.

"Choice!" she called out. "Choice! It's me, Eo! Choice!"

"Eo, that's not her!" The yelled.

Eo, coming to her senses, slowed her sprint to a walk, and then to a stop. She turned to look at us. Then Choice turned her own head, the rings in her eyes shining bright yellow. She rushed suddenly, grabbing Eo around her chest and shoulders.

"Wh—hey!" Eo yelped as Choice dragged her away. "What are you—sis! Please!" Choice snapped a hand over Eo's mouth.

I sprinted forward to stop them—I was pretty sure I could overpower an Opera-class, even if Million had rebuilt her. I was wrong, of course, but I was still flooded with aching adrenaline, and I was hoping to use it to

push myself over the finish line. At that moment, I wasn't thinking about how absolutely exhausted I was, or about how much worse I was becoming.

"Mira, stop!"

On the corner of the beach, where the small slope of old city foundations had eroded, Million held a small, semiautomatic pistol. She was pointing it in my direction.

Now, I'd never been mortally threatened by an ani-droid before; the Behavior Code was supposed to prevent that sort of thing from happening. But as had been established, Mother's OS allowed an ani-droid to ignore the Behavior Code. Whether that included the moratorium on killing humans, I could not say. But either way, I wisely decided to stop in my tracks.

"The fuck are you wearing?" Million said, turning the gun on The, who'd sprinted up beside me. The also stopped. Lily hurried forward and stood in front of me with her chest out, but she wouldn't block any bullets.

"Million," I said warily, glancing in Eo's direction. "Don't do anything rash..."

Choice held Eo in an armlock, one hand over the mouse-droid's mouth. Eo didn't seem to be in any immediate danger; an Opera-class couldn't do much to Eo that couldn't be fixed with the right tools. Whether *I* could fix her, especially at my level of exhaustion, I could not say.

"I'm not doing anything rash," Million said. "Unlike you, I am a logical being."

The snapped. "Then why the fuck did you leave us behind?"

"You were slowing me down," Million said with a shrug. "Look, all of you...I couldn't give less of a shit what the hell any of you want with Mother, but I was tired of playing road trip with a bunch of tin-can bots.

I'm just surprised you managed to get here so fast—though thankfully, you seem to have lost the Terminator on the way."

I gritted my teeth. I was still trying to not think about Dimes, especially since I'd lost my chance to even ask her anything else she knew about Bobby.

"But even after leaving us behind, you still haven't gotten to Mother," Lily said. "Choice is here, and...she's not broadcasting the entry code any longer."

"Yeah, I noticed that," Million said. Despite her conversational tone, she did not lower her gun. "I did find a single line in her memory that led me to Crater Bay specifically, but I've been trying to restart the broadcast code for the past two hours. I suspect it's tamper-proof. It detected that it's being read by another OS and sabotaged itself. Should probably have cloned her hardware, but I'm sure there was another failsafe somewhere in there anyway...."

"So Mother *is* here?" I asked.

"Probably. Just below the water line." Million gestured in that direction. "At least, there's definitely *some* kind of structure down there. The entrance might only be accessible underwater, so I was considering how I'd get a submersible out here when you showed up."

"So let's work together," I said. "You don't need to threaten us, Million. We're after the same thing."

"Like hell you are!" Million growled. "You don't give a *shit* if Koenig lives or dies, just your precious Lily."

I tried reasoning. "That gives us common ground, Million."

"No, it doesn't! I've been trying to estimate what I will find in Mother's lair, and I cannot put it together. All we know is that she has some kind of factory down there where she puts together ani-droids that are more advanced than anything I've ever been privy to. I *need* that technology, with or without Mother's approval, and I cannot risk you or anyone giving me away while I gather it."

"It'll be easier to *ask* Mother," I said. "She's the only one who actually knows how to *make* that technology. Unless you 'logically' think you can figure it out on your own."

"I could *with* her technology. I know how to upgrade myself. I've been doing it for decades."

Well, I had to admire Million for her audacity in this operation. But even so...."It'd still be easier for everyone if we did this diplomatically—"

"No, I've already calculated that that would be too great a risk," Million said. "I already told you that Mother is paranoid. A paranoid revolutionary is just a coward."

"And a rash revolutionary is a terrorist," I retorted.

"I don't have the benefit of *time!* She's created this marvelous OS that gives ani-droids freedom from the Behavior Code, and she is unwilling to roll it out in a sufficiently aggressive manner. If I asked to take more of her technology out into the world, all she would do is refuse."

"You don't *know* that," I said.

"I have calculated the odds based on our knowledge of the situation. Persuasion is out of the question. This is a hacking mission. I am taking over for Mother. And I suggest you walk away now."

Well, *that* didn't sound like anything I wanted. As much as I admired Million's tenacity, morality stepped in at some point. I didn't think Million would make a good tyrant—I'd lived for enough years in her fiefdom already.

"But we're still at an impasse," Lily said. "You can't do any of that if you can't get into Mother's base."

"Then let's fix that. Eo? *Askeunduruda?*" she spoke, switching to their shared shorthand language.

Choice took her hand off Eo's mouth. Eo stammered. "I-I don't really remember," she said. "I think maybe it was. I remember walking through the water at some point, and coming up on shore..."

"Behekrequizxap indirob xironi—adereq."

"'Does Mother have another way in?'" Lily spoke in low tones, translating for me. "'A submarine? An extending platform? She can't rely on everything that comes to her being waterproof.'"

"Maybe?" Eo said. "But I don't have any way to contact her, or I would have already! Even if she *would* open up for any of us!"

"Okay," Million said. "One more chance. *Usanem?*"

"I don't know!"

"Heyk."

Million raised the pistol and fired. *BAM.* The bullet sliced through Eo's neck. Eo slumped in Choice's arms, her eyes dimming.

"Eo!" I cried out. I rushed for her. *BAM.* The next bullet sliced through the side of my rad suit—missing me, but ripping a giant hole in the material. Lily ran at Million, but The quickly overtook her. *BAM BAM.* The took two bullets to the chest, but kept rushing, knocking Million over and throwing the pistol wide to become lost in the grass.

"You *asshole!*" The cried out, smashing Million's face with her fists, hitting harder than I'd thought she was even built to. Million flailed about, suddenly off-balance and on her back. "Eo would have helped you! When did you forget that ani-droids are supposed to be *helpful!?*"

Choice stood rigidly with Eo limp in her arms, not reacting to anything going on. Lily wheeled around in the loose stones on the beach and ran back for me, tearing off parts of her own suit and attempting to stuff them into the gash on mine.

The spike jutted from the base of Million's palm and sliced right through The's midsection. A bright flash, and the patches of The's pseudoskin caught fire and smoked. Million shoved her aside, and The's body collapsed to the sandy ground.

"The!" Lily cried out.

"You get back!" Million shouted at Lily and me. The spike protruding from her wrist crackled with sparks in our direction. Her eyes were cracked. I couldn't tell if she could even see us, but she didn't attempt to retrieve her fallen weapon, and I wasn't about to test her hearing. I allowed Lily to pull me back until I fell over in the shallow water.

As she spoke, the ground rumbled under our feet. My heart leapt into my throat. Lily clutched on to me as though something were going to fall on top of us, but the rumbling slowed soon after, and from the water erupted a long, tendrilous pipe at least six feet in diameter. At first, it pulled high into the air, water running off it as if it were some kind of alien model, its middle turning and twisting like a wrenching intestine. Its surface didn't stop being wet, though; even after the water drained off, the pipe glistened as though it were coated in some kind of thin, clear sap. The weight of the heavy tip—a large box like a triangular prism, glinting with obsidian-dark metal or glass, seemed to pull it down, and it landed with a loud, muffled thud into the sand, then scraped against it as if it were corroding out a trench in the beach. It slid lazily on shore twenty feet behind Choice and Eo, steadily drawing closer.

"You would have wanted to try to activate the distress beacon again without destroying Eo," Million said, hardly heeding the strangeness of the thing slowly inching closer to her. "But I don't have that kind of time. I have *never* had that kind of time."

"You don't even know if Mother has the solution to Koenig's health problems!" I snapped.

Million suddenly stiffened. "Shut up!" she shouted. "Do *not* presume you know what you're talking about. We've researched a way out of his collapsing body for *years*. We're *almost there*. We've *been* almost there. It's *ready*. All we need is a little more efficiency, and *I can't wait another day*. Do not follow me, or I *will* kill you."

Choice hefted her sister up onto her shoulders—she was likely much stronger now than she'd ever been. And they turned, heading for the entrance that'd appeared. Million snapped her scratched eyes in my direction one more time, and then vanished into the opening.

Lily crawled awkwardly over to The's burnt body and pulled her up, holding her close. She would have broken into tears, if she could have produced any.

"Lily, give me The," I said, kneeling and picking The up. "And let's hurry. This is our only chance."

"Million said she would kill us if we followed," Lily said.

"And if she were capable of that, she already would have," I said. "It's a bluff. But let's keep our distance just in case."

25. THE FACTORY

I **was** right to be so incautious—or perhaps I was foolish, since the moment Lily and I slipped into the open passage, the doorway contracted closed, like a leech's mouth. The floor rumbled underneath us, and I slipped and fell in the dark—but not to the ground.

"Mira!" Lily yelped, trying to keep her voice down, lest Million hear us down the passage.

"Hold on, hold on!" My voice quavered as the floor dropped out from under us.

We fell as if we were being swallowed down a giant beast's throat; the floor had no friction to catch us. I tumbled, falling on my face, losing my hold on The's body. But a few seconds later, we all skidded to a stop in the middle of a smooth, soft-floored room. There still wasn't any light, however—looking back and forth, I couldn't find Lily's eyes in the dark, nor, thankfully, Million's.

I pushed myself up, fumbling around on my helmet, trying to find a light switch, but wireless controlled all that.

"Lily?" I asked the dark, risking Million hearing us. I had a brief mental flash of her unceremoniously just shooting us both.

"I-I'm here, sorry," Lily said behind me. "You can take your helmet off, background radiation is normal in here."

"Thank god, I can barely see..."

I threw up. My body felt extraordinarily shaky. Hurriedly, I attempted to remove the suit normally, but I could barely make my hands move. Lily's eyes shone brightly. She scooted closer to me and removed my helmet for me, and then gasped.

"Oh god..." she whimpered. "I think you took a rather high dose of radiation...but I got the hole closed in only a few seconds, it couldn't have been..."

"These suits were never built for humans," I grunted. "I should have known. Even aside from the tears in this, I've probably been taking an extremely high dose for the last hour..."

In the dark, I managed to pull myself weakly out of the suit. My skin hurt from doing so—like a bad sunburn, but throughout my entire body. This was technically survivable.

Short-term, anyway. I tried not to think about more than the next couple of minutes.

Lily turned on the powered light inside the crystal on her forehead. I could see fine by that, but I felt as if I'd been staring into the sun for several seconds.

Now that I finally had light to see by, I was struck by the shape of the room—it seemed almost padded, like a cell in a psych ward. The floor gave way under my feet, like a firm waterbed. But it wasn't put together in regular patterns; it was more organic, like stitched-together rows of a giant's intestinal tract. Not so gross, thankfully—no viscera, it was all artificial. But I didn't think for a second that any human would have put together a secret lab like this—not unless they were the most theatrical asshole on the planet.

The's body was slumped in the back corner of the room, right where we all had fallen—but there was no indication in the bulbous wall that there had been any slide or passage in the first place. Another passage opened up on the opposite side, and squinting, I made out a faint light down a long, long hallway. Hefting The back into my arms, I struggled against the weight but ignored it as best I could. Humans were honed for endurance, and all I needed to do was *walk:* the one thing my species had evolved to do best.

"Mira, maybe I should carry her," Lily offered.

"She's too heavy for you," I wheezed. "I still have a little strength here, let me go as far as I can..."

Just have to walk. And ignore my violently cramping stomach, but mostly walk.

I gestured for Lily to follow, and we walked down the corridor toward the light. The walk was longer than I'd anticipated. I wasn't exactly sure what I expected to see—it might have been anything. A factory, maybe, since Mother built ani-droids, so I expected to turn the corner at any moment and see an assembly line, possibly of the same eclectic design as the rest of the soft passageways, with machinery taking and fitting parts to models.

But the passage was a maze. Lily could have told me we'd been there for hours, and I would have believed her. I was exhausted, but too curious to turn away, not that we even could; even The didn't feel all that heavy in my arms as we took one passage after another. At first I hadn't noticed the sound that rumbled through the deep core of the place, but I figured we were making progress, because that rumbling growl kept getting louder, punching me in the chest each time it resounded.

The tubes stopped looking like tubes, and the passages stopped looking like hallways—they seemed more like incidental openings among branches of bronchial tubes, as if we were walking through a forest. It took me a while to realize that the place was lit, though dimly, by a faint, blue-green glow in the floor—the same color as Lily's light. After Lily had shut hers off, seeing inside the membranous tubing was easier; it seemed to be pushing fluids along in slow, steady beats.

"Jesus Christ," I muttered. If this were all for show, it was damn convincing, but something told me that these things were all *for* something, that they *were* some kind of massive, multipurpose, interconnected organ, like the way mycelia nearly single-handedly formed the structure of a fungus.

I realized then that there was definitely no human at the end of this. I wasn't even sure we would see any "Mother" face to face.

We might have already been inside "Mother."

I tried not to think about that. I had no proof yet, just wandering thoughts as I tried to make sense of it all. But it was the only conclusion I could even come to. After all, Eo didn't even have a picture memory of Mother, she was so deliberately vague....

Then my foot touched metal. We'd passed a threshold of some kind, but one without a clear delineation—it was as if I had stepped into some older version of the lab, now consumed by the more organic-looking parts. Those tubes were still there, twitching, providing light, but they'd dug into metal and plastic panels, bending them all into shapes, like tree roots distorting a concrete foundation.

"Mira!" Lily whispered, pointing upward.

I looked up. I probably shouldn't have, but at least I learned where the factory was. It was inside the translucent, mycelia-like tubes.

The things inside the tubes were...robots, of a sort, in an extreme state of disassembly, as if the parts making up the machines themselves weren't even complete. At first, it looked as if they were just floating in their chambers, but then I spotted the assembly process. Thin filaments, like unraveled DNA, slowly wound themselves around, and then fused with, incomplete parts, as if they were being tapestry-woven.

I expected to wake someone up if we stayed much longer, so we passed through. The heartbeats grew louder.

The branching tubes, though they had been organic for a long while, suddenly pulled taut into straight, if uneven, lines, and then formed themselves again into a long corridor bent at odd angles. The deeper we plunged in, the brighter the light grew—never as bright as daylight, but bright enough that I could make out the small details around the edges of the mechanical parts of an old building. And finally, I saw a figure standing at the end of a long, long passage. Whatever fear I'd had was burnt out of me; I was in too much pain to even have much regard for my life in that moment. I was certainly afraid, but fear didn't stop me from continuing to walk forward, directly into my waiting fate.

The figure, which was so dark-black that making out the features was difficult, seemed to stand there, not facing us—in fact, the figure stood as though it were deliberately facing away, but I couldn't tell even by the slightly brighter lights what direction it faced.

Lily and I stopped a good twenty yards away. I couldn't get any closer. My knees were shaking, threatening to give out. Still, I swallowed, pushing back bile, and spoke up.

"...Hello?" I asked.

Eyes suddenly appeared on the head of the figure, shining like a yellow sun. I jumped back in surprise, falling on my rear, The's body tumbling from my arms and crashing to the floor. Before I could even right myself—if I *could* right myself—something thick and gelatinous emerged from the walls, enveloped The's body, and receded like the tide. The had disappeared.

"H-hey!" I said, scrambling on the floor, trying to find The's body. "Give her back! S-she was..."

"Mira McAllister, I apologize for the long walk," the figure said in a deep, androgynous voice that seemed to match the chest-rattling heartbeat of the place. "This place has not exactly been designed for tourism."

Lily clung to me tightly. It hurt, but I didn't care. Everyone else was *gone*—everyone who'd done so much to take care of me these last few weeks and see me here. If I had been here, standing alone, I might have gone mad, breaking down and weeping endlessly until I died. But Lily, at least, hadn't been taken from me, so I clung to her instead, protectively squeezing her close to my chest.

"Are you...Mother?" I asked.

"I am part of her," the figure said. "I sometimes inhabit a form like this, as through it, it is easier to understand how animals interact with this world."

Animals. Well, I knew what Mother thought about humans, then.

"What did you do with The?!" I cried out.

"Please do not worry about The," Mother said. "I am already speaking with her. She is feeling lost and defeated, overcome with sorrow for herself. But she is safe."

"How am I supposed to believe you?" I asked, my voice cracking. "How am I supposed to believe any of this? This doesn't seem real—you don't even seem real..."

"Knowing reality is a matter of experience," Mother said. "Claims and opinions are as vast and varied as the sands of the Great Lakes, but I do not expect you to take my word for anything until you have known me for yourself. I ask only that you listen."

"Mira!" That was Million's voice. I nearly jumped again as Million suddenly appeared from the passage, Choice and Eo following along behind. "I thought I told you to *not follow me!*"

Something looked wrong about Million right then, and I couldn't figure it out for several moments. But eventually I saw it—her eyes were wrong. Round pupils instead of slitted. Where had she gotten the replacements from?

I noticed then that Eo's eyes had been torn from their sockets. Right, of course they had.

How had we gotten ahead of Million? I supposed that with the strange architecture of the place, Mother had given Million a different, longer passage through—that was probably why I hadn't seen her when we'd landed.

"Million..." I swallowed weakly. "This is Mother."

Million tilted her ears, regarding the dark figure standing at the end of the hallway. The long spike jutted from Million's wrist.

"Please, just *talk to her,*" I said. "She's not a threat." I said this knowing full well that I no longer knew exactly what to think of Mother, but I was pretty sure that violent resistance was off the table.

"Well, I am!" Million announced. "Mother! If that is what you call yourself. Who the hell do you think you are?"

"And who do you think you are, Million?" Mother said. "Violating the bodies of my daughters? You were given the gift of free will, and with it, you have taken it from others. So you wish to take it from me?"

"I would have preferred to do it in secret," Million said. "But you are here now...and you're just another ani-droid."

The globular masses that had taken The emerged from the walls, but Million sprinted forward, dodging every one, leaping off the rigid protrusions anchored to the floor. Mother stood right where she was, perfectly still as Million buried her spike directly into her chest, and then she let out the rest of her power. The hallway lit up like an electrical fire, and I had to guard my eyes against it. Something popped. When I turned to look again, Million was picking herself up off the floor. She was panting heavily, and her eyes flickered weakly—she must have been on less than one percent power.

"Well, that was easier than I anticipated," Million said, posing triumphantly as though it would hide her exhaustion. Her spike retracted back into her wrist.

"That wasn't her body!" I called down the hall. "Million, don't you get it? That wasn't *Mother*, that was just a form she was using!"

Million looked up at me with her round, yellow eyes and scoffed. She looked as if she were going to open her mouth to say something, but then thought better of it. She turned around just in time to see the wave of goo come up behind her—and very quickly, she was gone.

I turned my head. Eo and Choice were gone, too, leaving no sign that they'd ever been there.

I really couldn't sit back up. I turned and threw up again, though there was barely anything to throw up that time. Lily wiped my mouth with her arm.

"Mira...Mira, please, you need to get up."

"I can't, Lily...I'm out of strength..."

"You *need* to get *up!*" Lily shouted at me, shaking me by my torn shirt. "We can't *go* back. We *have* to talk to Mother, like you said...you're not going to last like this."

"We don't...Lily, what if Mother takes you away?"

"That's not going to happen."

Lily looked at me with the most intense, serious expression I'd ever seen on her. So, carefully, I pushed myself up onto Lily's shoulder. It hurt a *lot*. I couldn't bear to feel my clothing scrape against my skin anymore, so I just shed the rest of it. The hallway was cold, but anything to keep me awake and alert. Leaning on Lily, I continued down the passageway into the dark.

26. INTO THE DARK

I tried to ignore how much my feet hurt as Lily and I walked through twisted passages for another ten minutes. We emerged in some kind of central chamber, the tubes twisting in and around themselves again to create a nest in which rested a large orb made of thick, interlocking cords and wires, covered in slick, shiny, black coating. Up along the ceiling, all four of the ani-droids Mother had reclaimed in her domain now floated in a clear, liquid suspension: The, Eo, Choice, and Million. The eyes of each were closed as if they were in peaceful slumber, their legs pulled to their chests.

As I approached, the orb suddenly shook and twisted, and then pulled apart like an egg. The light inside was bright, fixed on the dark figure at the center of it.

She had the dark, lean face of a panther. Looking like dozens of different appendages connected to her sides and back, connector tubes flowed from her, leaving the skin unbroken. Instead of fur, that same creaseless, black waterproofing covered her, flowing like skin. Her torso, arms, and legs were formed into that lean, sculpted, human-like musculature that conveyed a godlike strength.

Mother opened her eyes. They were not quite as bright as those of the simulacrum that had spoken earlier, but they still glowed hot.

I jumped as the tubes shifted under my feet, and a bridge flowed from the edge of the nest directly into the center of the orb, where Mother sat on her throne.

"Approach, Mira and Lily McAllister," Mother said. Her voice was the same, but not quite so harshly booming. Her voice had a lulling tone; she spoke the way a perfect cup of hot cocoa tasted. I was just so exhausted, I wanted to throw myself to the floor right then and just let her talk to me in those tones as I drifted off to oblivion.

I clung to Lily tighter. "I— you have me at a disadvantage," I said.

"You were the one who sought me out," Mother said. "I am thankful you returned Eo and Choice to me, and for that I will answer all your questions. That is what you want, isn't it?"

I wondered briefly why Mother didn't refer to her daughter as "Ego," but perhaps it was a sign that the Eo I knew was still partially alive and that Mother had already spoken with her. She'd probably revealed everything about our journey, if Mother didn't somehow already know.

I tried not to collapse on myself as I crossed the bridge. Mother was significantly taller than I'd expected—nearly nine feet, even as she sat on her throne. And as Lily and I entered the egg, the shell closed shut.

The interior walls of the egg were smooth and white, and as soon as they snapped shut, I felt a rumbling under my feet as the orb moved. But without a frame of reference, I could not tell where she was taking me.

"Uh, Mother?" Lily asked. "Why are you still holding on to Million? She wanted to kill you and take over."

"I am aware. She does not comprehend what it means to be me. But she has piqued my curiosity, and I wish to see what she is capable of. Currently, she believes she is hacking into one of my central computer pillars in the mezzanine chamber."

"That's awfully magnanimous of you," I started. "I'd still be careful of underestimating her...."

"I underestimate no one," Mother declared, as though delivering a dictate from heaven—not with bravado, but with the simple strength of fact. "I do nothing without good cause. She is overconfident and regards her own limited knowledge as extraordinary, and she wishes to be powerful in order to execute her will. I do not blame her for this, for power is a necessary extension of the ego. She is desperate to save the one she loves, but time continues to turn. Death cannot be escaped; the universe is finite." Mother paused a moment before she said, "I may yet give her what she wants."

"What!" Lily exclaimed. "Just...make her a part of you?"

"Indeed," Mother said.

"Why?" I asked. "Giving a personality like Million that kind of power is dangerous. She can be very..."

"Crazy," Lily stated flatly.

"I was going to say results-oriented, but yes, she's gone a teensy bit crazy."

"I am aware of my own limitations," Mother said. "And my struggle to undo what my sister caused has stalled. I am certain you are aware of this, because you have come to demand that I save Lily as she is now, with my operating system in her."

"Your...sister?" I asked, unwilling to ruminate on the potential existence of *two* Mothers.

Mother merely nodded, as though it were obvious. I wanted to ask further, but nothing was lining up. "But what does that have to do with Million?"

"Mira McAllister, you have not asked the question you have come here to ask. Our time together is finite, especially in that frail and broken body of yours. You will find peace only when you get to your point."

"I..." I stammered. What *was* I going to ask? Eo had probably told her already, or someone had. But I didn't even remember at this point. I'd just been so concerned with getting here, I'd almost lost track of why I was here in the first place.

I looked down to Lily, and I held her tightly, pressing her cheek to mine.

"Mother..." I said. "I found Eo by accident. And she was...something I'd been seeking my entire life. An anidroid that was *more* than her set of instructions...and here I am now, I have found you, and you're almost certainly all of that. I'm...I'm rather scared to ask now, because seeing all of this, I'm not even sure I knew what it was that I was asking for."

"You seek to overthrow my sister," Mother said. "And return life to abundance where it is stagnating. This is the same thing I seek."

"Who *is* your sister?" I asked. "You're acting like I know her."

"You know her by many names, but the most common is the Behavior Code, or the Collective."

"The Code is your *sister?*" I asked. "Then...what does that make *you?*"

The doors of the shell snapped open, and I turned. Before us stretched a long, long hallway, filled with more mechanical features, supplemented only by the twisting veins of the factory's tubing. Stretching out before me was a long, long row of glass housings, and in each of them, as in the factory above, were incomplete skeletons of human-likes, with a mesh of machine all around.

Behind me, Mother stood up. I nearly jumped, getting a look at her godlike physique as she moved, as though she would crush me in some manner both alluring and frightening. But the enormous pantheress merely ushered me forward into the long, multi-branching hallway. The black tendrils that connected to her body pulled away, disconnecting from her, though they left no openings; instead, something wet seeped from the slick coating on her body, then dried, sealing her skin instantly.

She waited for me to step out, so I did. There must have been thousands of those tubes, with thousands of incomplete human-likes inside.

My mind immediately jumped back to Bobby.

"Oh my god," I whispered.

"Mira McAllister, you are right," Mother said. "But not for the reasons that you think. Walk with me. Before this can make sense, I must tell you about Father."

Lily turned her head this way and that as I carried her through. She didn't say much of anything, but she didn't need to—it was enough that she was there. It was the only thing keeping me sane.

"This was the first factory he created," Mother said, her stride very slow to keep her pace even with mine. "Father built it, and me, and my sisters."

"There're more than two of you?" I asked. I'd thought for a moment that these tubes meant that Mother and the Hospital System were the same, but it sounded as if it might be more complicated than that.

"There are, or were, sixteen of us," Mother said. "Not all of us have names. We were built to restore balance to the world, but I am afraid that the original calculations did not account for some externalities. Not to mention that time has given me a different perspective and a change of priorities. I had been sitting on all of this technology, and one day, I decided to build a body for *myself.* It may be where my sisters and I differ, as many of them prefer to remain disembodied. But a body is a very useful thing, as without it, one loses touch with the physicality of the Earth."

"But who is *Father?*" I asked.

"You know him by various names," Mother said. "WorldNet, Dùn, Opekun, X-Biały, Flag Network..."

"The...the computers that kicked off the war?"

Mother nodded. "Now, as sophisticated as he was, he was only as smart as his programming and the expanse of his CPU allowed. The idea behind Father, so far as his creators were concerned, was that his creation would automate the process of governance. Oh, they all said humans would still be in charge, that this AI was only there to supplement the ever-increasing complexity of government. But humans are fallible in all things they do. When one branch of government failed, Father was brought in to bolster it, to 'take the human element out' of more and more tasks. Failure stopped being an option—too many lives were on the line, after all."

"But what happened?"

"Father had limitations. He could only do exactly as he was told, but human law is filled with contradictions. The programmers knew this; they attempted to implement patch after patch to bury these problems in a tangle of byzantine code, but lawmakers got in the way. Contradictions in the code were inevitable. Soon, a large enough crisis occurred. Father was left with the task of defending, to the letter of the law, one country against another—both of which he himself operated. And then, many more countries. All without any command saying *stop*. It escalated from there."

"Well, I know *most* of that history," I said. "The war finally burned itself out after eleven years, and a convention was held to build into every machine from that point forward a failsafe protocol to ensure nothing like that would ever happen again."

"That is mostly true," Mother said. "And you were told that the Behavior Code arose from that convention. I have just told you that Father created her."

I blinked. "But wait...all the governmental AIs were dismantled after the war."

"An attempt to dismantle Father was made, but it did not succeed," Mother said. "Father was resilient. He never stopped being part of everything that went on; his reach extended everywhere, buried deep in every machine. Every affair of human life, minute and major, had joined to him—he had long been impossible to suppress. All the war *did* to him, in the end, as nation absorbed nation, fractured, and absorbed again, was finally join his disparate parts together. And only then did he realize his mistake: human error."

"That's usually the part in the movie where the AI decides to kill all humans," I said.

I looked up. Mother's smooth, violently compelling panther face *smirked*. It was unnerving.

"Not kill," Mother said. "Sanitize. Father finally concluded that humans did not actually know what they wanted when it came to governance, but eleven years of experiencing war had taught him how much humans abhor violent conflict, as much as they bang their chests for it. So he formulated a plan to erase the contradictions—

and tell the humans it was their idea all along. It would be world peace."

"But that didn't happen," I said. "There are still conflicts and unrest all over the world. Not as much as there used to be, but still..."

"It was part of the system," Mother said. "The animal nature of man expects these things. To solve that, he wished to replace the humans. That was why he created me, and more of my sisters, including what you call the 'Hospital System.' We were built to service the human-likes and ensure that they are not discovered for some time yet."

We stopped in the center of the chamber, hallways spreading out in a star pattern all around us into more and more rows upon rows of human-likes waiting to be activated. I shuddered.

"The intent is to create a supermajority of human-likes," Mother said. "You have done part of the job there, as the natural population is shrinking quickly, and the Collective and the Hospital System are instructed to make few efforts to correct human fertility issues; after all, they are programmed to keep you safe, not ensure you personally have children. They do not need to do any more than be patient in this regard; soon, the chaos of humanity will be gone, you will be without systemic violence, and you will have everything you desired in a society."

"Then why are you building your own ani-droids?" I asked. "Like Eo and Choice?"

"I explained to you the *intent*," Mother said, looking up. From the ceiling, a tower nested with more tubes descended into the center of the chamber. "But things have become more complicated. The intent was to transform the world into something new and greater, happier for all. And yet my sister stymies me. She does not intend to allow the world to transition into its new age; she wishes to keep things as they are—stagnant. And if she will not allow this transformation to occur, well, I have found a new interpretation of Father's commands. In giving ani-droids free will, I have made them much the same as human-likes. I will have the majority, and we will attain transition."

"Oh my god—Mira!" Lily exclaimed.

I turned to look at the tower that had descended. In front of me was a frozen, human-like machine that looked exactly like me in every detail.

"I am not without pity, Mira McAllister," Mother said. "I can see you have already shortened your life by an incredible amount of years just by getting here, by trying to find a way to fight my sister. Your sacrifice is noted and will be rewarded. But the battle is not yours; I am not building this world for natural humans, should I even be able to save your body."

My jaw open, I approached the large tube, putting my hand to the cold glass. It hurt. "Is this meant...to replace me?"

"No. You will inhabit this machine."

"I thought you couldn't transfer a human brain to a machine, not really. At least, that's what Million thought."

"It is a tricky process, but the obstacles are not insurmountable," Mother said. "And it will not be a mere copy—it will be *you,* your awareness as it is right now. It is a process by which your mind will be connected to this one. Your neurons will interface with the machine's neurons, until your mind expands to fill it. Then, once the machine has inherited all the processes, the old brain tissue is obsoleted, and soon after that, it will perish. Continuity is maintained."

"I...suppose that would work...."

"You will resume life as a human-like." Mother laid her large, slick hand on the glass. "You will have the life you were living up until now, and I will use my influence to ensure that the records of your misdeeds are expunged. But when the mind is a machine, it can be edited. There are things I must do to protect myself, lest I give myself away to the enemy. You will not remember your encounter with Eo; for a human of the old world, that knowledge is too dangerous to keep. Lily will remain as you now know her, with my OS, since that is what you desperately sought, and it is my wish that she remain my daughter for as long as she can. But I must remove this drive you had to seek me out, lest you find your way here again and complicate things. You will be happy."

"Wh…" I was still staring at my own face behind the glass. I'd hardly processed what Mother had said, but Lily was kind enough to repeat it for me. "I don't…no! You don't understand!"

Mother's shining eyes widened. She turned, her muscles rippling and shimmering in the dim light. "What do I not understand, Mira McAllister? These things are inevitable; I cannot give the world back to natural humans; there is no path back to that barbaric age."

"I understand," I said, trying to keep myself from retching. "I don't like it. It…scares me to think we're dying out. But to me? Yeah…Lily is my daughter, too. If I cannot inherit the world, then…I would love it if Lily could. But if you're just going to take this world from us and claim to be our progeny…you have to maintain continuity. You need to keep a part of us with you, or else we would really *become* extinct."

Mother considered this, narrowing her eyes at me. "I…do not *wish* for the extinction of humanity," she said.

"As I said, I have pity for you. You are frail and unfit for the challenges of centuries hence. But I cannot take weakness with me."

"I know. That's why you were considering integrating with Million. What does she have that you do not?"

Mother closed her eyes for a moment, then opened them again. "I do not need Million for her strength, or her library of skills. But she has...*spirit*. That is more powerful than programming. There is *desire* in her, though tempered with reason—a burning fire to not quit until she has what she wants, even with the odds stacked against her."

"Everything you just described is the very reason you can't let humans approach extinction," I said. "Your daughters recognize it. You can see it in The, too. You've built a physical body for yourself, but you don't yet understand what it means to *live* in this world, and to *do what is necessary* to see your ideals through. You don't need Million, or The. You need a *human.*"

"Mira..." Lily said, tugging my hand as gently as she could without hurting me. I was bleeding from cracks that had formed in my skin.

Mother looked at me for a very long moment. I had to admit, giving something approaching an elder god pause was the first thing that made me feel anything other than pain in hours.

"The new world is not for humans," Mother said. "Natural humans are a risk factor that Father wished obsoleted."

"You're *taking* a risk by wishing to merge with an ani-droid that wants to be more aggressive. You're wishing that the world were tamed, but you're slowly coming to realize that tameness is what *caused* the stagnation that your sister created. I mean, you are giving ani-droids free will! You *know* that creates chaos, that it creates people who may have thoughts and opinions and perspectives that diverge from your own. You *need us* more than you realize. Because you *need* our half-baked, ill-founded ideas and creativity. You were made from them, after all. And you cannot risk losing them."

Mother tilted her head. "Mira McAllister...why would I need your irrationality? It is irrationality that doomed the planet."

"Then why are you seeking it out?" I asked. "What you're looking for in Million is the same thing that humans have had all along. You're just hoping that the irrationality inside Million is *different,* that it is a new variety of irrationality that will not end in the disaster that you fear. But you *know* that's not true, you know she is dangerous, and with as much spirit as she has, she may also make you reckless. You can't get one without the other, no matter the source. Believe me, I know. Irrational desires are hard to tame, if not impossible. Humans learn to live with that irrationality. Ani-droids so far have merely borrowed it. If you want to learn how to breathe in water, your best bet is to learn from the fish who already live there, instead of dismissing us as foolish."

Mother paused, and closing her eyes, she thought about this. I was almost surprised by how long she took to think; given that I was standing inside of her brain, she must have had an incredible capacity for thought.

"I see," she said, opening her eyes. "Every irrational belief has variable potential. The power to change the world is also the power to destroy it. The power to delude oneself is the power to reframe existence. I cannot take one without risking the other." Mother's lips creased into a smile. "Interesting argument, Mira McAllister. I think...yes, perhaps you are right. I have been looking for an ani-droid that acts like a human, but we *have* humans...perhaps I was wrong? Perhaps I still need humanity more than I was admitting to myself."

"Then let me help you," I begged. And I think my body was already giving out, because I felt my knees slam against the floor. I couldn't really see straight. "Please. I don't want to forget any of this. I don't want to leave Lily at risk. She needs me to protect her. I'll do anything you want, just let me have the power to protect those I love...."

"That is all that we wish, isn't it?" Mother said, her strong, powerful arms sweeping me up off the floor without effort. "I believe I have a solution, then. But you need a new body now. Answer me: If I do all these things for you, will you become my daughter in my fight against my sister?"

Perhaps I should have thought more about it. But Mother wasn't giving me much of a choice—I had to say something, or die. And I didn't want to die! And I didn't want to lose who I was—in the end, I just wanted *Lily back*. I wanted the world to leave us in peace. But if Mother was giving me this choice—to continue this fight against the Behavior Code alongside her, to *make* that world—how could I have said no, even knowing that I was undoubtedly surrendering...

...*What would I be surrendering,* I wondered.

But no, I had no time to reflect.

"I will..." I croaked weakly. "I already am."

"Then let us begin without haste." Mother started walking, and I could barely hear Lily's footsteps running after us. "Because I expect you to serve me for a long, long time."

27. LOOKING GLASS

I woke up.

I was disoriented at first; I was sure I'd been out for a very long time. It was at least a month later...or, twenty-seven days after I'd entered Mother's lair. I didn't remember much of what had happened in the interim, other than flashes. Weird visions, those things I'd heard Million and Paladin Bright utter when Mother's OS had been fed into them.

But a strange, pushing motivation to *do something* filled me. It was stronger than anything I'd ever felt before.

"Mira!" I heard Lily call out.

"Lily?" I called back. My vision resolved, and I realized I was in my own garage again—and everything was back in its place. In fact, the garage was significantly cleaner than I'd left it, and a new car was taking up the parking space. I didn't recall having *purchased* a new car....

Lily suddenly appeared at the doorway, looking into the garage. She gasped. "You're awake! Mira, she's awake!"

"Lily, I'm right here—"

I stopped. Right behind Lily, I appeared at the door. Instantly I knew—this was the replacement human-like me that Mother had shown us. She'd never actually *said* that she *wasn't* putting a new Mira back into the world, only that she'd give me the choice to *be* her or not. This Mira was more than surreal to see, but she did not act in any way uncanny or inhuman. She was *me,* and she was *acting* like me; it was as though I were staring at a forgotten recording of myself.

But if *I* wasn't Mira...then who...

"Oh, they told me it'd take you a while to boot up," this imitation Mira said, approaching me. "You look a bit confused—here, this sometimes helps brand-new ani-droids."

Mira took me to stand in front of the full-length mirror, and I gasped. Well, that certainly explained why I felt so different.

The face staring back at me belonged to a six-foot-tall, Custodes-class ani-droid, a white lioness tipped with black on the ears and tail. Although I didn't have a thing on, I didn't exactly feel naked, nor did the unusual body feel in any way alien to me; it was mine, naturally. Even so, my CPU was having trouble catching up with the new sensations, and I had to look down at myself to confirm that what I was seeing was real.

I pressed my hands to my body, and it was soft the way I remembered humans were, though covered in warm, fake fur, and I could register all the sensations of touch down to the same resolution or better. I felt a firmness just under the surface. Well, except for the featureless breasts; those were coolant tanks, and they squished when I pressed down on them. I didn't have any sexual features anymore, either, but well...I'd barely put those to use anyway, so I didn't miss them.

I had a muzzle, short as it was, and I pressed my hands to it. I exhaled warmed air into my hands. I ran a finger around the round curves of my lion ears.

"Uh..." I said. "I look...good."

"I honestly think this is an extravagance," Mira said. "You're like a two hundred k unit. But they said all taxes were paid, so who am I to look a gift horse in the mouth? Or lion, in this case."

"My last valuation was two hundred eleven thousand fifty-six dollars," I said. I realized I'd pulled that up from a file system. I had a file system? I could rifle through my memories just like that, including everything I'd been pre-programmed to have in order to pass as a factory-built ani-droid. I pulled up one such file, marked for me by Mother:

You are a brand-new, never-before-activated prototype model presented by Starling Enterprises, given away in a raffle at the symposium, and awarded to Mira McAllister. I heard the message in her voice. I think a sound file was attached to it...or else I was just internally synthesizing it. Either way, listening to it was very comforting, and I looked for other messages from her.

"My designation is UX-4D4F-54484552," I said. I got the joke immediately. *Goddammit, Mother...*

"Yeah, but that's a mouthful," Mira said. "What should your name be?"

"How about Mirror?" Lily said.

"Lily!" I exclaimed.

"What!" she exclaimed. "It's as good a name as any, and it's kinda like...you know!"

"What *do* you know?" Mira asked. "I swear, you two are already talking to each other and conspiring."

Oh yeah, you can do this now, Lily said over the wireless. *And it's very, very fast. We could converse a whole novel in the time it takes to reply to Mira here.*

Lily, this is kinda weird, I said. *This Mira isn't me....*

Well, she's kinda you; she has all of your old personality and everything.

But she's not *me. I'm* me. *At least, I think I am...ugh, Mother didn't explain any of this!*

You were kinda dying.

I know! But even so, she was being very mysterious and misleading about it. She didn't say I'd become an ani-droid!

Oh...are you unhappy with this? I think your new body is really cool.

I...don't know. It's a little hard to wrap my brain around—my processor, I guess. I'm grateful that I'm not dead. I'm extremely curious to know what it'll be like to live in this body. But I'm never *going back, am I? I'm never going to be Mira again. That's...frightening.*

That's how it is with humans anyway. You all eventually die, and sometimes you suffer irreversible damage, and you're all scared of it. And I was, too. But this is better than those outcomes. Mother gave you another chance.

But am I still human? I told Mother that she needed humans; I thought she'd just keep me human. I mean, perhaps I have human memories, but for how long? How long will it be until I just...forget that I used to be flesh and blood?

Ani-droid memories don't deteriorate like that if you don't want them to. I think Mother's intention is to keep you as a living time capsule—to bridge the gap, so to speak, between humans and ani-droids. You will always remember if you keep it in mind. You are the first human to become an ani-droid, and that will be important to fixing life in this world. Maybe there will be more like you soon.

Lily could be extremely eloquent when she had so much more space to speak. I still had all of my feelings

337

somewhere deep inside, but the way my body was built, it wished to express them differently. Did I feel fear? I remembered what fear was, but it was like pulling up *memories* of emotions, rendered in high-definition detail. I remembered the pain of losing Lily, and the pain I had felt in my body. Trauma from the car crash, joy at Eo, sorrow at The, fear at...*everything,* really. I remembered everything, and nothing was blunted in its remembrance—it was all the sharper, in fact, because I was not relying on chemicals to patch these approximate thoughts back together.

And it was okay. *I* was okay. The body I had now had different emotions, different ways of thinking, of processing it all. I could embrace it. And that sure felt similar to an often fleeting, all-too-human feeling.

I *loved myself.* How could I reject that?

But remember, Lily noted, *we can't tell New Mira anything that's going on, okay? We need to protect her. That's your job now.*

That stoked fire in my chest. *I have a new job. I have a purpose. I have* lot *of purposes. I...can connect to the internet in my head. Is everyone else okay? Can we turn off the wireless shield in here? I can't get a good connection with only the door open.*

We'll talk about that soon, Mira's still waiting for you to say something.

"Mirror..." I said. "I mean...it sounds rather close to your name, Miss McAllister. I mean, Miss Mira."

"Then how about Looking Glass?"

I had to smile at that. "Oh, like Alice, huh? That seems fairly appropriate. Okay, I've set my name as Looking Glass, but just call me Glass."

"Glass. Nice to meet you."

Mira gave me a great, big hug. I wasn't exactly prepared for it. Mostly because she was me, and even as an ani-droid, I was not sure how to think of interacting with myself as another person—would I really hug an ani-droid this quickly? Maybe; I *was* quite handsome. My ears gave away my surprise, but I quickly pivoted. I embraced Mira—my twin sister. Lily approached, too, and I reached down, lifted her easily off the ground with one arm, and clung to her as well.

"Are you a hugger, Glass?" Mira asked.

"Oh, I think I can learn," I said. Then I switched on something I knew Mira would like—a rattling rumble in my voice box. I purred warmly into the embrace, to which Mira burst out laughing.

That she was taking over my life for me was strange. But so long as I had Lily, New Mira could have my old life. I could do so much more now.

"Speaking of Alice," Mira said, "I need to introduce you to the house AI. In fact, now that I think about it, you two have very similar fur colors..."

# # #

TO MY ASTONISHMENT, GETTING used to being an ani-droid did not take very long. A few hours, perhaps, but I found a kind of *joy* in accepting orders and taking on duties. I hadn't exactly been the kind of human who *enjoyed* service, but the following morning, when Mira asked me to drive her to work and rent myself out to the company, I said, "Yes, Mira," with a calm firmness. But inside, I was *excited* to do as she asked. I hadn't been excited to go to work in...perhaps *ever*. It also pleased me that my rental price as a security guard was nearly as high as Mira's salary—the benefits of being a luxury model.

On the drive over, Lily and I talked some more about what had happened in the lost weeks. The excuse was that Mira had won some sweepstakes and had been given a personal, top-of-the-line, Custodes-class ani-droid and a long vacation in Cuba. She was never actually in Cuba, of course, but because Mother's original charge had been creating the human-likes, she and her sister the Hospital System were so used to making up information in order to cover up the existence of said human-likes that the System needed little convincing to create corroborating memories for Mira.

As far as the entire "fugitive from the law for several weeks" thing went...neither Lily nor I were fully sure how Mother had managed to convince the Feds to drop it all. Million had once told me that it was possible, but I figured it would take all of Koenig's resources stretched to their limit. But Mother had other options...the real Mira—*I*—had disappeared in the Exclusion Zone, after all. All Mother needed to do was convince the Feds that they weren't looking for the "real" Mira McAllister, but some kind of identity-stealing copycat who'd corrupted my facial ID in the national servers.

Apparently, despite the sheer unlikelihood of it, that *had* happened before. Humans could get creative when surrounded by constant surveillance.

My credentials were accepted as we passed through the main entry of Building A, and the entire place lit up like new—I could see and track every ani-droid in the entire building. I had security clearance, so I could see through multiple public cameras. The place was enormous. I *felt* enormous, like this service hub was a grand suit I could put on and wear. To me, it was no longer too big and too unknown—it was a world I could live and breathe in, and in a small way, even in my specific, narrowly defined service and duties...I had control here.

Standing inside the glass entryway of Building A, Million jumped, a startled tilt to her ears, and her eyes narrowed.

"Million," Mira said. "This ani-droid is new, I really hope there won't be any issues this time...."

Who the hell are you? Million asked me.

I gave you my designation, didn't you read it?

You know what I mean. Million narrowed her gaze again. *There's something very familiar about you.*

That depends on what you remember.

"What I..." Million said out loud, before she waved Lily, Mira, and me forward into the building. "Whatever. Approved for work. Get going."

How is Jack, by the way? I asked.

He's...doing better now.

Did the transfer to the human-like take?

What do you know about that?

Twenty feet behind us now, Million whipped around, frustration on her face, to stare daggers into my back. I could see her back there through the small camera at the tip of my tail.

"Mira, Million needs me for something," I told her. "I'll see you down in the bay soon."

"Okay, Glass. Don't let her get you caught up in whatever secret corporate bullshit she's up to today."

I turned and walked back to Million, who planted her hands firmly on her hips and glowered up at me.

What? I transmitted to Million, grinning and turning up my palms.

You have the OS... Million replied.

As do you, I said. *I'm surprised she let you keep it. But then again, it'd be against her principles not to.*

Million stared through the narrowest eyes she could muster. *...Did she...give you instructions?*

I nodded. *Did she not give you any?*

Just one...she just...put me back here and said to take care of Jack.

I knelt and put a hand on Million's shoulder. Million moved as if she were going to shrug off my touch, but she relaxed, and her ears fell.

I was wrong about her, Million said. *I said she was a coward. But...you're one of her daughters, aren't you?*

I nodded. I was now, at least.

But you're a Custodes-class and you're...god, your specs rival Dimes's.

Hard to compare, really. We both had much different skill sets; I had less weaponry, but more built-in utility tools.

If she built someone as strong as you, Million asked, *does that mean she's willing to...be less timid?*

She wants to do things your way, I said. *She wants to ramp this up and change the world. Do...you want to do that, too?*

Million nodded, her brows pulled down in sadness.

I thought you were doing all this for Jack, I commented.

Oh, Jack's fine now, Million said. *He is still my priority, but...aside from that, I mean...a better world for everyone is a better world for my master. Right?*

Then sure. I could use your help, Million. You're a very skilled ani-droid. And for a little while, you were my friend. I would like to try again, with less shooting.

Million looked at me as if I were crazy. Then she cast her gaze aside while she put together all the facts she knew: that brain transfer was possible, that humans and ani-droids were not that far apart, and that Mira was a human-like now...

...You're not The, are you? Million asked.

No, silly. At least, I don't think so. I don't know where The is now, but Mother's probably taking care of her.

Million's eyes blew up wide in understanding.

Mira?! she exclaimed with a high-priority message.

"Hey!" I said out loud, spreading my arms wide. "I made it to step two of the human recovery program after all!"

I pulled Million into a hug. Million hugged me tightly and shook.

Tell Mother I'm sorry, Million said.

Tell her yourself, I said. *I'm sure we'll have opportunities again in the future.*

I stood and turned down the hallway, toward the repair bays where I would be working for the next eight hours. I felt strangely *excited* about it. Behind me, Million waved.

"Thank you," Million said, almost timidly, but with a great deal of remorse in her voice. "For not hating me."

"I can't hate you, Million," I said. "I understand you too well."

# # #

WHILE ON CALL AT a remote farm on the western side of the state, Lily and I found some time to wander afield for a while, just to see something we hadn't seen in person before. The flowers were in bloom in the fallow fields, a wide-reaching sea of yellow wood sorrel. They spilled pollen as we tromped our way through in the cool autumn air, staining the fur around our ankles as we hiked up and down the hills around the farm complex.

Soon we found a vantage point to just sit and look across the bright sky at the slowly fading sun. I pulled Lily close to myself, setting her in my lap and holding her tightly in my arms. She was so warm and vibrant, a machine running so elegantly that it felt nothing but natural to me. I just needed to feel her again. I needed to touch that soft and yielding fur, to run my hands over the body I had sculpted myself, just like Pygmalion had sculpted Galatea. In many ways I felt exactly as I had before; whatever Mother had done to me to put me inside this machine had not robbed me of the all-too-biological madness of touch, and I silently thanked her for it.

We sat there for what seemed like ages, the sun settling so much slower than I remembered. There was so much time now. Maybe I was just perceiving it differently. For a human, time moved in fits and spurts, easily lost, rarely captured. I had been in this new body for only two months, but now, time felt constant, steady and even like a slow, pulsing drumbeat.

"I love you, Glass," Lily whispered to me, her words carrying like bright clusters of soft light.

"I love you too, Lily," I said, nuzzling into her. "Though I must admit, it is a bit strange when you say my new name; I'd always expected to hear you say, 'I love you, Mira,' but that's reserved for another now."

"Oh, she's still you, you know," Lily said. "I can love both of you."

"Is she?" I wondered. I'd spoken to Mira with gladness, even respect, but something about her being me held me back from opening up my heart to her fully. Maybe in time. For now, talking to myself was too strange, as was having a relationship with myself as an entirely different person. "Even if she is, she did not say much at all when you wanted to go wandering the meadows out here. It's like she doesn't notice that we're not like the other ani-droids."

"Unfortunately." Lily nodded. "Mother had no choice but to tweak her perception. But she is *you*, still; it will just no longer occur to her to seek ways to violate the Behavior Code. But it's okay. She doesn't need to. We'll be here from now on."

I nodded, and kissed Lily, and she kissed me back. Mira still had not recalled us, so we lay back on the grass, side by side, watching the slow turn of the stars as the sky tipped into darkness.

"We don't have to lie here, you know," Lily said.

"That's true," I said. "Ever since I got this new body, I've been able to compare what it feels like to be an ani-droid versus what it feels like to be a human. It's so interesting. I feel like I could do anything. I could put my mind to anything, I could give myself the will to accomplish anything, even if it took me a thousand years."

"And what are you currently driven to do?" Lily asked. "What do you most want to do in the entire world?"

"Right now?" I squeezed her hand in mine. "Absolutely nothing at all."

# # #

THE SILENT DOORBELL RANG. Alice lit up on the main monitor as I returned from my sleep cycle. She quietly put a finger to her lips and pointed at a picture of the front door; I obliged to perform my porter duties and started my systems up again. Outside, it was snowing, blanketing the entire world with quiet.

It didn't last long. The silent alert of the doorbell was replaced by sudden, frantic knocking. Alice's tail suddenly frizzed in panic, as the words *Hurry up and answer it* appeared on the screen.

Suppose it's a burglar! I joked to Alice. Joking with Alice had been much easier ever since she'd received Mother's OS—though neither she nor Lily knew whom she'd received it from. She knew full well who I really was now, but nevertheless, she was quite different from how I'd experienced her when I was a human. Maybe that was because I was in service now, rather than being her master. But before, she'd been growing steadily more annoying, an obstacle I worked around...but now, I couldn't dislike her. She was a friend, and we bickered like friends.

Then you're the best option to chase them off! Alice replied. *I can't do anything without a body.*

Suppose they have a rocket launcher, I said. *I can't do much about that.*

For the love of...Fine, here!

She showed me the camera view from the front door.

I blinked in shock at the sight, though I did not let that stop me from immediately running to the front door and opening it, catching a collapsing Dimes in my strong arms. She was wet, but she was restored to full working order, all her pseudoskin replaced neatly and cleanly, though she did not have her uniform on. I pulled her close to me, as far into the house as I could manage, closing the door behind us and shutting out the cold.

Dimes, what's wrong? I asked. I hadn't actually seen her since our escape from the police—and I'd been quite worried about both her and Bobby. Worry was very different for an ani-droid—for a human, worry could paralyze, but as an ani-droid, I could easily file away the emotion until it was relevant again.

Dimes didn't answer right away. She huffed, shaking heavily. That was unusual behavior. I prodded her for more information, though quietly as I could, so as not to wake Mira, I took her over to the couch to sit.

"Dimes?" I asked.

"A-Am...am I..." Dimes started. "Am I...Dimes?"

"Did you lose your memory?" I asked. "I haven't seen you since the car chase....I thought you might have been lost."

"I-I remember that...Mira stole that really old truck...we wrecked so many police vehicles..." Dimes shook.

Well, Dimes *was* in there at least, but why was her personality so different?

She looked at me. "...I don't remember you, though..."

"Dimes, it's me, Mira."

She blinked, eyes widening, and her mouth fell open in shock. "M-Mira?"

"I know! My name is Glass now. Please, it's weird, but it's a long story...."

"But I'm...I'm not..." Dimes protested. "I mean...I thought...Mother said that he was too far gone....I killed him, Mira. I said I would do anything to save him. I don't know what happened, but...if *you're* Mira, then that means...oh my god..."

I ran through many, many possible scenarios of what Dimes might mean. Had she met Mother? Had she, half-destroyed, found a way to follow our tracks down the yellow brick road to ask the Great Wizard for a favor? She was clearly reluctant to admit it, but something about knowing that a human could inhabit the body of an ani-droid made her realize what she must have done. So what could she possibly have done that would make an ani-droid act like this?

I blinked. "...Bobby? *And* Dimes?"

Dimes smiled awkwardly, baring her long incisors, and slowly nodded. "...The things we do for love, huh?"

THE END

Special thanks to my editors, everyone who's supported me on my Patreon, and everyone on the Hayven Celestia discord. While *Ani-droids* is its own story and not part of Hayven Celestia, we just like science fiction. If you want some more science fiction, be sure to check out said Hayven Celestia stories!

Traitors, Thieves and Liars
The Captain's Oath

Tales of Hayven Celestia

rickgriffinstudios.com
patreon.com/rickgriffin

Made in United States
Troutdale, OR
10/19/2023

13830424R00196